# THE CONTRACT

Also by Sheila Grinell
*Appetite*

# THE
# CONTRACT

A NOVEL

SHEILA GRINELL

SHE WRITES PRESS

Published 2019
Printed in the United States of America
ISBN: 978-1-63152-648-0 pbk
ISBN: 978-1-63152-649-7 ebk
Library of Congress Control Number: 2019939202

For information, address:
She Writes Press
1569 Solano Ave #546
Berkeley, CA 94707
She Writes Press is a division of SparkPoint Studio, LLC.

Interior design by Tabitha Lahr

To Pax and his family

*The highest result of education is tolerance.*

–Helen Keller

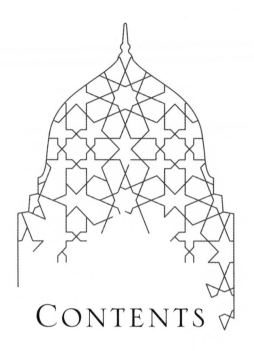

# Contents

# QUALIFICATIONS

1

They stepped out of the Jetway into a marble-walled corridor leading to passport control. Joanna pulled a roller bag, and Ev lugged an equipment case across the tiled floor. They followed two fit-looking young men dressed in athletic wear. Jo felt worn and grimy in comparison. She ran her tongue over the crust that had formed on her front teeth during the eight-hour flight from London to Riyadh. The gate agent at Heathrow had warned that mouthwash with any alcohol content would be confiscated, so she had jettisoned it before boarding. What else, she wondered, didn't she know about Saudi Arabia that she should?

"Tell me again, when are we meeting the interpreter?" Ev asked.

"Not now. His name's Peter, and he arrives tonight from Cairo." Jo had already told him twice. Ev didn't attend to detail, except when building one of his models. He'd been her business partner for ten years and husband for five; she kept lists for both of them.

They followed the athletes around a bend in the corridor, and the queue came to a halt. Ev shifted the messenger bag containing his notebook and drawing tools to his other shoulder. Jo used a bungee cord to secure her briefcase on top of the roller bag. It contained their travel documents—documents were always safer in her keeping than in his—and their correspondence with the potential client. They'd come to Riyadh to present their company's qualifications to design a museum for children. And to see if they could work in a country under Shariah rule.

Ev took a few sheets of paper from his pocket and put them in the messenger bag. He had spent most of the final leg of their thirty-two hour journey from Oakland doodling. Jo wondered if he had sketched something charming for tomorrow's pitch, or if he had been sulking, still resenting the trip. She wanted to placate him.

"Did you notice the flight attendant's cap? Half a scarf draped from ear to shoulder makes it look Middle Eastern without getting in the way." On questions of design, they never disagreed.

"Yeah." He looked straight ahead.

"Are you going to ignore me the whole time we're here?"

"You know I think we don't need this job."

"And you know I think we do."

Ev thought she wanted to make a pile of money because she couldn't stand being in debt. True, but she had a better reason. This job could catapult them into the ranks of designers who command big fees and get celebrated in the *New York Times*. She wanted one undeniable, top-tier win. She was forty-eight, and it was time to make her mark.

She lowered her voice. "You're not going to be rude, are you?"

"These people don't believe in reason. I won't know how to talk to them."

"You think Americans believe in reason?"

"They should. The Founding Fathers did."

"Ev, this is business."

"We're here, aren't we?" he said, as if to end the discussion.

Sure enough, she thought, for better or for worse. She was gambling that he'd come around once he got a chance to build something. She didn't dwell on how she'd feel if he didn't.

The queue resumed moving, and passengers from further forward in the jumbo jet merged into the crowd. They found themselves behind a family: three small children in Nike jackets, a portly man in a business suit, and two women shrouded in black. The women wore *abayas,* loose garments like graduation gowns, over their clothes; their heads were wrapped in scarves with a flap of cloth in front of the face so only their eyes could be seen. Jo wondered if they had sat face-covered all the way from London. One of the women appeared to be youngish: lithe, with jet-black beading along the edges of her garment. The other, squat, might have been the grandmother. Or perhaps a nanny, if money were plentiful. She and Ev had designed children's museums outside the US before, in Denmark and Brazil, and had needed to make only minor tweaks to their US-style plans, children being children. But here, where a woman must be accompanied by a male guardian, how does a mother explore a museum with her child? The pit of Jo's stomach contracted. They were vying for a job that might be impossible to execute to their standards: how do you encourage curiosity in a place where thoughts are policed?

The corridor led to a cavernous room with two signs overhead, one in Arabic and one reading "Immigration" in English.

Inside, past a gateway labeled "Foreigners," a crowd of short, rough-looking men massed in front of a counter marked "First-time Entry." An orderly line of suited men stood in front of "Business— Diplomats." Jo pulled Ev over to the end of the Business line. There was no other woman in sight. She wondered if she should cover her hair with the scarf she had packed for the purpose. She thought about the mail-order abaya in her bag. Should she duck into a ladies' room and put it on over her travel clothes? She wanted to show the proper respect, if only she knew how.

In a minute, a man in uniform, perhaps a soldier, walked toward them, pointing to Jo.

He said, "Lady, visa?"

Jo nodded yes and extended her passport opened to the visa stamp. He examined it, walked away with her passport in hand.

Ev whispered, "I guess you get special treatment."

"Or deported."

"This is one for your memoirs."

She shushed him, watching the uniformed man until he disappeared behind a barrier. She steeled herself: the Saudis knew how to pump oil, but they didn't know how to design museums for children, and she did. They needed to let her in.

The soldier-guard returned, empty-handed, and beckoned her to follow. She reached for the roller bag, but he waved her off. In a panic, she sought out Ev's eyes. Everything important lay in the briefcase on top of the bag. She begged him silently to take care of it.

Ev saluted her.

He could be so cavalier!

She marched behind the soldier-guard toward First-time Entry. He pushed in front of the crowd and indicated a scanner on the counter glowing laser green. A clerk with downcast eyes showed her a card with pictures of where to place one's fingers and walked her through the fingerprinting process without touching her. The soldier-guard said "lady" and pointed to another man with epaulettes on his uniform.

She presented herself.

"Mrs. Dunhill? You are alone?" He scrutinized her passport.

It's Ms. Dunhill, married to Mr. Dana, she thought reflexively. "My husband is over there in line."

"Follow me." He stepped behind a barricade into a glass-walled cubicle and sat behind a desk. There were no other chairs. She stood facing him.

"Why do you come here?" He frowned.

"My husband and I own a design company. We were invited to bid on a job." She wanted to avoid saying anything controversial, whatever that might be.

"Who invited you?"

"The name of the government agency is on the papers in my briefcase." She pointed past the barricade.

"Why do you have multiple-entry visa?"

"Is that wrong? I sent our passports to a courier company that sent them to your embassy in New York. They came back as you see. I'm sorry, I don't read Arabic."

He stared, as if doubting her truthfulness. "What is your plan?"

Were they in trouble? "If we get the job, we'll come back, but I have no plan."

He examined the visa again. He picked up the phone receiver on his desk and spoke to someone. She stood there, frozen in place while he talked. Was this job already doomed?

He replaced the receiver and looked her up and down, the sides of his mouth drawing down in evident distaste.

He glared. "There is no selling. Or you go back to America."

She nodded. She struggled to stay silent.

He opened the desk drawer and removed a stamp. He marked her passport and handed it back to her.

"You wait. There." He pointed down another corridor.

Feeling like Alice at the rabbit hole, Jo stepped out of the cubicle and down the indicated aisle, unfrozen arms and legs twitching. She reached a row of benches against a wall and took a seat near a young woman in an abaya, but with uncovered face, sitting beside an older woman and man. The young woman acknowledged Jo. Her eyebrows were darkly penciled in the shape of a chevron, and her teeth were very white. Jo leaned back; where was Ev when she needed him?

After a minute, the young woman leaned toward her. "English?"

"American."

"How do you do? I am English teacher." She pointed. "My mother, my father."

"Can you tell me what is going on here?"

"We are waiting. A small problem. You are alone?"

"My husband is still on line."

"Ah, your husband. It is not good to be alone."

"Do many people speak English here?"

"Only a few. I must work harder." The woman chuckled at her own joke. Pointing to Jo's disheveled curls, she added, "You have pretty hair."

"Thank you." How odd, Jo thought, relaxing an inch. She had expected to be treated formally in this most conservative city in a conservative nation. "You are a teacher, you say?"

"Yes. High school."

"Isn't it unusual for a woman to work?"

"Girls must study. The nation needs teachers." She clasped her hands in her lap. "I love my work."

Jo wanted to ask a hundred questions: Do you work full-time? How did you become a teacher? Are you married? Where did you learn English? She settled for, "Do you have a family?"

"Four children. Maybe more, *Inshallah*."

Who watches four kids while mom works at a high school? Perhaps Saudi women had more options than she had imagined. Options that she and Ev could build on—if they got the job. She relaxed another inch.

The woman leaned closer. "This is my parents' first trip to Riyadh, and I must help them."

"Have you been here before?"

"Yes. For my education. But many people do not leave their home town, especially older people." The space between her eyebrows contracted. "I am concerned. Your husband must guard you."

"I'm sure my husband is trying to find me."

Music issued from inside the designer purse at the woman's feet. She fished out a smart phone, said, "Excuse me," and held an intense conversation. Or an ordinary conversation that sounded intense to Jo's ears.

A knock on the wall. The officer with epaulettes stood frowning at her. Ev stood beside him towing their luggage. She rose and gathered her purse.

The teacher placed her hand over her phone and said, "Your husband?"

Jo nodded.

The teacher addressed Ev. "You must not leave your wife alone. Some men, they will misunderstand. They will think she has no value to you."

The old woman reached for her daughter's arm with both hands, as if to stop her talking. The teacher addressed Jo.

"Welcome to Saudi Arabia."

The officer moved away.

Jo leaned into Ev, relieved to see his smile. He passed the roller bag handle to her; the briefcase, thank goodness, had remained attached. He'd kept everything safe. Ev took her elbow and steered toward the exit doors, whispering, "Sorry it took so long. The guard kept walking up and down the line saying something I couldn't understand. I finally figured out he was looking for Mr. Dunhill. I pulled out one of our brochures to show him he wanted me."

"I was worried you wouldn't find me." She swallowed to release the catch in her throat.

"What happened to you?"

She whispered, "I got fingerprinted. The officer who brought you took me into his office and warned me not to sell anything or else."

"Did you provoke him?"

"No! He was hostile from the start."

"What about that young woman?"

"She has four children and loves her work as a high school English teacher. My mind is boggled."

"I figured you'd find someone to talk to."

"She found me. She asked twice about my husband. She wants you to protect me."

"You don't need protection."

Jo suppressed a flash of annoyance. In Ev's mythology, Jo was invulnerable. He said she could handle anything and deferred to her in practical matters, big and small. She had learned over the years that if she called him on it, she would get nowhere. "Optimistic," he would say; "oblivious" she would think.

But maybe things were different here.

They passed through Customs unimpeded. Out beyond the security doors, they walked along a rail behind which a scrum of men in bedraggled suit jackets bore placards in their hands. Jo looked for a "Dunhill + Dana + Design" sign. Seeing none, she led Ev to a lounge area with a coffee bar advertising internet access. They sat in plastic armchairs to wait for the escort they'd been promised.

People bustled around them, getting coffee and cola, lugging suitcases and jackets, talking noisily. Jo extracted a compact from her briefcase and examined her face in the mirror: jet-lagged, plain, and unadorned. She had always gotten by on smarts and grit. She would do so here. She took a deep breath and stuffed the compact back into the briefcase. The test was about to begin. Not the presentation she and Ev would make to the review committee—they knew how to present their qualifications. No, the test would be learning the ropes of a society that repressed women yet where the potential client, the deputy director of the agency that had summoned them, was female.

White-robed men ambled by, sometimes trailed by families. Little boys and girls bounced along, appearing to complain when corralled, just like at home. But the taller girls, already in black, walked sedately. Jo had been assured that the client intended to treat boys and girls equally, but seeing nine-year-olds in abayas made her itch under her skin. She rummaged in her bag for her scarf, a subdued blue rather than black. She covered her hair, tying the ends around the back of her neck; the airport clamor dimmed.

She concentrated on the task at hand: looking for their escort. In the scramble to submit their qualifications to bid on the job, she'd had little time to bone up on Saudi protocol. She'd read the State Department advisories but nothing else. Of course, she'd seen plenty of images of Saudi leaders in the media, darkish men with prominent noses clad in sunglasses, checkerboard headdress, and a long, white shirt. Would a driver wear the same outfit as a pol?

Minutes passed. She wondered if there had been a miscommunication. She pulled out her phone to call the client, but she had no bars and the Wi-Fi network required a password. More minutes passed; Ev doodled while she fretted. She reached for the equipment case and unzipped it. Ev looked up from his notebook.

"I'm going to Skype them," she said.

"Relax. They'll track us down."

"Maybe the driver can't find us. Let's ask the barista for the password."

"Nah, we haven't been here all that long."

"So we sit here for hours while the driver goes back to his office for instructions?"

"There could be traffic or something. Wait a while." He closed the notebook and tucked it into the messenger bag at his feet.

She zipped up the case and sat back. She would wait another fifteen minutes, no more. She retied the scarf over her hair. She would not invite the ire of another bureaucrat.

Ev nudged her arm. "See that guy over there?" He pointed to an older man in a white headdress. He carried a magazine, peered right and left as he strolled. His knee-length white shirt—a *thawb*, the State Department called it—stretched tight over a pot belly. "Is that our brochure in his hands? Maybe he's our guy."

Ev waved and caught the man's eye. A smile broke out and he waddled toward them. Coming close, he pointed to Jo's scarf and then her picture in the brochure, shaking his head and smiling. Ev laughed. "He means he didn't recognize you. Thought you were a local."

Evidently this was their escort, dressed like a prince. Perhaps he was a prince. She'd better not make assumptions. After all, on one of her first jobs, the paint-spattered person who'd picked her up at the train station had turned out to be the agency's director. She extended her hand to the roly-poly escort. He ignored it. He pulled out the handles of their bags and motioned them forward with a tilt of the head. At last, she thought with relief. They were back on track.

They followed the escort through the terminal out to his car, a limo like any other. They settled into the back and Jo turned to look out the window, tinted blue against the Arabian sun. As the escort navigated out of the airport onto a highway, a highway like any other, a little thrill passed through her. The skyline did not look like any other: scattered tall buildings in hazy colors, signs in a graceful, cursive script. She wanted to learn enough about this culture to create a place where boys and girls could expand their horizons, and where mothers could experience the twenty-first century in a new way.

But first they needed to get the job.

Ev said, "I wonder who else is interviewing."

"My very thought. I expect we'll find out."

She glanced over at him, peering out the window. He looked intent. She hoped he would develop some enthusiasm and turn up the charm for the review committee. Ev had a way about him. He made clients comfortable because they sensed his lack of malice. When it came time for toughness, as it inevitably did, Jo took over. Now, even if she'd have to cajole him, she'd get him to perform because, bottom line, she wanted to win.

On this June morning, the Riyadh sky looked like milk. Jo sat at a window in the chilly hotel lobby, wrapped in black, waiting for the interpreter to finish his breakfast. He had arrived the night before too late to meet. Outside it was already over a hundred degrees, and palm branches swayed in the wind. Ev said the sky's color came from sunlight scattering off dust kicked up by the hot wind. All that white overhead made her squint. She had stocked her purse with eye drops, just in case. She tightened the head scarf under her chin—it kept sliding off her curls—and stared out the window. Cars passed, but no people. A limo lurked in the hotel portico, the driver thumbing his phone behind closed windows. Her nerves felt frayed. By jetlag, of course, and anticipation. One always felt jittery before pitching a new client, but in an abaya? The head scarf blocked her peripheral vision; the shrouding might cramp her style.

The interpreter approached and sat beside her. He offered his hand.

"Mrs. Joanna, good morning. Please call me Peter. My name in Arabic is too hard to pronounce. I should mention the men here will not shake your hand, but you can feel free with the women."

Jo sized him up. Fifty-five, bit of a belly, cheap suit, nice tie. An Egyptian, "the best of the best" according to one of the trustees at a previous client who did business in the Middle East and who had insisted they use their own interpreter rather than rely on a local. The trustee had said his guy was rough around the edges but smart and savvy, worth every extra penny. Which meant airfare from Cairo and a room at the hotel.

"Peter. Have you worked on cultural projects before?"

"No, I do mostly legal and business. But I am engineer by training, and I read your materials on the plane last night. No problem." An educated voice, mild accent.

"Have you worked in Saudi Arabia before?"

"Of course. Here, in Jeddah, in Dammam. I know these people. They are different to Egyptians because they were nomads not so long ago. I can help you. If you are not pleased, you tell me to go home."

"I don't understand 'nomads.'"

"I will tell you . . ."

The elevator dinged and Ev stepped out, notebook and computer beneath his arm, projector slung across his shoulder. Peter rose, hand extended.

"Doctor Everett, good morning. We use first names here after a person's title."

Ev said, "I'm not a doctor. I'm not even a bachelor."

"Your interviewer may call you 'doctor' to show respect. If he does, please do not correct him."

"Right. You're an expert in protocol?" Ev looked annoyed.

"Not expert. But there is a great deal of diplomacy in my work."

Ev turned to Jo. "All set. We won't need to plug in."

She stood. "We should go."

Peter went to hail a taxi and they followed him out of the hotel. When the cab arrived, Jo grasped the abaya and the long skirt she wore beneath it in one hand and swished clumsily into the back seat. Ev sat beside her and slipped their good luck talisman, a spherical stone they had found at the Shenandoah River, into her hand. He didn't get nervous at pitches; he left uncertainty to her. Peter climbed into the front seat and conversed volubly with the driver. She would have to get used to the harsh sound.

The taxi traveled quickly along wide, uncrowded streets lined with multi-storied, stucco-faced buildings. Air conditioners protruded from windows. Small windows, flat roofs, cheap construction like other expanding cities in the warm places in the world. They turned into a street of storefronts with signs in graceful Arabic and bold Roman letters, then into the driveway of a modern office tower. The cab stopped and Peter negotiated with the driver while Ev handed her out. The lobby was lined in marble and bone chilly. They took an elevator to the sixth floor. As they stepped out, Peter whispered. "Let your husband start. Then you can talk."

A man in white robe and checkerboard headdress greeted them. "I trust your journey was uneventful." He extended a business card to Peter.

Peter said something in Arabic and gestured to Ev. "This is Mr. Everett and Mrs. Joanna."

"How do you do? I am your chairman today. Come meet everyone." Perfect American English.

He led them into a conference room with a shiny oval table. Seated along the far side were six other men dressed similarly but with distinctly different faces. Jo wondered if they came from different regions. The chairman sat at the head of the table and gestured for them to sit opposite the committee. As Peter pulled out Jo's chair, he whispered, "The chairman is an Aramco executive on loan to this project. You know Aramco? The Saudi oil company? Good."

Mr. Aramco introduced the others by name and title—impossible to remember—and asked them to speak. One at a time, through Peter or in halting English, each explained what he hoped the future children's museum would accomplish. While one man talked, some of the other men fiddled with their head gear, flicking the checkered cloth over their shoulders the way a teenage girl might flick back long hair. One man removed his headgear entirely and, after smoothing the cloth, repositioned it and the crown-like cord that secured it back on his head. Jo would have thought such fussing to be impolite.

As the men spoke, her chest began to contract: they had too many goals, and the goals were too grand. Serve every child in the Kingdom of Saudi Arabia, from infant to elementary school; lay the foundation for a career in renewable energy; improve the preparation of elementary school teachers; lead the world in research on early learning; contribute to a positive image of the nation's future. Most clients wanted too much at the start, and gradually you schooled them in reality. Jo worried that these men could not be schooled; what reasonable person would even *dream* of teaching toddlers about renewable energy? She hoped the female boss knew better, so she took a chance on interrupting.

"May we also hear about what the deputy director expects? Will we be able to meet with her?"

Aramco said, "She is listening." He pointed to a speakerphone in the middle of the table that Jo had not registered. A female voice crackled from the speaker: "Please continue. Tell us about your firm."

Jo felt her cheeks start to burn. How embarrassing to miss a cue!

Ev looked at her with raised eyebrows. She nodded. He started the projector and launched into their standard pitch. He displayed photos of their most successful and innovative projects, quoted testimonials from owners, showed video clips of children having a fine time. He stopped abruptly at the end of the video segment. Jo stepped into the gap. "Do the gentlemen or Madam Director have any questions?"

Peter translated a long reply from the man with drooping eyelids: "We know about your work, and it is very good, but nothing you showed us relates to the goals we have for our children. How would you address our requirements, which extend beyond American children's museums, even the famous Indianapolis, which belongs to the past and not the future?"

Jo was taken aback. She had not expected the man to know the scene in the US, let alone to share her secret opinion of one of its most venerable institutions. She should recalibrate. "We would expect to have extensive dialog with you to discover, together, how your wonderful vision could be implemented for your audience. We don't know enough yet about family habits and parents' expectations for a museum visit, or even if they have expectations. Our first steps would be to listen and learn."

A conversation erupted in Arabic. Peter sat quietly, face neutral, while the men seemed to argue with one another, waving papers clutched in hands. Jo worried they objected to her statement. Impatient clients sometimes said, "Why should we pay you to learn? You're supposed to be the expert." Or they didn't have the money to spend on visitor research. This client was neither hasty nor poor. Perhaps these men knew their goals to be only aspirational. Jo glanced at Peter, still impassive, and Ev, doodling, while the conversation roared on.

She didn't dare interrupt again.

Aramco spoke and they hushed. He stood. "We have another interview now, but please join us for lunch at twelve forty-five, after prayers, in the restaurant across the street. I hope you will be comfortable in the lobby until then."

They rose. Peter and Ev shook hands with each of the interviewers. Ev gathered his notebook and the computer gear, and they stepped across a cool marble hallway into an atrium where several clusters of armchairs surrounded coffee tables. In a corner, a young man in street clothes tended a bar. He approached after they had settled down, asking, in lilting English, if they would like coffee or tea or a cold drink. Peter leaned over and whispered, "Pakistani. All the daily work here is done by foreigners. Indonesians, Filipinos, Uzbekistanis. From the Muslim nations with too many people and too little money."

"What about Mr. Aramco? Isn't he a Saudi?"

"Yes. He is representative of the owner, the king. Management is Saudi. But Westerners do the technical jobs. Your client wants to change that."

"Why renewable energy? What about medicine, or computers, or a thousand other things?"

"Think what would happen to this country if they ran out of oil." Peter's eyes glittered, as if he relished the prospect.

Jo bridled at the hint of animosity. Clients deserved respect, until they proved they didn't. She made a mental note to filter Peter's commentary as . . . prejudice? Or cynicism? But could she, herself, respect these costumed men who wouldn't shake a woman's hand? She leaned across the coffee table. "They didn't seem to like our presentation."

"Oh, no. They really liked your answer about dialog. They were arguing how to go about it. There is always much discussion at these meetings. They all like to talk."

"When will we get to ask *them* questions? There's so much we need to know." She didn't hide her disappointment.

"You Americans are too fast. They like process here."

The waiter brought juice for Peter and Ev and water for Jo. They sipped and the men sank back into the cushions. Ev seemed content to sit without speaking. Jo's head ached from jetlag; she had slept little in the short night. She leaned back in her chair and gazed at the atrium skylight, feeling tired and cold. Colleagues had told her that even if they did win the job, getting the final payment out of Saudi Arabia might take years. She missed the comfort of her own culture. And her own bed.

Peter's voice roused her—she must have dozed off—saying it was time to meet their hosts for lunch. He led them out into the white heat. They crossed the street mid-block, and Ev headed for the restaurant door. Peter pulled him back saying, "We must use the family entrance for Mrs. Joanna." He led them around to the side of the building and into another door that led to a foyer shielded by a screen from the lobby proper. Mustachioed, foreign-looking waiters pointed the way to a private room.

Evidently they were the last to arrive. In the center of the room, the committee members had divided themselves between two white-cloth-covered tables. Against the far wall a long buffet bore a phalanx of chafing dishes and platters of cold foods. Mr. Aramco waved them toward three chairs at his table. Droopy eyelids sat at the other table, with two European-looking men. Jo caught her breath: she recognized Phil Owen, a competitor, a smarmy Brit who had made his reputation as a designer by knocking everyone else.

She turned to Ev, who said, "Yeah, I see. You sit." Ev loped over to the other table to shake hands with Owen and the other European.

Jo whispered to Peter, "Can't stand that guy. If they're foolish enough to select him over us, they'll get what they deserve." Phil

Owen made her teeth hurt. He snowed clients with trendy rhetoric and never measured the impact of his work. Yet good, earnest people hired him, again and again. Instead of her and Ev.

Peter whispered back, "Don't worry. You have the better table. The others do not have good English."

Ev returned to the table, and the chairman invited them to help themselves to the buffet, ladies first. Peter's eyebrows shot up and he winked at Jo. So, she thought, in Riyadh, ladies do not go first. She decided to exploit her privilege. She adjusted her head scarf, then slowly surveyed the buffet. She helped herself to a meat-and-rice dish and one of the salads that looked familiar. Ev followed, loading his plate with a little bit of everything, his love of experimentation trumping his lack of interest in food. Usually Ev just needed to fill up while Jo sought the proper combination of nutrition and calories.

They ate. The chairman, who seemed in the best of spirits, led them in chitchat. After a bit, Jo asked him about the other table. He said the committee had scouted the world and narrowed the field of potential consultants to two. Jo should be pleased to have risen to the top. Indeed, she said, she was. For the rest of the copious meal, he said nothing more about business. Jo, too, confined herself to chitchat, giving up the effort to impress. Ev tasted all the dishes on his plate, one at a time, making no particular effort to talk. When they stood to leave, she glared at Phil Owen and swept ahead of the others into the family lobby.

In the cab back to the hotel, Jo let loose. "Why did they parade Owen in front of us? Is it some kind of test?"

"Mrs. Joanna, you must understand," Peter said. "This is the way of nomads. At the table, all are welcome. There was no offense intended. Did you see how many dishes there were and how much was left?"

"So?"

"They will throw it away. Every meal, they will serve too much and throw it away. Nomads must always show they have more than enough to feed all who stop at their tent. These people have not lived in tents for generations, but the custom persists. It is a question of honor. You are being treated honorably."

Or arrogantly. Not much difference between honor and pride in this part of the world, Jo thought. She sat in silence for the rest of the drive.

In the hotel lobby, they agreed to meet later for dinner and a little sight-seeing. Jo wanted to visit a mosque. Peter said you can't go into a mosque but you can go into a shopping mall, and you should. There would be no families in the evening, but they would see the women spending the money their husbands got from the government. Ev said he'd rather look at desert architecture. Jo bit her lip and let them plan the evening. She craved a nap.

Upstairs, abaya draped over a chair, she stretched out on the hotel bed. Her limbs felt heavy, her brain fuzzy with fatigue. And frustration. Usually by this point in an interview process, she'd have picked up clues to the potential client's character. Here she could guess at nothing. She didn't know who really was in charge, where the money came from, how long it took to make decisions, or how success would be defined. She wanted to get Ev's take, Ev, who saw the world through rainbow glasses, a different color every day. She could rely on his singular vision back home because she could place it in context. But here? Her mind flashed to the rest of the crew waiting for them back in the office in Oakland, four employees needing to hear that their bread would be thickly buttered this coming year. She needed to think clearly. No, she needed sleep.

Jo had met Everett Dana in Atlanta, where she'd gone to make signs for the 1996 Olympics, two years after college. Their paths crossed one spring day on the lawn of the Fernbank Natural History Museum during a solar eclipse. Little had she known that the chance encounter would lead to a partnership, first in business and then in love.

The lawn that afternoon teemed with people lined up at telescopes to look indirectly at the sun. Over against a fence, a row of booths caught Jo's eye. One table was covered with little boxes in jewel colors. She walked over and picked up a shiny red box. A rubber eyepiece, like you see on binoculars, was stuck to one of its faces, so she raised it to her eye and was dazzled by the view: a kaleidoscopic scene that sparkled, like sunlight winking around the edges of leaves. When she pivoted, the colors spun. She pointed the box up at the sky and down at the ground: both views scintillated. She turned the box over, searching for the source of its brilliance.

A man in a hoodie sitting behind the table said, "You seem to like it."

"How does it work?"

"Do you want a hint?"

She examined the box again, tracing its ruby surface with her finger. "I give up. Where's the light source?"

He pointed to the sky. "A periscope. You'd figure it out if you took it home. Not complicated, really."

"If I took it home I'd reverse engineer it and sell it to the museum's gift shop."

"That would be wonderful. Would you really?"

"Only if you wouldn't sue me."

"Why should I sue you? The more people play with sunlight the better."

She thought, this guy's not for real. "Aren't you selling these?"

'Yes, to get money to make more. I want people to appreciate sunlight. What better time than at an eclipse?" His hands opened wide like a benediction.

What an oddball. "People *do* appreciate sunlight."

"Not enough. It's the source." He fumbled in a pocket and removed a card. "Last one. I've got more sun stuff at my place."

She took the frayed card: a line drawing of a winking dog and the legend "Everett Dana, Lone Wolf Studio."

"Bye," she said and trudged toward the museum entrance, heels catching in the soft grass.

But the Lone Wolf's clever little box lingered in the back of her mind. Tinkerers like him could be useful in her world. So she decided to check him out.

She drove to his address in a poor part of the city. He led her into the garage behind his house. It was unheated and smelled like grease and metal and dust; a dim light filtered in from above. He closed the door behind them and asked her to stand quietly. He pulled a chain hanging from the ceiling, something creaked, and the room filled with color. Slashes of neon green and yellow and fuchsia and blue rippled along the walls. He invited her to explore, enjoining her to step carefully in the semi-dark. As she moved, the colors played over her body. Again, she was dazzled.

"Should I guess this is some kind of sunlight?"

"There's only one kind of sunlight. I pipe it in and break it up so you can see its parts. You've come on a good day. Clouds spoil the show." He pulled out a chair. "If you sit still five minutes you'll see it change. The sun moves fast."

She sat, wondering if it were possible to package such a display. The colors slowly crept across the walls, moving like Day-Glo lizards. "What makes the colors so . . . luminous?"

"Good choice of word. They are lumens. Pure light, reflected off the walls and mirrors. You can't tell but the surfaces in here are polished so they reflect as much as possible.

"Mr. Dana, I . . ."

"Everett."

"Everett, do you ever build things on commission? Sometimes my clients want three-dimensional graphics. In color."

He laughed. "Can't bottle these colors." He gestured toward the door. "Want to see some other pieces? There's more in the house."

She followed him out of the garage into a room crowded with open crates containing irregular hunks of metal. He told her that he made musical instruments from detritus. His pieces had to sound like themselves, not like tinny approximations of familiar instruments. He took what looked like a fire extinguisher out of a crate and hit it with the heel of his hand. It made a low moan that lasted seconds, a metallic OM. She touched the canister ever so lightly to sense the vibration.

"You make inanimate things seem alive. How do you do it?"

"It's all just nature. Want a cup of tea?"

An hour later, she left Lone Wolf Studio convinced of his talent but unsettled by his dodges to her perfectly reasonable questions. Everything seemed to embarrass him. She decided not to patronize him. But his craftsmanship—that impressed.

Months passed. In a slow week, she volunteered to produce a brochure for a friend who belonged to a women's organization planning a museum for kids. It occurred to her that the Lone Wolf could help them. Kids would love his "nature" stuff, and they'd be safe handling it. So she wrote him an email outlining the challenge and suggesting he contact her friend. A few weeks later, he showed up at her door, toolbox in hand, offering to build whatever her friend needed. She thought him naive but decided to take a chance. She worked up a master plan, and he built models they thought would appeal to kids. Jo liked his use of simple materials. Ev appreciated her straightforward graphics, a style others called too spare. They developed a synergy that pleased them. The women's organization approved their design.

A month later, the women abandoned the project because they couldn't agree on how to raise money. But one of the women whose husband sat on the board of the local art museum persuaded the museum to include a room for children in their new wing. Jo and Ev jumped at the opportunity to fill the room. They worked quickly, and the synergy bore fruit.

A few days before the opening of the museum's new wing, Ev showed up at their rented studio with five kids of different sizes and complexions and instructed them to play with the nearly finished exhibits. He motioned Jo to stand beside him and watch.

"What are you doing?" she said. "They're going to make a mess."

Ev took her flailing hands in his. "Better now than opening night. I can fix it now. They're having a good time. Isn't that what we want?"

"No, we want them to learn color theory. Or Mrs. Moody may stop payment."

"We want them to play around so they *will* learn something. Mrs. Moody will get it."

Jo harrumphed and folded her arms.

They watched the five kids flow around the exhibits like liquid, easing around corners, spreading across surfaces. As the kids explored, they called to each other to come see something cool. They giggled and jostled to get closer to the displays. At the xylophone of found objects, they used the rubber hammers on the keys and not each other, as Ev had predicted. At the color wheels, they fumbled the controls; Jo realized she should change the label. In short order, the kids showed them how to make their good work even better. Jo had to admire Ev's instinct to bring them.

At the opening gala celebration, Ev in rented tuxedo and Jo in a secondhand prom dress stood in a corner of the children's room. They held their breath as men in black tie and women in long gowns sauntered in and picked their way among the displays. Jo had worried that the privileged party goers would scorn the simple exhibits she and Ev had geared to ordinary children. After a few minutes, though, the guests put their drinks down and plunged their hands into the displays, turning color wheels, matching puzzle pieces, hammering away on Ev's instruments. Couples called to each other to come see, just as the test kids had. When a chime rang to announce dinner and the room emptied, Jo felt the tension whoosh out of her. She turned to Ev, who was beaming.

He said, "We're all kids deep down."

"I think we scored." Her breath came deeper.

"You scored. I'm just the labor."

No, she thought, you're the genie. I rub the lamp.

When Ev leaned in to kiss her, she shushed him and said they should go to dinner in case Mrs. Moody needed them. In reality, she feared she'd kiss him back, which might interfere with business. Instead, she took his skinny arm to go join the crowd.

As she was driving Ev home later that night, Jo made up her mind.

"Do you really like the three D's mark?" She meant the logo she had produced hastily for the initial Dunhill + Dana + Design plan months ago.

"Yeah. Why?"

"Should we make it permanent, apply for a trademark?"

Ev sat up straighter. "Are you sober?"

"Completely. Mrs. Moody has connections. We do great work together and I think I can sell us." She watched his face out of the corner of her eye. Heart knocking against her ribs, she held her tongue. If she could corral his genius, she'd make something special happen. No one would ever take her for granted again, not her family, not her old boss. This was the way forward.

"Have you and Mrs. Moody been conspiring?"

"No. She asked me to write an article for one of her newsletters, which got me thinking." She was tempted to add the ten reasons he should jump at the opportunity, but with Ev, she had learned, less was more.

"I'll need my own shop. I need to be able to run a ripsaw at three in the morning."

"Deal."

He hadn't sounded terribly positive, but she'd risk it. She'd find the money to equip a shop. She was sure that together they could make magical environments that intrigued, and informed, and entertained in the best sense of the word. The prospect thrilled her.

In the second year after the business incorporated, they were invited to design an interactive art gallery in New York City. It was their first nationally prominent job, and Jo could barely contain her excitement.

Ten days before the gallery was to open, she went north to prep the client. When she arrived, she found him pacing nervously. He told her he had just discovered that the landlord insisted on his using a union shop to install the displays, and he hadn't budgeted for such a large expense. He was out of money, out of time, and facing a public relations disaster. Jo felt the bottom drop out from under her. Out of earshot of the miserable client, she called Ev.

"Don't come. Glover can't pay for installation, so the whole thing is off."

"What needs to be done?"

"The walls are painted and the floor is decent, but no power grid. I could kill him. I asked about installation a hundred times and he said 'Fine, dear, fine.' I could kill him."

"Tell him we don't need installation. I'll build the displays on site."

"That's too dangerous. You'll make a mess."

"I'll load a truck and be there in two days. I've got this."

He arrived as promised with two student helpers, three tool boxes, reels of cable, and the displays in pieces. Under Jo's tutelage, Glover told his landlord a story about "the artistic process on-site" that managed to appease him. Ev and crew worked around the clock to assemble the displays.

Fifteen minutes before the scheduled opening, Jo shooed the helpers out of the gallery, gathering up extension cords and empty coffee cups from the floor. She and Ev waited outside in the corridor while the guests crowded into the space. Peeking in, they saw that the exhibits functioned as planned. They collected their tools and slipped away.

Ev was hungry—he'd skipped meals to finish on time—so they picked up Thai takeout on the way to Jo's hotel. She spread the containers on the bed, and Ev attacked noodles with a plastic fork, scattering chili sauce on the duvet.

"Man," he said when he had slowed down, "I needed this."

"You deserve caviar and filet mignon. You saved his sorry ass."

"Prefer this." A piece of noodle was stuck on his lip.

"He doesn't appreciate what you did. He won't pay an extra dime."

"I don't care. I did it for you, not for him." He took another swig of beer. "I didn't want you to be disappointed."

How sweet Ev could be! "Wouldn't you have been disappointed?"

"Not really." He wiped his mouth on a paper napkin. "I like being your hero."

"I think you are my hero." Gratitude flooded through her, and something else.

He reached a long arm to her shoulder, a question on his face. She answered with her hand on his.

They made slow, sweet love for the first time since they'd met.

Afterwards, Ev left to drive his helpers to a hostel, as promised. Jo lay there, feeling heavy and content. She hadn't imagined Ev to be such a good lover. Would they love again? She'd prefer nothing change between them for the good of the business. She roused herself and went to the bathroom to clean up and discard the condom he'd left on the night table. Looking at the deflated rubber, she knew they'd crossed a threshold. She did not speculate about where it might lead.

They resumed working as before, but now they shared the occasional out-of-town hotel room, and their hands sometimes lingered an extra beat when they touched. Ev spent nights at her place now and then. If the staff sensed anything, they didn't speak up. Clients assumed they were a couple although neither wore a ring.

In the fourth year of the business, the neighbor who housed their shop put his place up for sale. After some dithering, they decided to move everything—office, workshop, storage, living quarters—to one property. Jo searched online for something big and cheap. A former classmate wrote that her artist uncle had had a heart attack and the family wanted to unload his house and attached studio. In California, close to the site of the Oakland hills fire, at a fire sale price. On the phone, the bank officer said he could arrange for Jo and her husband to assume the mortgage fairly quickly.

*Her husband.* Oh, what the hell, if she was going to marry, it might as well be to Ev. Four years younger and much poorer than she? Irrelevant. A known quantity, a decent guy. She told the bank officer yes. Then she told Ev. He kissed her hand.

They made a date with a justice of the peace. Right after the wedding, they bought the Oakland property and moved in. Soon they picked up some local clients, and business resumed its normal pace.

They worked hard. Jo sold clients on their services, accounted for money, and managed staff and contractors. Ev solved design problems in his unique way. For a client who wanted an environment based on a children's book about giants, Ev blew up a photo forty feet by thirty feet so that even parents felt tiny. A smashing success. For a client who wanted to stand out from the crowd, Ev suspended all the displays from the ceiling. A total flop: hardly anyone dared step past the entrance. Jo refunded the latter client and extracted a glowing testimonial from the former. She took it all in stride, becoming more skilled as a businesswoman with every deal. Successes outnumbered flops, and their reputation spread.

Their marriage flourished, too, as a union of opposites. Jo wore an antique wedding band; Ev didn't want a ring that would trap paint and grease. Jo managed their household like she managed their company; Ev was as grateful for good meals as he was for good clients. There was one sticking point between them: Jo did not want children. The eldest of four, she said she'd already done enough mothering. Her dreams did not include changing diapers and paying for orthodontia. Ev said he might like to be a father, but he did not insist. He told her he loved her just as she was, tender underneath.

Did she love him back?

In her way.

Ev seemed satisfied.

Other things occupied her time and attention.

At ten that evening, a hotel clerk brought a message to their door: the deputy director wanted to meet privately at one o'clock the following afternoon, and an interpreter would not be necessary. Jo realized they would have to delay their departure—and pay for another day in the hotel—but she wanted to see the woman in charge. Searching online had yielded little: the deputy director was one of only a handful of women in government in the Middle East, and her project was part of a national effort described only in generalities in the Saudi English-language press. Jo wanted to know if she had political muscle and if her interest in children's museums ran deep.

After breakfast, Jo sat at the desk in their hotel room and reviewed their pitch, wondering what the director wished to discuss. She wanted to impress the woman, of course, but she also needed answers to the questions that worried her. Getting a client was like dating; you had to scope out incompatibility before making a commitment, or else misery lay ahead.

Ev paced behind her. "I'm ready to go home."

"How about doing something for me? Think of a way to deal with renewable energy for four-year-olds."

"Ridiculous."

"Ev, they need to hear something from us."

"Okay. I wish I had my tools." He retrieved his notebook and pencil case. "Going for coffee." Ev liked noise in the background, preferably the whine of a table saw, but cafe clatter would do in a pinch.

She turned back to the computer screen. After all this time with Ev, she could not anticipate his thought process or predict the result, which she found both exhilarating and frustrating. Exhilarating when he came up with fantastic designs; frustrating when he ignored deadlines or the five times she made the same request. Eventually he'd honor her request, when its significance *to her* finally registered. Ev didn't see the world like most people. Raised off the grid by hippie parents in a West Virginia holler, homeschooled until high school, he had dropped out of community college and taught himself to work. You'd expect someone with his history to have peculiar ideas, but his peculiarity went beyond ideas to the inner logic of his brain. If he'd gone to a regular school, teachers might have caught on to his idiosyncrasy and taken some kind of remedial action. Instead, the child Ev had preferred to work with his hands. The adult Ev preferred to linger in his workshop where, it seemed, machines spoke to him. Jo had long since given up trying to get into his head. And it was okay. And occasionally it was terrific.

She focused on the PowerPoint slide in front of her; she'd rather be over-prepared than overconfident.

An older woman in abaya and head scarf greeted them at the reception desk at the Ministry.

"Are you the deputy director's interpreter?"

"Oh, no. She speaks English. Better than me. I am her assistant for many years." The woman took Jo's hand in both of hers. "I read your qualifications, and I am very pleased to meet you." She pressed Jo's hand between her soft palms.

"Thank you." Such a warm greeting. Would the deputy director be as positive?

The woman smiled broadly. "Please come with me."

She led them to a conference room off the lobby.

"Should we set up our equipment here?" Jo gestured to the table in the center.

"There is no need. The director wants to talk to you. Thank you for coming."

First time any of the Saudis had expressed appreciation for their responsiveness. Jo's shoulders inched down a fraction. She and Ev sat. His face showed his mind was elsewhere. Not a good sign. He'd been AWOL for a while in the morning, and she worried he wouldn't stick to the presentation they'd planned.

The woman sat opposite them. "I am happy to meet you. The director enjoyed your documents. So good for boys and girls."

"Should I address her as director or deputy director?"

The woman leaned toward Jo. "It does not matter. The director got her job because her husband is family of the king. But she has vision."

The door opened, and a middle-aged woman in abaya entered. She took in the room in a glance and seated herself at the head of the table. The director adjusted her head scarf and began to preside.

"Welcome to Riyadh. Is this your first visit?"

"Yes. I hope to learn a lot more about your country."

The director folded her hands on the table. "Your company is innovative, but you are small, without resources. How will you provide all the services we require?"

No pleasantries from this woman. "We collaborate with a range of companies who can do everything you might need, with the same high standards we have. I'd be happy to send you details about them and the museums we have built together, especially the ones outside the US."

'I am aware of your previous work. But here we must do more."

"In what way?"

"We must connect the learning at the museum to the teaching in schools. We need a *system* to accelerate the development of our children. We need to use twenty-first-century methods." She paused, looking into Jo's eyes, then Ev's. "I am only interested in exceptional design for my project."

"Yes, certainly. May I ask, have you seen a system you might want to emulate anywhere else?"

"No. We will develop a children's museum that leads naturally to better understanding and performance in school. It must be measurable."

What a tall order, Jo thought. "May I ask you about a concern of mine in that regard? Many museum exhibits and programs depend on social interaction, on opportunities for conversation or collaboration among visitors. We may not be able to design a full range of experiences where genders do not mix."

The director flicked her wrist. "That is not a concern. We know how to arrange it."

She addressed Ev. "You are quiet. What do you wish to tell me?"

"You shouldn't preach to little kids about renewable energy. Kids need to see something concrete."

Jo sighed inside. Ev on a tear.

The director asked in a bright voice, "In your opinion, what should you do?"

Ev stood and pulled a greasy chain from his jacket pocket. "I borrowed this from a bicycle at the hotel this morning. Watch." He placed the chain on a hook and spun it in a wobbly circle, around and around until it snapped into an arch that looked like a beak and then collapsed. "Ask a kid what she saw. Then you can let her feel it and guess where its energy came from. And where it went." His face glowed with the pleasure of his invention, just like a kid's.

"I see your point. Is there anything else you wish to say?"

Ev shook his head.

The director pushed her chair back from the table and rose. "I regret there is no more time to talk. I have another appointment. Myriam will see you out. I enjoyed your comments."

Jo's mouth snapped shut. Was that all? Why bother summoning them for ten minutes' conversation? She felt a flush of anger pass through her and was determined not to show it. The director had proven herself to be as arrogant as her male colleagues.

Ev picked up the unused projection hardware, and the assistant led them back to the lobby. Stopping at the exit, Jo asked Myriam to stay with them a moment to answer a few questions.

"What did the director mean when she said you know how to mix genders?"

Myriam nodded. "There is no problem. Boys will come three days and girls will come two days so they can all be free."

"But won't the girls need chaperones?"

Myriam smiled. "On girls' days, the female staff will be in charge. On boys' days and family days, the male staff will be in charge."

"Do you mean to say the museum will have two separate sets of staff?"

"That is our way."

"Does the director realize how expensive that is?"

"Of course. The director is a brilliant woman. She has PhD. She is very good with the politicians. She will get the money."

"But she couldn't get money to bring us here."

"You can charge later."

If there is a later, Jo thought.

Myriam leaned in. "You must realize it takes patience to make change in my country. Patience and cleverness. The director has both."

"Yes, but we learned very little about your requirements. We need to know a lot more."

"The director must be very careful with information. There are people who do not want her to succeed. I cannot say more."

"Can you tell me why the committee asked us to focus on renewable energy?"

Myriam raised her hands and touched fingertip to fingertip. "My country is expert in energy. We have graduate school of petroleum studies in Damman. We want our children to work in all forms of energy. So they must be inspired to learn. My words are not clear."

"Your words are clear, and I respect your government's desire to diversify. But we fear the topic is too abstract for young children."

Myriam nodded. "That is why we need your help." She turned to Ev. "Mr. Everett, how did you make the metal bird? I want to show my son. He studies physics."

Ev put down the equipment case and pulled the chain from his pocket. He spun it until a beak formed and collapsed. He offered it to Myriam, grease and all, but she demurred. Jo fought to hide her distress.

As Ev pocketed the chain, Phil Owen strolled over, grinning like the Cheshire cat.

"I see you're here, too. Playing games with the client?"

So, the director's next appointment. Jo's voice took on the arch tone Ev disliked. "We had an excellent conversation." She busied herself with the equipment case. Ev cupped her elbow in his non-greasy hand and they walked away. Jo waved thanks to the loyal Myriam.

They sat silent in a taxi. Ev lowered his window, and hot city air flooded in. Jo's chest contracted. Damn Riyadh. Damn the director. Damn Phil Owen. She should have taken the goddamn chain away from Ev. She erupted.

"Why couldn't you follow the plan?"

"Myriam liked the demo."

"Myriam doesn't pay the bills."

Ev said nothing.

"I should have left you at the hotel."

The taxi careened around a corner, sending the equipment case to the floor. Ev retrieved it. He settled back onto the banquette. Jo sat rigid.

He said, "Are you sure I'm the one you're angry at?"

"You're the one who just blew three grand, and maybe the whole job."

"Maybe that's the right outcome."

Neither of them spoke for the rest of the diesel-scented ride.

At the hotel, Ev said he had to see a man about a bicycle. Jo, condescending, said she'd transport the hardware. Up in their room, she threw off the abaya and shook off her shoes. She sat in the chair beside the window, squinting against the sun at the beige-and-white buildings lining the street below. Her pulse slowed. Perhaps Ev hadn't blown the interview; he'd given the director a dose of their style, an honest if graceless one. Maybe it was Phil Owen's appearance that had pushed her over the top. She'd known the s.o.b. was competing for the job, with all its contradictions. She didn't really believe boys and girls could explore freely behind a wall of taboos.

A rap on the door; Ev's muffled voice: "Is it safe?"

"It's safe."

He sat on the bed, attentive.

"I'm sorry."

He nodded.

"Maybe we should let Owen get the contract," she murmured.

"Is that what you want?"

"No."

"I know. This job is your baby." He rose. "I'll start packing up." He went into the bathroom.

What a know-it-all, she thought, but he knows me, all right.

She leaned back into the upholstery. Surely the director could have been more collegial. On the other hand, *if* they were offered the gig, and *if* Ev would do his magic, she could test the woman's resolve. Jo did not consider herself a subversive, but if the director meant what she said about playing in the twenty-first century, she needed radical help.

Back in Oakland, Jo steered the station wagon beneath the eucalyptus tree that overhung their driveway and switched off the
headlights. When they'd first moved in, she had wanted to cut down
the tree because the falling nuts clunked on the windshields of clients' vehicles. But Ev had insisted such a mighty creature deserved
respect. Jo had countered that it wasn't native. Its forebears had been
imported from Australia to shore up the gold mines. Ev had replied
the species should be congratulated for immigrating successfully.
He loved trees, called them noble and benign beings, the pride of
evolution. So they'd kept the tree, nuts and all, and every damp day,
its odor permeated the property. It had rained hours before their
arrival, a rare event in summer, and as she opened the driver's side
door, the pungent aroma signaled "home."

The house they'd bought in a hurry was perfectly functional
although quirky, sort of like Ev, Jo often thought. The realtor had
told them the house was designed by Bernard Maybeck or maybe
Julia Morgan, which intrigued them. The house turned out to be by
neither iconic Bay Area architect, just a solid example of Arts and
Crafts style. Brown wood-shingled exterior; multi-paned windows;
a peaked roof that jutted beyond the walls, giving shelter from rain
and sun. They had ripped out interior walls on the ground floor,
except for the kitchen and bath, to make one large work space
and a semi-private cubby for meetings. They lived in the rooms

above, reached by an improbably cantilevered staircase built by Ev: a sunny bedroom, a spare room containing their TV and Jo's stationary bike, and a generous bath. Behind the house, a patio led to a glass-walled studio containing Ev's machines and supplies. Clients seemed to enjoy watching Ev at work behind the glass, protected as they were from the noise and dust.

Although it was late, all four staff members were waiting in the office to hear the news from Riyadh. Becca, a recent college graduate, did the graphic design that Jo sold to clients since she no longer had time for it. Andy, the IT guy, worked nights on the websites that constituted a steadily increasing share of the business. Carlos, a draftsman, and Diane, Jo's sister and part-time book-keeper, had hung around to find out if the Saudi project was a go. Jo scanned their expectant faces; only Becca frowned.

Jo said, "Thanks for waiting. I don't have much to report. We didn't get a chance to ask questions. I don't know much more than I did before."

Ev said, "I got an idea for a one-man demo that I'm going to work up. Could be a demo or a stand-alone exhibit."

"Please, not now," Jo said. "I'm tired and these people need to go home."

"Of course. I need to get some rope and stuff." Ev picked up the roller bag and headed to the staircase. "Good night. *Manana*."

Diane said, "When are you going to know?"

"I can't say. We haven't been invited to submit a full proposal yet."

Diane slung her colossal purse over her shoulder. "Well, I'm glad we're still in the running. Gotta go." Diane usually arrived at work breathless and left in a tizzy. Younger and larger than her sister, she carried a huge bag that overflowed with clothes, food, papers, whatever. In the office, she tallied sums neatly and entered them in QuickBooks meticulously. She seemed to lead a sloppy, hurried personal life but an exacting professional one, as if two distinct people. Diane kept the candy bowl on her desk full; the rest of the team liked her.

Carlos and Andy muttered something and prepared to take their leave. Becca hung back while the others walked into the night. Becca leaned toward Jo and spoke urgently.

"Why can't they tell you anything? I think you're being bullied. We should stop wasting our time on them." Becca was a tall young woman, gently tattooed. She wore minuscule skirts over tights and layers of tank tops, and sometimes when she hunched her shoulders, as with so many tall girls who want to appear shorter, the top of a breast emerged at her neckline. Yet her designs were clean and cool.

"If this job comes through, we could do the most important work we'll ever do. More important than amusing rich white kids in the suburbs."

Becca fired back, "You'd prefer rich Saudi kids?"

Jo suppressed impatience. "Those kids' moms walk around with cloth over their faces. Even if we pried up the veil a little, we might make something happen. We could give the next generation ideas that change their lives."

"And you think the government would let us?"

Jo sat at her desk to signal the end of the conversation. "The government is run by people. We're dealing with people. Until they prove otherwise, I will give them what they say they want."

Becca slowly packed her messenger bag. "I think you're being naïve. I can't believe I just said that."

Jo laughed. "You have to trust me. Go home. We'll talk tomorrow."

"I'll do the work, you know."

Jo smiled through her fatigue to reassure the girl. "Good night."

As the door closed behind Becca, Jo unpacked her briefcase. She returned her passport to its accustomed place beside her checkbook and sat back to think. Becca, short fuse notwithstanding, might be right. It might be impossible to do the kind of work they loved to do in Saudi Arabia. But everybody on staff needed a paycheck, especially Diane, a single mom ferrying a handicapped child to endless doctors' appointments. She feared disappointing the staff, and herself. They had formed a cohesive team. When big jobs came and Jo brought in free-lancers, the regulars mentored them, and the job got done efficiently. She was proud of their esprit as well as their product.

Things had not always been as good. Two years back, in a flurry of bravura in response to praise for their work in Brazil, Jo had made a business move that, in retrospect, she shouldn't have. The error still resonated.

D-Three, as they referred to the company internally, had been collaborating with a print shop in Walnut Creek to make wayfinding graphics for a retail chain when the print shop's owner, a man with a temper, divorced his wife and planned to leave the Bay Area. Wanting to continue the project, a massive assignment from their first big commercial client, Jo offered to buy the owner out for a price that she considered a steal, and he agreed. She wanted to position D-Three to offer clients the whole package—design *and* production of all their graphic needs—at a reduced cost. Ev went along, saying he trusted her entrepreneurial instincts. She spent a month negotiating with the bank and lawyers, and then took over the reins at the print shop. They finished the commercial project on time and on budget, to Jo's great satisfaction. Then she turned her attention to the print shop itself. At first, she handled it without much strain, shuttling between Oakland and Walnut Creek to approve drafts and sign checks. Then the idea to expand the business entered her life in the person of Skinny Flynt, as the staff later came to call him.

Chris Flynn had credentials: two years at each of two name-brand New York advertising agencies. Approaching thirty, with long hair and a skeletal body, he'd come to the Bay Area because his mother, who now lived in El Cerrito, was ill, and he needed freelance work to tide him over. Jo liked his credentials and his energy; he'd either liven up the old-timers in the print shop or scare the stodgiest away, either of which would be good. She offered him a commission on any new jobs he might bring in. He got to work with purpose: he canvassed every likely business in five East Bay communities, with modest success. She offered him a base salary to supplement the commission.

Then he approached her with an idea.

"Look," he said, pointing to the list of people he had contacted, "these guys don't need printing, they need customers in their stores. They need marketing! You could do it for them. You've got it all, the graphics, the printing, the IT capacity. The only thing missing is analysis. And some software for fulfillment."

"You're suggesting I start a new business?"

"No. Modernize the one you have. No one else around here can offer anything close. These guys don't want to trek to San Francisco to meet with an underling at a big firm. And they don't trust folks on the peninsula. Opportunity is knocking."

"Surely there are marketers in Oakland."

"Yeah, but not with the graphics and business chops you have. I've seen what well-designed messaging can do. I'll help."

"I'll think about it."

She did, and she talked with Ev, who told her he didn't like Skinny Flynt, period. Annoyed at his refusal to open his mind, she called their lawyer, who could see no reason not to proceed. When Jo ran the numbers, the prospect looked iffy. But she wanted to proceed; she wanted to leap into the future, as forecast by Chris Flynn. So she offered him a generous share of any new accounts he could bring in and got busy studying marketing. She left Ev in charge of the design business.

The new venture seemed to blossom. She bought the necessary software and called in a consultant to train her and the staff to use it. She accompanied Flynn to sales meetings; they gave a good pitch, had a few nibbles. The nibbles turned into two small jobs they managed to fulfill, and then Chris reported a big fish on his line, a medical equipment manufacturer with sales subsidiaries across the country. Jo flew them to Pennsylvania to meet the manufacturer at its headquarters. Chris gave a brilliant pitch, and they left, excited and encouraged.

Over the next four months, it seemed the big fish played out the line, dragging Chris to sales meetings at all its branches, while Jo continued to trawl around the Bay. The print shop began to suck up all her time; she would return to the Oakland house in the evening to see Ev still behind the glass in his workshop. Most nights, she fell asleep before they could talk. If he missed her company, he didn't say.

Then Chris returned from the last of his sales trips and walked into her office, an unreadable expression on his face.

"They're going for it. Targeted marketing from the central office tailored to each site. A million-dollar account, for sure."

She jumped up from her chair to hug him, but he caught her arms and seated her.

"I don't know how to say this so I'll just say it. They want me to handle the account. In-house."

"What does that mean?" She felt herself flush.

"I'm leaving D-Three. I'm sorry it worked out this way, but it's too good to pass up."

"So you'll contract the work with us?"

"No. They want me to run the campaign in house. I've already done half the research."

"On my time." She wanted to slap him.

He backed away from her. "Listen, I tried. I've known the CEO's family for years, that's how I got my foot in the door in the first place. I tried to swing him your way. But he's made up his mind." He looked chagrinned. "You knew I planned to go back East eventually."

"All I know is you led me on. All those trips to the branches. You must have thought me a sucker."

"No, no. I honestly thought it would work out. I'm very sorry it didn't."

"Not sorry enough to refuse the job offer." She could not contain her anger, or the shame breaking through it. How foolish she had been to follow a callow man's lead. "If you have no other business to deliver, get out."

On the drive back to Oakland that evening, she squirmed behind the wheel, worried about Ev's reaction. She knew he wouldn't say "I told you so"—he didn't keep score—but he might criticize her for barging into a field she knew nothing about. And he would be right. He might accuse her of letting a fancy man get into her head. Yeah, but he didn't get into her bed. Ev would know that, wouldn't he? Contrite, she stopped at a supermarket close to home to pick up the makings of a meal. Over the pasta,

Ev took the news calmly, and she blessed him silently. He told her they needed her back in Oakland. The next day, at her desk in the office she discovered why.

In the nine months she'd been chasing modernity with Skinny Flynt, the design side of the business had floundered. Ev had taken on no new clients, because no one who'd sent a query had appealed to him. She had known he wouldn't concentrate on sales—nothing managed to hold his attention for long except his models, and Jo herself—but not a single new client? And he had fulfilled only half their contracts. Evidently, he'd been playing with new ideas in the shop while their crew idled. Two techs and the accountant had quit, and the books were a mess. She discovered they were out of cash, with two mortgages, a loan repayment, and payroll coming due. In a panic, Jo appealed to the bank and was told they'd advance funds if she would divest the print shop. So she made plans to sell it to the employees as quickly as possible.

At first, she'd been furious. Why hadn't Ev told her about the problems? When she'd checked the financial statements, the bottom line had seemed okay. Now she knew why: he hadn't bought materials or paid a full staff. For weeks she woke regularly at three in the morning to rehearse the litany of his errors and, truth be told, her own. She should never have left him in charge. He couldn't manage a picnic. She worried the design business might have been dealt a fatal blow. She could make peace with losing the print shop, but the damage to D-Three terrified her. Their livelihood, and their identity, hung in the balance. She began to question Ev's ability to function as a full partner. She spoke to him only when necessary; they stopped eating meals together. He retreated to his machines.

Over the next few months, thanks to Jo's dogged persistence, things slowly righted themselves. Jo paid the bills with the bank's cash, and they sold copies of Ev's old exhibits to a group in western Canada that wanted to open a museum in a hurry. The partial crew went back to work full-time. Business began to feel normal except for the giant loan hanging over Jo's head. Her parents' ineptitude had taught her to loathe compound interest. She swore to repay the loan in record time.

Then, one day, Jo's sister showed up saying she was thinking about moving to the Bay Area and did Jo have any advice? For as long as Jo could remember, Diane, her baby sister, had needed help, and Jo, the eldest sibling, had provided. Tuition, finding jobs, finding doctors for her nephew and paying them . . . With a sigh, Jo realized she would continue to provide. She offered Diane a part-time job, out of conscience rather than affection, and the fact that D-Three's books now needed keeping.

Diane and her teenaged son arrived two weeks later with a jumble of clothing, equipment, kitchen tools, and a slobbery dog. Jo reacted with disgust to Diane's mess, but Ev embraced it. He helped Diane and her special-needs boy find a cheap apartment, settle in, make order, and feel good about the move. He built a dog run out back behind the studio so Diane could bring her family to work without, he said, getting in Jo's hair. He invited her nephew into the studio and helped him finger the tools. Jo saw his attentions work wonders for the boy, and her resentment began to thaw. She admired the underlying tenderness that made Ev an inspired designer for children, and, she remembered, a good lover.

Over the next few weeks, life at the D-Three house got better: Diane's conscientious bookkeeping lifted one of Jo's burdens, and Ev emerged from the shop to talk whenever Jo wanted him. They landed a complex job: a kids' museum to be operated by an existing science museum without competing with the latter for the four- to eight-year-olds who might be comfortable in either place. Jo and Ev worked closely together for months, solving one problem after the next. Her love for him returned. As a bonus, the job finished in the black. As did the next one, and the next.

Then they were asked to submit qualifications for the Saudi project, a world away.

Jo rose from her desk and turned off the light. She hefted her purse, fattened by the checkered headgear she'd had Peter purchase for her nephew, and made her way to the stairs in the blue glow from the router. As she climbed, she felt determination descend on her shoulders. These good people who had waited to greet the boss deserved her fullest effort. D-Three had made such progress since the print shop snafu. She would not let things backslide. She would keep her eyes open and scope out the Saudi deal. This she knew how to do.

In the morning, Jo woke to the sound of muffled voices below. The clock displayed a red 9:48; evidently Ev had let her sleep in. She washed, dressed, and descended the stairs. There was Ev, standing in the middle of the office, whirling a loop of rope on a contraption that looked like an old-fashioned spinning wheel. The loop expanded and then snapped into a beak-like shape, as Carlos and Becca watched. She skirted them, heading to the kitchen to make a cup of tea. Ev called out, "*Hola*," and resumed spinning.

She stood at the sink to fill the tea kettle. Ranged along the windowsill in front of her were eight tiny terracotta pots containing Ev's experimental garden. When they'd arrived in Oakland, he'd decided to grow saguaro cactus from seed. Why? To nurture something tree-like, he'd said, that would still be portable in case of fire, and to remind himself that California lacks water. He'd germinated the glossy black seeds in a makeshift greenhouse, producing tiny, succulent, green gems with a miniature tuft of spines in the middle. After a year, the seedlings looked cactus-like, and he transplanted them into the pots. At five years, they were a whopping four inches tall. Ev admired them every time he watered. Jo shook her head; she hoped the spinning experiment would not last as long as the cactus experiment.

As she took a muffin from the fridge, she overheard them.

"I used a chain in Riyadh," Ev said, "but kids can't handle chain. The little ones poke their fingers into the links. I may need to abrade the rope to make it more flexible."

"What's Riyadh like?" Becca asked.

"Weird. In the men's' bathroom, there's a bank of hooks on the wall just behind the door. The toilets are squatters, so the men have to take off their robes to take a shit. Jo says there's hooks in the ladies' too. The Saudis have a dress problem."

Carlos grasped the rope and fingered it slowly. "Where's this idea come from, anyway?"

"Knots."

Calling out from the kitchen, Jo said, "Have you ever pulled a power cord or a hose and accidently made knots in it? Ev thinks that's how organic molecules evolved from the primordial soup. The next step is life."

"Heavy," Carlos said.

Diane burst through the front door, leading her son. "Sorry I'm late. Found out Joey's school was closed for maintenance when we got there." She sat the boy at her desk and tucked her bag beneath it. Joey shook his head side to side, got up and ran to Jo and hugged her. She'd taught him to play Chutes and Ladders once, at least a decade ago, and he'd had a thing for her ever since. Jo remembered the checkerboard head gear—Joey loved hats—and led him to her desk. She fished the headgear out of her purse and draped her nephew's head. Joey beamed. Holding his head with both hands, he let his mother take him back to her corner and settle him down again. Diane mouthed "thank you" to Jo. The two women joined the others standing around Ev, watching the rope spin.

"Is this for the Saudi job?" Diane asked.

Ev said, "It could be."

"The Saudis want to prepare toddlers for careers in renewable energy. Imagine *that*," Jo said.

Diane looked doubtful. "Do little kids understand the concept of energy?"

"No, too abstract," Ev said. "Got another idea. I'm going to the studio."

"If we're asked to bid, we'll think of something to satisfy them." Jo turned to Becca. "We're smarter than the competition."

"But don't you have to do what they want?" Diane said.

"Yes and no. Let's discuss this after lunch. I need to get to my email." Diane didn't understand business, Jo thought. Even Ev was savvier.

The staff dispersed. Jo made a cup of tea and took it to her desk. She powered up, and as Outlook populated, she glanced outside. The sky was a clear blue, and the eucalyptus leaves shimmered in the breeze. It was good to be home.


Jo had been seven when Diane was born, and her brothers had been four and three. There had been another baby who died that no one talked about. After Diane's birth, her mom went back to work full-time for her dad, and there were no more babies and little joy.

Before Diane was born, when Jo helped care for the boys, it first felt like a game. Mom would ask her to do something adult, and she'd manage to do it. She once overheard Mom tell an aunt who questioned the wisdom of entrusting babies to a five-year-old, "Joanna understands everything I say," and Jo swelled with pride. After Diane arrived, the family called the two girls "Baby Sister" and "Big Sister." In time, the nicknames morphed into "Baby" and "Sister," and Jo's duties steadily increased. The game stopped being fun because it never stopped. She changed diapers and fed bottles when Mom was on the phone or buried in paperwork. After the boys came home from school, she broke up their fights and portioned out sweets. She had the run of the kitchen because Mom knew she would keep it tidy. She learned to distract the boys with television so she could mop the floor. She learned to operate the washing machine and hang out the clothes. Diane toddled around behind her, clutching a doll.

Her parents praised Jo for mothering the kids, and for a while she was content with her role. A problem developed, though, as Diane grew. It seemed the rules changed: pretty, little Diane had privileges Jo had never had, and it didn't seem fair. Diane got presents, and frilly dresses like her friends', and she had no chores to speak of. It was as if their parents were too worn down by their work and the sheer size of the family to discipline yet another child. Jo's resentment built, but she didn't let it show. She escaped to school, hanging around her teachers after class. It was a small school in a small town, but it opened the door to a wider world, and Jo gladly walked through it. She went to high school in the next town over, took after-school jobs when the boys were older. Eventually she made it to Virginia Commonwealth University on her own nickel.

Senior year in college, when Jo called home at Thanksgiving, her mother had begged her to talk sense into Diane. Her mother said Diane had fallen in with a reckless bunch and was cutting school. Her mother sounded beside herself, so Jo went home for the weekend to put things right.

Diane, at fifteen, no longer looked like a pretty little thing. She was wide-hipped and buxom, with blonde hair teased high. She wore tight black jeans and bright lipstick. A cigarette lighter protruded from her back pocket. She slouched and spoke to her mother with as few words as possible. She seemed happy to see Jo, though, and followed her out into the backyard where, Jo expected, they could talk.

They brushed fallen leaves off a bench and sat side by side. Diane played with her hands, transferring her four rings one at a time from one finger to another. Jo wondered how to begin the conversation and stared at her own hands.

Diane said, "How come you're here? Don't you like college?"

"I like learning how to make a living. Different from Mom and Dad."

"Yeah, I'll say."

Jo decided to be straight with her. "What have you been up to? Mom's worried."

"Mom doesn't like my friends. She thinks they're a bad influence. She acts like they control me. They don't. I'm doing what I want to do."

"What do you want to do?"

"I want to have fun! I don't want to turn into Mom until I'm old." She pushed a loose strand of hair behind her ear. "Everything is gray and tired here. Mom and Dad, the house. It's no way to live. Not for me."

"Mom says you're cutting school."

"You remember Central High? I'm not missing much. I told Mom I'll graduate. I'll have the grades. She shouldn't bother you about it."

"What do you do when you cut?"

A soft smile spread across Diane's face. "Hang out. Listen to music. You know."

"Do you drink?"

"I don't like alcohol." She looked into Jo's eyes. "I like weed. Don't get ballistic on me, I only do weed."

"And what else do you do?" Jo began to think her mother's worry justified.

"Oh, whatever. Some of the guys are older. They have their options." She resumed transferring her rings. "I hate it here. I'm going to leave."

"Where will you go?" Jo thought Diane had it easy, too easy to understand the impact of leaving home.

"My friends will take care of me."

Jo forced herself to speak calmly. "That's not enough of a plan."

"You got out of here fast."

"I worked hard for it, and I went to a safe place."

"Well, I'm not as smart as you. I have to do it my way." She stood. "I'm getting cold. Can we go in now?"

Jo nodded and followed Diane inside. Diane was no dummy, but her parents had spoiled her. They were about to reap the rewards of their carelessness. After dinner, Jo took her mother aside to say she had no leverage over her sister, but she'd call to check up on Diane from time to time. They'd just have to hope for the best. It pained Jo to leave her sister behind in that dreary house in her present state of mind. But she had to finish the year at VCU to assure her own escape.

Diane graduated from high school and ran away the next day. Her boyfriend had urged her to, she told Jo much later, and she hadn't known how to say no. She did not communicate with the family for a year, and they did not ask the police to find her. Jo kept her concern about her sister in the background because her job demanded attention and there was nothing to do for a girl who didn't want to be found.

Diane showed up at her parents' home one evening, dirty, tired, and close-mouthed. She slept in for weeks, gradually regaining

SHEILA GRINELL ⟡ 69

color in her cheeks. One morning, out of the blue, she called Jo to ask for help finding a job. Jo told Diane to get an associate's degree so she'd be employable. Diane said she didn't have money. Jo offered to pay tuition—she was starting her own company at the time and could barely afford to—and Diane agreed. She enrolled in the nearest community college and began to study, according to their mother. But after eighteen months or so, she dropped out, pregnant. Jo's disappointment, when she heard the news, bordered on disgust. She kept sending money because her mother begged her to, but she gave up feeling she could influence Diane's future. Lord knows, she'd tried to teach Diane to be responsible all the years she'd been in charge of her. Evidently Diane hadn't learned.

When the baby was born, something was wrong; he didn't cry or wave his arms although he had ten fingers and toes. They had to go to Richmond for a diagnosis, and it took a while to figure out the chromosomal disorder—not an inherited disorder, something unique to him—that stunted his development. Jo wondered, pointlessly, if Diane had done drugs at the wrong time, but she said nothing. Diane cried herself to sleep at night, but she devoted herself to her son's care. She got a part-time job and bought a clunker of a car. As the baby grew, it became clear that she needed help dealing with him. Mom and Dad had no extra money and no extra strength, not with the business as bad as it was. The boys were off doing their thing. So Diane called Jo, who agreed to come home for a weekend to make a plan.

Diane picked Jo up at the train station. They embraced, and Jo took a good look at her sister. She looked . . . okay, hair in a ponytail, no makeup, sallow beneath her eyes, and restrained in demeanor. As Diane drove home, she talked only about her son's progress. She said she'd been taught how to do physical therapy for him. Twice a day for twenty minutes, and he loved it. A nurse's aide came once a week, from the State, and checked him out. She had found lots of advice online. There was so much to try, she felt things would work out if she could get some help. She stopped talking abruptly.

Jo asked, "Does Mom help?"

Diane glanced at Jo. "She takes him for a few hours at a time. She says she's too old for childcare. I'm not sure she ever liked it."

Jo had to agree. "So, what do you need?"

"I need to be in two places at the same time." She sighed. "I need to work, and I need to take care of Joey."

"Where's Joey's father?"

"He went back to Grundy, to his folks. He's messed up."

"Can't you get help from him?"

Diane sucked in her breath. "He needs help himself. He comes from coal mining people. They don't understand."

"What do you mean, 'coal mining people'?"

"They're poor and plain and traditional. They don't approve of me and the baby."

"Well, if they're traditional, don't they want him to take care of his kid?

"He has nothing to give right now. I can't ask him."

"But you can ask me." Resentment filled her chest. Evidently it was okay for Diane to screw a loser because her big sister would bail her out.

Diane looked straight ahead. "I'm sorry." She drove the rest of the way silently. Jo withheld comment, not trusting what her angry gut might prompt her to say.

Their parents waited on the sagging front porch, grim-faced, as if braced for a fight. Jo put her roller bag in the bedroom she and Diane had shared as children and followed the family into the boys' room, now devoted to Joey. Against the wall, a hospital bed with raised rails, cables leading to a monitor, a cart holding a jumble of braces, bottles, cotton balls, tongue depressors. In the center of the room, a padded playpen with a small figure lying inside. He was dressed in a blue-and-white sweat suit, and he lay still, looking peaceful. Diane lifted him in her arms and turned toward Jo. She picked up Joey's hand in hers and laid it against Jo's cheek. Diane said, "Here's Aunt Jo. She cares about you, too."

Jo felt a pang—a flash of love, then fear. Love for Diane, despite everything, and fear that Joey would never heal. Diane would wither, and they would all suffer. Jo cringed and recoiled.

Diane said, "It's okay. You won't hurt him. You can hold him."

"No, I'm clumsy with babies. Maybe later." She left the room shortly to calm herself.

After dinner, Jo held Joey in her lap as they sat making plans. She offered to help find specialists and additional caregivers, and to pay for them, provided Diane contributed and stayed clean. Diane looked relieved and tried to embrace her. Jo brushed her aside. In the morning, they parted well, and things stayed amicable for a while, until their mother called to tell Jo that Diane had been seeing the baby's father again, and who knew what they were up to. Jo called her sister immediately.

"Why are you seeing him? Is he going to support you? Or are you getting high?"

"He has no money. I want Joey to know his father. That's all."

"Mom says you've been seeing a lot of him. All for Joey?"

Diane sighed. "I need someone to talk to who's not Mom or my boss. I have no one else."

"That's totally stupid. You know he's a loser."

"Nothing bad is happening! I would never endanger Joey!" Her voice shrank. "I just need some comfort once in a while. He's my friend."

"What do you call 'comfort'?"

"Jo, please."

"Are you lying to me?"

"I never lie to you. Don't you know that?"

"I can't stomach it. If you keep seeing him, count me out." She hung up. She could taste her disappointment, like an acrid coating on the tongue, and she swore to butt out of Diane's life. Diane would never do right by her. Diane didn't care.

She did not completely abandon Diane, of course. After their father died, everyone treated Jo as "the man in the family." She continued to pay for Joey's treatments for several years but held herself aloof. Diane eventually got a degree and a decent job. Jo visited a few times to satisfy herself that Diane and Joey were safe, which was all she dared hope for. The sisters lost touch after a while, for a long while. Jo's resentment faded in the press of business. Then Diane showed up in Oakland with a gangly teenager who reasoned like a nine-year-old and adored his mom. And Jo gave her a job. A job she did to the best of her ability, bless her screwy little heart.

# PROPOSAL

7

You could always find good Italian food in Oakland. Immigrants from northern Italy had coalesced there around the turn of the twentieth century. In California's Mediterranean climate, they grew familiar crops and sold the produce. They established restaurants and delis, some of which still operated. After the 1906 earthquake, more Italians and many people of means came over from San Francisco, the latter settling in the foothills on the eastern edge of town. The city divided into "the flatlands," where ordinary workers and successive waves of immigrants lived, and "the hills," where the fortunate enjoyed fog-free views of the Bay. The D-Three house stood at the edge of the flats, at the base of the hills, and D-Three sometimes fraternized with gentry, sometimes with hoi polloi. Jo attended museum and gallery openings, while Ev collected olive oils in various colors and flavors, ranging the bottles on top of the kitchen cabinets. Most of the time, Jo and Ev stayed home, she running the business, he tinkering.

This morning, Jo came downstairs early to make a blow-up of the Saudi RFP that had arrived via email the day before, after a month of silence. It was a request for a proposal to define a children's museum in the capital that would later support satellites in the provinces. Everyone on staff had read it. The language was grandiose and formal and so unspecific that a bidder could answer with boiler plate and brags. Unwilling to vamp, Jo and Ev had discussed their options and finally decided last night to invent a scenario to show how D-Three thinks. Their proposal would constitute a model of their design process rather than a conventional bid. She was betting the Saudis would appreciate their integrity.

Last night, preparing for bed upstairs, Jo had fretted about the competition. She'd told Ev she expected Phil Owen to trot out the glamour, to flaunt the fact that he had taught in two European capitals and could arrange interviews with museum directors in London, Paris, and Istanbul. She'd wanted to counterpunch. Ev said it wasn't necessary because Owen hadn't talked to a kid in a decade and he wouldn't know what to say if he ran into one. Imitating Owen, he puffed up his cheeks and got in her face. He called her "young lady" and offered to shake her hand. Jo took his hand and bit it. Ev dropped the Owen face and chased her around the bedroom. He caught her and tossed her onto the bed. He covered her body with his, and they began to undress each other. They slid into lovemaking and afterwards into sleep. It sometimes happened that way, work segueing into love, although most of the time Jo tried to keep these parts of their lives separate.

To prepare for the staff meeting that would soon begin, Jo tacked the RPF blow-up onto the wall next to the white board and assembled a pile of colored markers. She underlined three sentences in blue, the ones she wanted the staff to keep foremost in mind as they ran through the design procedure. She felt in her element. She went to the kitchen and put on a pot of coffee and another pot of hot water and listened for Ev upstairs in the shower. In deference to their ancient water heater, he was supposed to turn on the washing machine, into which she'd loaded their soiled sheets, *after* the shower. And he was likely to forget. Not that he'd forget their pleasure.

Carlos was the first to arrive, carrying a platter of antipasto and two loaves of bread for the team to share for lunch. He said he figured they could use a little nourishment because you need to feed active brains. A squat, wide man, a second-generation Mexican–American who looked like a dock worker, Carlos had a light touch with a pencil. He illustrated D-Three's documents with unexpected whimsy. He'd been a construction laborer before attending tech school to learn computer-aided design, and he shared Ev's feel for materials and tools. He had a pretty, young wife, two daughters, and an older son he also loved to brag about. He was a family man, and D-Three was family.

Andy arrived next, cutting school to spend the morning with them. At the start of a project, Jo usually sent someone to photograph an established museum that could be considered comparable. Then they'd use the photos for inspiration. It was Andy's turn to travel, and, evidently, he wanted to, classes be damned. Whenever Jo prodded him to finish his degree, he complained the teachers and equipment were out of date. Jo urged him to finish anyway. He ignored her advice, and she exploited his availability, with only a twinge of guilt, because he was so good at coding. Looking sleepy, Andy slouched past her to the kitchen. He put two green teabags in his mug, filled it with hot water, and sat at his desk.

Becca arrived with an odd expression on her face. Diane entered at her heels, brandishing a bag of cookies. When the two women had deposited their belongings at their desks, Jo called out to Ev, still upstairs, and then walked over to the white board, red marker in hand. The staff pulled up chairs in front of her. Ev ambled in, with wet hair and the distracted look that signaled concentration on some internal matter. He pulled up a stool as Jo wrote a column of words at the left edge of the board: WHY, WHO, WHAT, HOW. She shot Diane a look that said "ready to take notes?" Diane's role in a brainstorm session.

"We're doing a scenario. The best topic, given Ev's current fascination, is tops. Tops as toys, as craft objects, as science lessons. Kids love playing with them. There could be a cultural connection. You know, the Sufi whirling dervishes? The proposal is due in two weeks." She wrote "playing with tops" on the board.

Becca said, "Why so soon? Normal clients would give us a month."

Jo let the comment pass. "Let's make some assumptions. Say we have a fifteen-hundred-square-foot storefront in a shopping mall in a hot, dry, city with no children's museums, maybe no museums at all, and only one small zoo nearby. I think we need to first show the community what a children's museum is like." She wrote "demonstrate" on the board next to WHY. "The client can't expect people to patronize something absolutely foreign to them."

Ev said, "We need to invite kids to spin things and let their brains spin."

Jo winked at him. She wrote "engagement."

Carlos said, "We'd better spin their bodies. Give them a gyroscope or two."

Jo wrote "excitement."

Andy said, "Why gyros? Riding a bicycle teaches you plenty about angular momentum." Andy had studied physics before dropping out of school the first time.

Carlos said, "Yeah, but it's not special."

"I'll call over to Cal and ask if there's research on kids and tops." Cal meant the educational psychology group at the university whom they consulted whenever they started work on a new topic. Jo insisted on grounding their imaginations in data.

Becca said, "Let's show a variety of tops from around the world."

Jo frowned. "Not sure they care about the rest of the world. The RFP states they don't want your typical collections. Let's move on for now."

Becca said, "So they don't want a museum."

"Most children's museums don't have collections." She picked up a green marker and poised it beside WHO. "Remember Spock's dictum, 'it's not about stuff, but for somebody.'"

Diane asked, "The baby doctor said that?"

"No, his son. One of the early thinkers about children's museums." She didn't want to waste time educating Diane. "In fifteen hundred square feet, we'll have room for only one age group. I suggest we do five- to seven-year-olds. Maybe their parents already think about careers. You remember they want us to prepare toddlers for careers in renewable energy." She pointed to one of the underlined sentences.

Ev said, "Be nice. But I agree. Older kids can do spinning games."

Jo wrote "five to seven" on the board.

Becca asked, "What about the parents?"

"They can spin the bottle." She paused; no one laughed. "The little ones will come with family. The five-to-sevens will come in school groups as well as with family. Boys one day, girls the next."

Becca asked, "They're segregated?"

"They go to separate schools."

Andy asked, "Is there an IT angle?"

"I don't know." She moved the green marker to point to WHAT. She addressed Andy. "I think you should go to that place in Calgary, the kids' museum inside a science center. Take pics and talk to them about apps. Maybe there's a career app already."

Ev said, "Don't push the career thing."

Jo flashed back to the last time Ev had ignored a client's directive. The client was a manufacturer of specialty equipment. For a geology convention, he had asked Ev to make weather maps for all the planets. Instead, Ev built a model of the Earth's atmosphere, complete with wind, in which you could fly a tiny kite and feel "convection" caused by a hidden heater. The client was incensed and refused to pay. At the time, she'd been angry at Ev for not listening. Later, she'd admired Ev's ingenuity; his piece would have garnered far more attention than a bunch of maps. The client had been too rigid, not sophisticated. Unlike the Saudis. Next to WHAT she wrote "experiment with tops" and, in parenthesis to denote secondary status, "careers." She turned to Becca.

"Can you find out what the kids study in school, ages five to seven? And anything you can about the teachers." She pointed to another underlined sentence. "The director wants us to connect to the curriculum. Her assistant might be helpful. I'll send you her email. Carlos, get everything about gyroscopes and anything that spins at other museums. And find out if anyone has a top-making activity. We'll reconvene Friday morning to discuss HOW." She tapped the marker on the word.

The staff dispersed, replacing chairs behind their desks and tables. Ev stretched off his stool and came to her.

"What's my assignment?" He tucked a lock of her hair behind her ear.

"Keep on inventing. I'm thinking we should go all the way. Ask them to set up a gallery somewhere so we can mount a demonstration and check out how families behave around the exhibits. How about you sketch what a demonstration might look like?"

"Okay." He pecked her cheek and walked away.

She went to her desk and opened her Contacts. She rolled up her mental sleeves as the screen populated. She always liked the early stage of design, when every idea exuded potential. Your excitement mounted as you added each new discovery to the collective concept. And then the team resolved the unruly accumulation into a singular, elegant notion that you would spend the next six months of your life amplifying and adjusting. This time, Jo felt an extra buzz: it might be possible to operate as a fifth column to infect mothers and daughters with disruptive ideas. She picked up her phone to call her contact at Cal.

Early the next morning, still dressing, Jo heard Becca enter the office and call up to her, asking to use her computer. Jo pulled on a shirt and went downstairs to find Becca seated at her desk.

"What's going on? Why do you need my computer?"

"Mugged on the bus. I preferred giving up my tablet to being knifed. I want to make notes on what I learned about Saudi schools while I remember." She held her hands over the keys, looked straight ahead at the screen."

"Look at me. Are you all right?"

"Of course not. Oakland's a cesspool. It never gets any better. I would move if not for this job."

"It has gotten better. The Black Panthers give tours now instead of rioting."

"Can I just get on with it? Working for the Saudis is bad enough."

Jo motioned Becca to move aside. She typed in her password, asked "Are you physically hurt?"

Becca shook her head and took the seat Jo vacated.

In the kitchen, Jo made tea and wondered how long it would take for Becca to come around. The girl puzzled her.

Rebekah Howard had first come to D-Three for a summer internship as an undergraduate. She'd found Jo's name at the alumni office at VCU, where she studied design, and made a cold call. She roomed with three students in Berkeley but spent most of her time at Jo's side, watching every move and following instructions to the letter. When she graduated, she asked for work and Jo hired her on the condition that she visit her parents at least once a year. Jo didn't want to be *in loco parentis,* even figuratively. Becca came from an old Yankee family that, apparently, had money enough. She was the middle child, a gangly girl with mousy blond hair. She'd had to learn to speak up for herself, first at the dinner table and then out in the world. She trooped around like an Amazon, but she was easily bruised. Jo didn't mind her sharp tongue, Ev liked her work, and you could trust her to follow through.

Jo put down her teacup and went to look over Becca's shoulder while she typed.

"Your buddy Myriam was helpful," Becca said.

Jo read:

- Schools are elementary, middle, secondary as in US—only a few kindergartens.
- Some student populations in big cities are large, but majority of schools are rural and tiny (less than 100 pupils) because each tribe requires its own school.
- Subject matter in elementary is Arabic language arts and Islamic religious studies, with only a smattering of math, science and art; other subjects don't start until 4th grade!!!
- Afterschool programs for older students (mostly boys) exist in some cities.
- There are two types of teachers: older, experienced ones who focus on classroom management; younger ones trained in progressive methods but lacking materials. They do not get along.
- Transpor. . . .

Jo interrupted, "They don't make our job easy, do they? I have no idea how we can connect to that curriculum."

"According to Myriam, that's not a problem because the teachers know how to relate to the modern world. She says the real problem is transportation. Poor women in the countryside don't have access. Even where there are buses, the more conservative parents won't let their girls ride for afterschool activities."

"Then we'd better concentrate on school groups."

"Didn't you say you wanted to reach the unreachable? You're compromising already."

"Don't be silly. Anything we could do would be a plus."

"Or it could be so compromised it reinforces the orthodoxy. It could be window dressing to make the patriarchs look progressive while they hang onto control. There's danger here!"

"Do you know something I don't know, or are you objecting on principle?"

"Just look at the RFP! *Support the national STEM initiative and the ten-year economic plan.* We're talking toddlers!"

"This is a government project. It's bureaucratic language."

"Ev doesn't like it." Becca grimaced. "Sometimes I can't tell if you're a Pollyanna, or you just blinker yourself, like the way you live in Oakland but you really don't see it. And that whole business with Skinny Flynt."

"You're way out of line." Even now, Jo flushed with shame. "So how would you handle it, with your superior principles?"

Becca looked surprised. "I'm not being superior. I'm trying to psych out the deal. . . ."

"Finish up. I need my computer before the meeting." She turned away to hide her pique. Ideology was a waste of time. People should quit bellyaching and get to work. Or get out of the way. Politics had no place in business.

She'd stubbed her political toe in those early days in Atlanta. A casual "girl-to-girl" talk about contraception with the wife of a museum trustee had led to her losing a job because her views were "insufficiently balanced." She'd sworn off airing her views then—better to be silent than hungry—and managed to keep her nose clean. She told only Ev what she truly believed. She took a defensive posture that no reasonable person could call hypocrisy. She felt herself to be incorruptible.

Noise at the front door. Carlos's and Ev's voices blended in the hallway. Soon the staff meeting would begin. She went to the white board and erased yesterday's notes. She pulled the cap off a green marker; the familiar acid smell comforted her as she wrote the date at the top of the board.

That evening, spinning scenario finally outlined to her satisfaction, Jo prepared for bed. Ev had not yet come upstairs. Still in his studio doodling pinwheels and windmills. D-Three had had a productive brainstorm, and if they suspended work on their other jobs, they had enough time to flesh out the outline before the proposal came due. She felt good about it. As she loosened her clothes, Becca's challenge emerged in her mind, disturbing her, not because Becca had mocked her—no, she could count on the girl's good will in the long run, but what if Becca were onto something? With some clients, you ran the risk of their turning on you six months down the line, or a year, or even two years into the work. They became afraid to offend some segment of the public, or afraid to spend enough money to finish the job properly. She didn't expect cowardice from this client, and she didn't expect them to run out of money. But should she anticipate being manipulated for some ulterior purpose?

She heard a scratching sound, Ev strumming his fingers on the bedroom door. Jo thought his courtesy unnecessary—it's okay to enter your own bedroom unannounced, she had said time and again—but he persisted. She told him to come in. He sat at the foot of the bed and untied his sneakers. She sat beside him.

"Becca and I quarreled this morning. She said I'm being bamboozled by the Saudis. The project could be political cover. Do you think she has a point?"

Ev shrugged and took off his socks.

"She implied you agree with her."

He stood and pulled his T-shirt over his head. "There's no way to know."

Jo raised her voice. "She's so absolute. So exacting."

He sat to remove his jeans. "Becca never got enough hugs."

"What does that have to do with anything?"

"She's a good kid." He headed for the bathroom. Over the noise of water filling the sink he called, "I need to go to the hardware store first thing tomorrow."

"Take your time. It's Saturday." He would, she knew, have nothing more to say.

She lay back on the bed, hearing the medicine cabinet door squeak as Ev followed his bedtime routine. She resented his nonchalance, or what seemed like nonchalance but was actually his reluctance to continue talking. He refused to engage with political or strategic questions. Sometimes she thought him incapable of reasoning like an adult. But the flip side, his ability to sense the world as it appeared to children, earned their living. For a nanosecond, she speculated about what if they hadn't married. She'd be running a different kind of business, for sure. Would she be happier? An unproductive line of thought.

She roused herself and continued undressing. Becca's doubt had wormed into her head. She hoped sleep would defuse it.

That night she dreamed about Chris Flynn, who morphed into Robbo, her first lover, who said something oblique and walked away from her, as he had in real life. She'd thought she'd put the affair to rest, but there it was poking up from below. She felt uneasy, and, somehow, ashamed at still caring about the loss of Robbo.

It had happened in college. Jo's parents had respected hard work, and she did, too. In high school, she added McDonald's and then KFC to her daily load of childcare and homework. Pretty girls got distracted by boys and clothes; Jo saved pennies and did well enough to pay in-state tuition at VCU.

College widened her world. She focused on her classes and job, but other peoples' experiences intruded. She discovered there had been holes in her upbringing; she kept her own counsel. When Sally Ride flew into space, she cheered for spunky, hard-working women everywhere. When *TIME* magazine nominated "the computer" as man of the year, she thought "this is the way forward." But she soon discovered she lacked aptitude for computers. She found a way to hitch her star to technology anyway by majoring in design. It turned out she was good at using a computer to graph information. She was also good at finishing projects on time.

Jo did not attack her social life with the same vigor. She didn't learn how to drink or flirt. She didn't play sports. She had no money for clothes. She got around campus on an old bicycle with a rusty basket, unlike her roommate's shiny car. She felt like an outsider, nose pressed to the ballroom window, bewildered by the dance. When dorm-mates invited her to join them, she claimed no interest. They mistook her standoffishness for disdain. She knew better. Junior year she challenged herself to get in the game. She decided to find a decent guy and sleep with him, like the other girls on her floor. She began to daydream about which of the men in her classes might accept an invitation to coffee. She had almost settled on a poetic-looking guy in a literature class when one of her teachers intervened. It seemed the design department was throwing a party for alumni who would be in town for a conference. The teacher suggested she come to scope out working in the field. She agreed.

The night of the party, without consciously planning to, she dressed in her only filmy blouse, leaving it partially unbuttoned. At the design chairman's home she asked for a glass of wine and sipped slowly, surveying the crowded room. After a beat, the department secretary, a myopic young woman who leaned into your shoulder when talking to you, came over. She whispered, "Do you see who's here?"

Jo shrugged.

"The boss is gloating. His favorite alum brought a fancy architect. This guy's hot. In all the magazines. Named Roberto something-or-other but he's American. I'm going to talk to him." She swayed a little and reached for the back of a chair. Jo bent to help her sit. As she straightened, a short, slender man with long, graying hair pushed back behind his ears approached. The secretary giggled.

"Do you need assistance?" he said looking into Jo's eyes. "Please call me Robbo . . ." nodding as if to apologize, ". . . silly nickname from childhood."

"I think she'll be okay. We don't usually party here."

Robbo raised his eyebrows. "How can they teach design without partying? You are missing something."

"Drinking?"

Robbo laughed. "No, celebration. Every culture celebrates in its own way. A designer must make room for it." He crossed his arms in front of his chest. "Would you come to dinner with me in, say, half an hour? I haven't eaten all day."

A hundred thoughts raced through her head. The secretary gave a little moan, and that clinched it. "Sure," she said, "I haven't eaten either."

She got tipsy at dinner. Robbo encouraged her to talk. She confessed to feeling isolated at VCU. He told her he had always felt so. She asked about his work. He said it kept him humble, made him realize he couldn't do anywhere near as good a job as the Designer of the Universe. When she blanched, he laughed, saying he was paraphrasing Buckminster Fuller. They began to speculate about uses for geodesic domes, each more far-fetched than the last. After the meal, he put her in a cab to go home—he said he had another appointment that evening, otherwise he would have accompanied her—and she wanted to cry. Her head turned so hard it spun for days.

He called her mid-week. It seemed he would be spending the next three months in Richmond, working on a commission. He invited her to party with him. She had never expected an elegant man to notice her, let alone like her. He told her he could show her love she'd never dreamed of. She wanted that dream. She spent a week high on the thought of him, juicy as never before. They met for coffee and drinks. He said he found her refreshing, so talented and attractive yet not the slightest bit spoiled. She found him intoxicating beyond words.

So she offered herself to Robbo, and he took her. After the initial embarrassment, she luxuriated in his attentions. She wanted to practice love Robbo's way. Several nights a week, she waited for him outside his rented apartment. She spent the night with him, happy and grateful for her good fortune. A man of the world admired her, a man whom the world admired. A grown man, who looked past the superficial and found her attractive. A man who valued her person, plain and simple. A man who could teach her so much.

Then Robbo finished his commission and prepared to leave Richmond. She begged to keep seeing him. He appeared disinterested. She asked for his home address. He said his wife would not wish to meet her. He had never mentioned a wife. And she had not thought to ask. She retreated, crushed.

She did not speak or write to him. For weeks after his departure she flagellated herself for having been so naïve. She reevaluated every flattering thing he had said. Exploitation, all of it. She'd been like a puppy; he must have been amused by her fawning. She suffered. She lost sleep and walked around pale and purposeless. She stopped riding her bike, she skipped class, talked to no one. Her social confidence, so recently won, bled away.

Toward the end of the semester, she screwed up her courage to go to the department office to look for a summer job. The secretary squinted at her, then stood up from her desk.

"You can use my computer. It's open to the job file."

Jo sat in the secretary's chair. The woman leaned against her shoulder. "You're looking a little better, I'm glad to say. We were all worried."

"What about?"

"Well, everyone knew Robbo's reputation. The boss told us. We hoped you wouldn't feel like a victim, although maybe you were."

Jo froze. She hated the thought that the design department had been talking about her. She hated their pity. She would not let this nasty little bitch wound her further. "Tell everyone I enjoyed Robbo's company. And he enjoyed mine." She hit delete and left the office.

In fact, the woman had done her a favor. Anger turned her focus outward. She vowed to finish her degree without any help from the design department, and over senior year, she kept the vow. She ignored her colleagues and got dinged for not participating in departmental activities, but she didn't care. She buckled down and figured out how to score well, and by graduation, the narrative in her head had changed from victim to victor. She called herself an independent thinker. The department had graded her "competent"; she had far more to offer than mere competence. Filled with ambition, she couldn't wait to prove it.

At her first job in the big Atlanta firm, she befriended the two other unconventional associates, a gay man and a grandmother returning to the workforce. They ate cheap meals together, and Jo read the books they recommended: Studs Terkel, Eric Hoffer, and other champions of the common man. She bought a better bike and committed to riding regularly. She didn't date, and when she got promoted, her ambition grew arms and legs: she needed more than material success, she wanted moral victory. When she left the firm to go out on her own, she determined to accept only projects that contributed to the public good, however loosely defined. She vowed never to give a client or colleague cause to say an ungenerous word about her. After she started D-Three, she swore to run the design office as democratically as possible, given the need for excellence. She would deal transparently with competitors and vendors. Nothing would ever blemish D-Three's reputation.

Over the years, Jo stuck to her guns. She preferred working on children's museums, she would say, because they offered the most potential to change lives. She accumulated data that proved museums helped children make significant academic gains. As the business grew and prospered, she became more and more convinced of the rightness of her approach. She did not let missteps shake her; she made a point to learn from them. The Skinny Flynt episode, for one, taught her to stick to basics. And Ev always seemed to approve, which mattered more than she would say.

But sometimes in an idle moment, she wondered if, deep down, there was rot at the core of her ambition. It had been born out of defiance, not out of passion. Truth be told, she cared more about proving herself valued in the design world than about inventing the next Helvetica. She'd always earned respect for her capacity to work hard, from girlhood on. It was her greatest strength. Ev told her the quality of work counted more than the quantity, but he didn't convince her. She wanted to prove to the world that she had mastered her discipline. She wanted to solve the most complex, visible problem possible. She wanted to create the Children's Museum of Riyadh.

Jo looked at the clock. 7:42. Ev had already risen. She got up and made the bed, the dream reverberating in her head. She dressed slowly as scenes emerged from the ether, and went downstairs to put on the kettle. Clearly, the argument with Becca had stimulated the dream. But why had it resurrected Robbo? Was there a connection, or was she simply upset at Becca? Nothing in this life was simple. She opened the fridge. Nothing looked good. She closed the door.

The kettle chirped. She turned off the burner and poured water into the waiting teapot. She set the microwave timer for five minutes and walked to the window. Behind the glass wall of the studio, Ev stood with his back to her, leaning over a workbench. She left the kitchen and slipped quietly into the studio—quiet because you never knew which dangerous tool might be in his hand—and watched him cut a thin piece of plastic with tin snips. She wondered how to begin talking about her mood. Ev didn't set stock in dreams.

The studio contained two workbenches back-to-back in the middle of the room. Machines lined the solid walls: a drill press, a lathe, a band saw, a welder. A cabinet of little drawers held screws, nails and other small parts whose names and functions Jo didn't care to know. A table saw stood in one corner, and lumber and sheets of plastic were stacked in another. Hammers and screwdrivers and wrenches lay around as if dropped at the end of a task. It looked messy to her, but Ev's mind worked differently.

He became aware of her and looked up. "Morning."

"You're starting early."

He rummaged on top of the workbench and picked up a loop of string with a button in the center. Turning to face her, he held one end of the string in each hand and pulled. The button spun, making a humming sound. "I thought we could get kids to play tunes with these, but it's too hard to restring the button."

Jo stepped closer. Ev's explanation would come.

"Look," he said, pointing to the notebook that lay open on the workbench. Spread across two pages was a drawing of a pole with a circular platform at the top and a crank attached at the bottom. On top of the platform a dog figure faced a cat figure. The contraption resembled a toy carousel splayed vertically.

Ev said, "Kid power spins the platform and the dog chases the cat." He turned the page, pointing to a diagram. "I'll put a cam under the dog."

Jo didn't understand the linkage. No matter. "What if a kid roots for the cat?"

"The dog never gets close enough to attack." He turned the page back to the drawing. "Kids can try different cranks with different gear ratios."

Jo visualized a five-year-old turning the crank. They'd have to find a way to protect other kids from getting their fingers pinched by the mechanism. Ev would get there soon enough.

"In West Virginia, people put whirligigs like this on weathervanes, and the wind spins them. I like the idea of spinning in the wind. Maybe we can use wind made from kid power." He raised one hand to the back of his head. "Got to figure it out. Could be too inefficient."

"Are you cutting out weathervane blades?"

Ev smiled. "You got it, wife." He reached out to touch her cheek. "I need help with woodworking. Know anyone local?"

"Couldn't Carlos do it?"

"I want a skilled craftsman. This should be folk art."

"You can do it."

"If I had the time."

She knew better than to challenge his judgment. "I'll look for someone. Do you want breakfast?"

He shook his head and picked up the tin snips.

She returned to the kitchen, unable to interfere with his pleasure. For Ev, there was no straight line to solving a design problem. She'd just have to watch and wait. She silenced the bleeping timer and rummaged in the refrigerator for a loaf of bread. She put a slice in the toaster, and as she watched its wires glow red, she thought about Ev's whirligig. In the end, it would be captivating, she was certain. Ev's work always lifted her up.

Her phone buzzed: Becca. So early on a Saturday? She swiped the phone.

"I hope I didn't wake you."

"Not at all. Is there a problem?"

"I'm the problem. I'm sorry that I mouthed off to you yesterday. I didn't mean to be insulting."

"I'm not insulted. But I am curious. What makes you so suspicious? We've dealt with bureaucrats before."

There was a pause, as if Becca were fighting for composure. "These people are different. Every time I see a woman wrapped up like that I cringe."

"The men's outfits are tough to wear, too. It doesn't make them liars. What's eating you?"

"It kills me to think we could be helping an oppressive regime."

"What about helping an oppressive regime do right by kids?"

"I don't want to fight, Jo."

"Neither do I. You let me worry about consequences. Suspend judgment until we get the facts, okay?"

"I will try."

"Thanks for the call."

Jo cut the connection. She felt pretty sure that Becca wouldn't be able to contain her disgust however much she wanted peace. Becca was short on tolerance. Jo would continue to exude calm. That's what you did for your young staff, whether or not you felt calm.

She poured a cup of now strong tea, took her toast to her desk. As she waited for the computer to power up, the dream flashed back into her head. With a start, she realized it wasn't Becca's comment that had conjured Robbo, it was the entire Saudi affair. She wanted the job—no, she craved the job—because it would be a culmination, recognition for all her years of sacrifice and struggle. And she needed to pay off the bank loan. Very soon.

What if they didn't get it? Her heart beat harder. She refused to pursue the thought.

Two weeks after the scenario/proposal had been delivered, word came that D-Three was wanted in Dubai. After having read both finalists' submissions, the Saudi review committee had decided to hold face-to-face meetings with the contenders, which could happen more quickly in the United Arab Emirates. Once again, no travel money accompanied the summons, so Jo swallowed hard and bought tickets for herself, Ev, and worth-every-extra-penny Peter to come from Cairo. Jo was pumped to go, like an athlete before a big meet. Not so Ev. He said he'd already done his bit in giving the committee a fine design to review. But he would follow her lead.

They arrived in Dubai the day before the scheduled morning interview. Peter met them at their hotel looking casual in jeans. As they registered, Peter told them he had organized an excursion that evening. He said his man on the ground had obtained tickets to tour the Burj Khalifa, the tallest building in the world. They would have to pay his guy a small premium for the hot commodity, and it would be polite to invite him to join them at dinner afterwards. Jo shrugged; she wanted to explore Dubai, where she could walk around freely in Western clothes, on her own, but Peter had already made decisions for them. As arrogant as the client. Too bad she needed him to interpret the language, and the Arab mind.

Peter's man, in thawb and white headdress, met them in the lobby fifteen minutes later, and Peter bundled them into the man's car. The man drove expertly through crowded streets onto a modern urban boulevard. He parked at a plaza with an upscale shopping mall on one side and an artificial lake on the other. In the lake, a long rank of water jets sprayed high to music, and above the mall you could sense more than see something looming overhead. The four of them entered the mall's air-conditioned, metallic lobby and joined a group of tourists being ushered toward an elevator. The driver waved to Peter and stepped out of the line. Peter followed Jo and Ev into the crowded elevator, which zoomed with eardrum-compressing speed to level 125. They exited into a glass-walled observation deck and a spectacular view of Dubai beginning to twinkle in the twilight. You could walk 360 degrees around the tower core and, in places, step outside the glass onto a patio in the warm evening air. Jo floated from one perspective to another while Ev investigated the armature supporting the deck's glass skin. Jo could see an avenue of garish skyscrapers in one direction, a flat, sandy landscape in another, and on all sides the gangly booms of construction cranes, the agents of Dubai's bizarre ambitions—where else would you find an artificial island shaped like a palm tree, made of sand and rocks dredged from the bottom of the sea?

Peter watched them with a grim expression on his face. Jo wondered if he feared heights. When they had completed a full circuit of the observation deck, he herded them into a long corridor that wound downward. Along the corridor's inner wall, graphic panels featured images of the construction of the tower, highlighting the faces of the people from 196 countries who had participated. You pushed a button to hear the recorded words of architects and carpenters, men and women in various dress, saying they were proud and humbled by their contribution to the grand structure. The faces were appealing and the graphics elegant, some resembling Islamic calligraphy. Jo was enchanted by the sheer humanity of it, the deliberate melding of Middle Eastern and Western practice and technology. Perhaps her potential client was also capable of such synthesis.

Peter's man awaited them in a restaurant near the base of the elevator. He spoke no English. The four of them took a table and ordered from an international menu. After the drinks came, Peter raised his glass.

"To success! Tell me, did you enjoy yourselves? Yusef did well, no?"

Jo said, "Yes. Is Yusef going to accompany us tomorrow?"

"Just tonight. He is Qatari. A friend from many years. Tomorrow I will be your guide. Do you see the fountains? They are beautiful at night with so many lights. Of course they are not made in Dubai. Dubai can only buy. From the Chinese."

Ev said, "Nope. Las Vegas. What you call the fountain was designed by a US firm."

Jo wondered how he knew that. She couldn't predict what he did or did not pay attention to. A few design magazines came to the office, but she rarely saw him reading.

Peter said, "The design, yes. But the Chinese can build it cheaper than the Americans. Let us not concern ourselves with manufacture. Not until after you win the contract." He sipped his juice.

Was there a message in that comment? Peter's motives eluded her. She said, "I assume you read the proposal. Any questions?"

"It is very clear and very good. Ah, here comes our food."

Over dinner Peter laid out his strategy for the interview, recommending that Jo and Ev alternate speaking. Ev should walk the committee through the scenario, he said, and Jo should discuss the business side of the design process. Silently, she agreed with him. He had their number, all right. She hoped he had the Saudis' as well. She asked about etiquette. He told her anything goes in Dubai. No one said another word about the Burj Khalifa or the Qatari's presence.

Back at the hotel, Peter and his friend disappeared into a hallway, and Jo and Ev went upstairs for the night. They unpacked and plugged in chargers. Jo wanted to rehearse again—their runthrough on the plane had been fitful—but Ev turned on the TV, flipping through channels, and she knew she'd lost his attention for the next little while. She made Keurig tea and looked out over the city. There was the Burj Khalifa shining in the distance with a thousand lights, a graceful, tiered spire, each tier more slender than the one below, anchored somehow in the sand. An elegant achievement, spiraling upward from the commerce at its base. It heartened her, proof that inspired design can raise the human spirit regardless of point of origin.

They sat in the lobby waiting for a limo. Jo had dismissed Peter after the abortive interview. He'd been just as stunned at the outcome as she and even more useless, fawning to the committee instead of confronting them. Jo had been royally pissed. Ev had silently packed up their things.

The interview had begun promptly, the same faces as before around a table, the same man in charge, only this time he had shaken Jo's hand. She had looked for a speakerphone. Seeing none, a chill had passed through her; she didn't know what the director's absence meant, and she didn't dare ask. After they had settled in, Ev began to walk the committee through the scenario, explaining the size and configuration of the demonstration displays, what family visitors would do, and how the team would collect data on people's reactions. Ev spoke with guileless charm, as always, and Jo thought surely the committee would respond accordingly. The chairman cut him off mid-sentence.

"Thank you, Doctor Everett. We understand your proposal. I want to ask about something your competitor has presented."

Ev looked at Jo. Jo looked at Peter, who raised an eyebrow in an otherwise expressionless face.

The chairman continued, "Owen Associates has proposed that before we proceed, we should do market research and develop a strategic plan. Responsible product development proceeds in such a manner in many industries. Doctor Everett, would you agree?"

A second chill passed through her. She interrupted Ev, "Yes, certainly. But you can't do market research without first showing people the product. People in Riyadh know very little about children's museums, so you can't expect to get good information from them. That's why we have proposed mounting a provisional display, so families can experience a sample of the product. And then you'll know what marketing questions to ask."

"Precisely. We want to create a sample of the product, as you put it. We want you to deliver the demonstration you have described for one hundred thousand dollars, and Owen Associates will perform the market research and produce a strategic plan. You will subcontract with them." The chairman leaned back, smiling, hands on his belly.

The thought of working under Owen appalled her. She backpedaled. "I'm delighted to hear that you want to do a demonstration. We'll have to revise our proposal to come in under a hundred grand. Perhaps it would be best for us to work directly for you?"

"But we want synergy, European analysis with American know-how. Our children deserve the best the world has to offer. We have made a commitment to Owen Associates. Please negotiate with them." He paused. "The commitment is for planning only. We want to see the results before we contract for the entire project. Think of this as a feasibility exercise. On all sides."

Peter said, "That is wise."

The chairman raised his hand to signal that the subject was closed. Peter stood, and D-Three followed. They shook hands, Peter glad-handing the committee, Jo desperate behind her smile, and left the room. In the taxi, Peter congratulated them on getting a piece of the pie. He said it was most important to get your foot in the door because riches will follow. Jo told him his services were no longer necessary.

Now Jo and Ev sat opposite each other in the chilly lobby waiting for a limo to the airport. She felt tired and disheartened. She glanced at Ev. His face had a faraway look that meant no use talking to him now. She brooded about Phil Owen. Some of their colleagues considered him a brilliant maverick; she considered him a self-serving prick, exploiting his Oxbridge accent and museum people's credulity. Years ago, when they'd first met, he'd asked questions about one of D-Three's works in progress, a seashore environment with wave table, tide calculator, and touch tank for anemones and crabs. She'd been proud of the compact "beach" they'd designed and flattered by his attention. He'd asked for the script, and despite a flash of doubt—colleagues didn't ask for scripts mid-project—she'd given it to him. A month later, he published a critique in an academic journal decrying designs that replace authentic objects with models and videos. He used their "beach" as an illustration, tearing it apart. D-Three's client did not see the article, but their colleagues did after Owen cross-posted it widely. Jo was forced to defend D-Three's work at conference after conference for years. She got good at it, developing a rationale backed by data from studies various researchers had performed, but that didn't take away the sting.

She bumped Ev's elbow to command his attention. "I'm sorry we came. Back home no one would change the scope of the RFP and force one competitor to subcontract with another. We were warned these people don't respect contracts."

"No one is forcing you to do anything you don't want to do."

"They want to steal our stuff for a hundred grand. It's a bait and switch."

"Maybe it's an opportunity. Build a couple of cool displays. Show them how to do it right."

"We wouldn't make back our investment. The boss wasn't even there."

He leaned forward and lowered his voice. "Hey, this could be to our advantage. Let Owen take the risk. He gets the bond, he manages the accounting and reporting."

"Owen is an asshole but he's no idiot. What makes you think he wouldn't pass any liability on to us?"

"He could try." He leaned back, making a tent with his fingertips, a sign that he'd said his piece.

The call to prayer issued from a loudspeaker somewhere outside, penetrating the marble lobby. A hush passed through the guests clustered there. Several men in thawbs appeared to excuse themselves to their interlocutors and then step behind a partition at the rear. The reception staff, men in hotel uniform, lowered their eyes but continued punching their computer screens. Must be foreigners, Jo thought. Then she chided herself for being presumptuous, like Peter. At the thought of him, despair at the amount of money they had spent on this trip welled up.

"If they knew what they wanted, why lure us here in the first place? They could have held *this* meeting by Skype."

Ev folded his hands. "Maybe Owen talked them into it yesterday. He's good at pitching his shtick. Maybe they didn't know what they wanted until yesterday."

"Do you really believe an Aramco executive doesn't know what he wants? They're immoral."

"They're different." Ev's voice was gentle, almost pleading.

"What do you know about them that I don't know?"

"I don't know anything about them. But I know you. You'll make it work."

One of the receptionists approached them, bowed to Jo. "Ms. Dunhill? Your driver called to say he'll be here at the end of prayers, in about a half hour. Is that satisfactory? I can look for a taxi if you are pressed for time."

"No, thanks. I'd rather sit here than at the airport. Ev?"

He nodded. The receptionist bowed and withdrew. Jo turned back to her husband. "Are you saying you want to proceed on their terms?"

"I think you'd regret it if we didn't."

"You want to play around in the studio. I'm the one who has to stomach Owen."

Ev reached over to touch her knee. "You're more than a match for him."

"Why have you changed your mind? You didn't want to make this trip, and you've been lukewarm all along."

"Because we can make it right. I like a challenge. And you want this one."

"But under Owen's thumb?"

"We'll solve the Saudis' problems. They need us."

"So do our other clients."

"They need us more."

"But they don't play fair."

"Who gets to define fair?"

"Not Phil Owen. I refuse to let him control us."

"He can't."

"So you say." She pulled out her phone, pretending to check email while she corralled her careening thoughts.

Ev might be unpredictable, but he had her back. They were connected underground, roots twining and supporting each other. She'd learned to stop and listen when her feelings hit a wall, to dig out the message lurking in his few words. He didn't have answers, but he sometimes pointed to a truth she'd missed. She trusted him as she trusted no other. Even when his interests conflicted with hers, he took her side, like the New Year's Eve she'd drunk too much and wanted to screw without her diaphragm. He'd said he didn't want to be a father by accident and slowed her down.

Did he have a point? Might an administrative layer between D-Three and the capricious Saudis help? If she could prevent Owen from interfering with their creative process . . . and the client had already sort of blessed their ideas. She would sleep on it. Ev had softened her spine.

Ev bent closer to her. "I'm glad to lose Peter."

She looked up from her phone.

"Last night when you went to the bathroom he invited me to go with him and his buddy. He said you can get anything in Dubai much cheaper than in Saudi."

"What did he mean?"

"I didn't want to find out."

The receptionist approached, saying that the driver had skipped his prayers to accommodate them and would be outside in five minutes. They gathered their belongings, Ev hefting the computer and roller bag, Jo folding their jackets over one arm and grasping her briefcase with her free hand. Inside the briefcase were fifteen full-color pamphlets beautifully illustrated by Carlos, designed and bound by Becca. Jo had been too distracted by the turn of events to distribute them to the committee. Feeling their weight, she asked the concierge to overnight them to Myriam, as a token of appreciation and so the director could see what a quarter million would buy, not the hundred grand they'd been allotted. This trip had not turned out as expected, and Peter had been worse than useless. Still, she hoped to salvage something that could launch them into the big time.

Jo rolled over in bed and glanced at the clock. They'd reached home late the night before, and her jetlagged brain didn't click into gear. Ev was not beside her. A package lay in the depression he had left in his pillow. He did this now and then, sent her doodads of his invention instead of love letters. She picked up the package and unpeeled the brown paper wrapping. It was a little cardboard box with a peephole. Looking in, she saw her own eye reflected again and again, seemingly to infinity. On the left, she saw the word "before" and on the right, "after." She lowered the box, puzzled but pleased. Ev would explain later. She could never anticipate his thinking, although she thought she understood how it had evolved. Despite his reticence, over the years she had managed to piece together the story of how he wound up on her doorstep one day, carrying a bag of tools.

The commune Ev's parents had founded on an old farm in a West Virginia holler had attracted a few dozen people who wanted to live off the grid. The communards had brought tools and supplies with them to turn a barn into a dormitory and shower. At first they shared everything, including sexual partners. That made everyone angry for one reason or another, so they settled into monogamy and soon sprouted a handful of kids. They grew vegetables and raised chickens, some of which they bartered for booze and books and other necessities.

Ev's mother taught the kids the basics. She showed no favoritism, although Ev could have used extra help when his eyes couldn't seem to locate the beginning of the next sentence in the first-grade reader. His mother said he didn't try hard enough. So he tried harder, and still, when she taught him arithmetic, his numbers never stacked in neat columns on the page. He stopped listening to his mother's lectures, retreated into the reaches of his mind. He was chided for daydreaming. His mother didn't realize he had no other choice. He confessed to Jo that he had always felt different from the others and kept to himself most of the time. He played no children's games.

Some of the communards gave occasional lessons in whatever occupied their imaginations. A sober man named Dizzy had brought a chest of hand-made carpenter tools with him, and he showed Ev how to saw and plane and finish surfaces. Dizzy let Ev handle his tools because the kid was careful and respectful of what Dizzy called their spirits, and Ev spent long afternoons puttering in Dizzy's corner. Ev loved Dizzy: he was gentle where Ev's mother was harsh, patient where she was demanding. Ev's first polished work of carpentry was a present for Dizzy, a case to hold a set of graduated wrenches. When Dizzy told him he needed to go to high school in the next valley over in order to become a superior craftsman, he got on the school bus with the others. He was twelve.

High school began as torture, Ev being smaller than the other boys and oddly dressed. But Dizzy encouraged him, and, somehow, he caught the attention of Mr. Irving and Miss Allen. Mr. Irving taught math and was amused by the unorthodox ways in which Ev approached problems. The kid couldn't do long division, but graphing came naturally. Mr. Irving did not understand how Ev visualized quadratic equations—and neither did Ev, shapes just materialized in his head—but he mentored him. And Miss Allen taught Ev to read, finally. She sat with him at lunch every day in a corner of the cafeteria and went over elementary texts syllable by syllable until he could read reliably on his own. The other students judged him a weirdo and ignored the reading lessons. Ev handed in assignments on time, and eventually the principal bent the rules— must have been at Mr. Irving's request because Ev's parents paid no attention—and Ev managed to graduate. So his mother decided to send him to a community college in a nearby city that had a dorm for boarders. She did not give him a choice.

Years later, Ev had told Jo, he realized he owed a debt to Mr. Irving and Miss Allen. He went back to the school to give each of them a magical rainbow periscope, like the one that had caught Jo's eye, but Mr. Irving had died. Miss Allen accepted the gift graciously, although she appeared confused by it. She thanked him for being her student, saying every remedial reading teacher deserved a pupil like him. Ev realized their gratitude was mutual.

At the community college, Ev found he could not take notes quickly enough. Miss Allen had taught him to read but not to write. When he wanted to capture a thought, the sentences seemed to fly up and down the page outside his volition. So, he stopped taking notes and flunked out. He did not tell his parents because he wanted to stay on campus, where he had made a new friend. The head of the physical sciences department had discovered that Ev could do anything with his hands and hired him as a lab technician. Ev maintained the equipment in all the labs and fashioned apparatus for faculty when asked. He lived in the dorm, auditing classes the physical science professors taught, having the occasional meal with his patron, who taught him to savor a good wine. After a while, his patron supplanted Dizzy in Ev's affections, so when the man suggested he branch out into biological science, he did. The theory of evolution captivated him, and he became curious about its genesis. So he read some history of science, which led him to European history. He haunted the library, developed a passion for reading. His technician's salary covered the little he needed to stay clothed and healthy. He was not unhappy. He felt he was seeing the world for the first time; he had transcended the grip of the commune.

And then he met Jessica. He was nineteen.

Before Jo and Ev married, she had asked him how many other women he had slept with. He blushed and said, "Do you want quantity or quality?" She said, "Both." He said, "A few, one," and told her about Jessica. He did not look at her whenever he spoke the girl's name.

Ev said he had noticed a girl in the library, sitting bent over her books, studying intensely. She had thick, dark hair that spilled down her back and a prominent nose. He watched her for weeks without approaching lest he interrupt, but in his fantasies he talked to her nightly. One spring day as he left the library he saw her sitting on the steps, eating an apple. Without thinking, he said, "Looks good."

She reached into her bag, pulled out another apple, and held it out to him. "I'm Jessica, who are you?"

"Everett. Dana."

"Which is it? Everett or Dana?" She stared at him with large, dark eyes.

"Dana is my last name. Friends call me Ev."

"Okay, Ev. Have a seat and tell me why you spend so much time in the library. You're always there when I show up."

"I come here after work. I work in the labs. As a technician."

He looked for the right words, didn't find them. "I guess I have a lot to learn."

Jessica laughed softly, and it pleased his ear. "So do I. My folks don't think so. They want me to give it up and go work in their store. Actually, my uncle owns the store but he has no sons, and my female cousins are slackers, so my parents think I'll inherit." She tossed the remains of the apple into the bushes and stood, gathering her belongings. "I have no idea why I told you all that. Maybe because you always look so forlorn."

Ev stood quickly. "May I walk you home?"

"That would be a long walk. You can walk me to the bus stop."

He did so. And every subsequent afternoon that spring he waited at the library, no longer able to concentrate on the Krebs cycle, for a chance to walk her to the bus. Jessica, he soon learned, was the daughter of Lebanese immigrants who had come to West Virginia to work for their wealthy relatives. She mocked her family's aspirations but seemed tied to them. Her uncle wanted Jessica to major in business at the university, but she wanted to study art. They had compromised, allowing her to take studio classes at the community college in exchange for a promise to "get serious" in a year's time. She told Ev she had no intention of keeping her side of the bargain.

Jessica had a lively mind; her sophistication dazzled him. She liked learning different things and prided herself on her ability to discriminate. Comfortable in her skin, she welcomed his questions and, up to a point, his naïve demonstrations of affection. He could be patient because she smiled so nicely when she rebuffed his inquiring hands. One day she insisted Ev take her to his workplace. When she saw the oversize barometer he was building out of glass tubing for a botany teacher, she said it was beautiful. So he built her one, telling the faculty member he needed to make a second apparatus to perfect the design. When he gave the barometer to her, she seemed to have forgotten her earlier comment. He stifled his disappointment and vowed to find another way into her heart.

Over the summer Jessica worked evenings in the studio in the art building. He waited outside for her, brought her a share of his dinner. And one very late night she went home with him to save herself the commute. He had become manager of the dorm and lived in a ground floor suite. They sneaked in, found it thrilling, and she let him pass the usual point. By the end of the summer, she was sleeping with him regularly. He never forgot to use a condom and was ready to marry. Jessica didn't want to commit; she had big things to do and places to go in pursuit of her dream.

At the end of the summer, she took him to see her final project, a mixed media piece, bright acrylic colors on a canvas from which the glass tubing he had given her protruded in arcs. He didn't know what to make of it or say, so he showed her a better way to affix the tubing. She got mad, told him he needed schooling in aesthetics. He promised to take an art class with her in the fall. And he did. He liked it well enough, and the teacher encouraged him. But Jessica hadn't liked his sculptures and picked fights. She said his pieces were boring compared to hers. When he received the higher grade, she wouldn't talk to him for weeks.

Jo asked Ev what he'd learned in that art class that led him to design. He replied he hadn't learned all that much, that most things slipped in and out of his head, except for structures. She asked what happened with Jessica. Ev said she went back to her family at the end of the semester, and there was nothing more to say.

But there was, and Jo got it out of him.

He had been inconsolable, missing Jessica in the library, the cafeteria, in his bed. He couldn't figure out what he'd done wrong. She'd said he'd done nothing wrong; it was just that she'd realized her uncle was right after all. She didn't want to slave away in obscurity for decades before being able to live in comfort—sneaking in and out of Ev's suite had lost its charm—so she needed a dependable degree. He offered to follow her to the university. She chided him about not being able to afford it. She left and didn't write.

In the spring, he stopped auditing the art class because her vacant chair made him blue. He stopped visiting the library because he still saw her in shadowy corners here and there. Then one day he saw a notice pinned to the cafeteria bulletin board that said the teacher who had commented positively on his clumsy pieces was giving a design seminar off campus. He went to the first meeting, joining three other students, none of them from the college, all of them older. The teacher started off saying that his only rule was they must produce. Ev resonated with his off-the-grid attitude. He went to the next meeting, and the next. He began to dig in to the work. He began going for a beer with the other students, and soon they pressed him to confess his troubles. They told him that Jessica had made a mistake and that he had a talent for design. He believed them because he believed in them. Gradually he let go of his grief.

She found him in the kitchen, misting his cacti. She handed him the infinity box.

"I love you, too, and I give up."

Ev's eyebrows arched in surprise. "Did you play with it?"

"Yup. So?"

He lowered the mister. "Humans are the only thing in nature that reverses the arrow of time. We can see into the past and the future." He grinned his best down-home, West Virginia grin. "I wanted to give you the gift of time. To work out the Saudi deal. Or drop it. I could go either way."

"Thanks," she said, patting his arm. "I accept."

# STRATEGY

11

Outside the open bedroom window: blue skies, dark green hillsides, a pleasant sixty-one degrees. So much more hospitable than Dubai. Jo sat in her reading chair, nursing a headache, smelling eucalyptus and sun-warmed wood. Her gaze drifted from the window to the drawing on the opposite wall, an abstract Ev had done years before: gray, black, and white lines of different thickness and orientation, like some mad architect's doodle. She'd liked it when he first showed it to her and had had it framed. Since Ev no longer drew, too busy working in three dimensions, she'd had no call to replace it. Nothing had changed in this room for a long time, which didn't particularly bother her. Her mind dwelled on the floor below.

She heard a truck pull up in front of the house. Glancing outside, she saw Diane greet a FedEx driver at the door. Now she had better get in gear. As she descended the stairs, Diane carried a parcel into the office. She stripped open the box, bouncing on her heels in excitement. As Jo approached, Diane pulled something black out of bubble wrap and held it aloft. An abaya. She measured it against Becca's shoulders. It was long enough to reach the floor and wide enough for two Beccas.

"Now we know you're an extra-long," Diane said.

Becca threaded her arms through the abaya's voluminous sleeves and flapped them, like a six-foot sting ray. Diane clapped her hands. Jo faced her.

"Why did you buy an abaya? You know I have one."

Diane looked surprised. "We'll need it to prototype the exhibits. Becca is so tall."

"*If* we prototype exhibits." Jo turned away, annoyed at Diane's rashness.

Becca followed Jo to her desk. She said, "I asked Diane to order this so I could see how it feels. Whether it gets in the way when a mother handles an exhibit or manipulatives. I figured you needed yours. I'll pay for it."

"No, don't pay. You can wear it on Halloween."

"Aren't we developing exhibits for the Saudis? Ev's working in the shop."

"Maybe, maybe not. We haven't settled on a subcontract with Owen Associates. Ev can't help himself. You can."

"I was trying to think ahead. I thought you'd be pleased."

"I know. Diane should have known better."

"Jo, it was my idea."

Jo waved her away.

Becca returned to Diane's desk and took off the filmy gown. Diane folded it and repacked it. She placed the package in her bottom drawer, mumbling about checking the return policy. Becca mumbled an inaudible answer.

Jo went to her desk and woke up her computer. A bond had developed between Diane and Becca that Jo would never have predicted, Becca being so strong-minded and Diane so vague. It had started a year or so ago when Diane brought her son and old dog to the office one day, leaving the dog behind to take Joey to his doctor's appointment. Becca babysat the dog, saying it reminded her of home. Over the ensuing months, Joey thrived but the dog sickened. Becca tended to it whenever Diane brought it round. One day the poor creature lay under Diane's desk, evidently in pain. At closing time, Diane didn't want to move it. Becca improvised a stretcher and transported the dog to the vet in her truck. Neither woman showed up during the two days it took the dog to die. When they returned, you could see a new feeling between them, expressed in frequent smiles and gentle comments and acts of consideration. Jo didn't question the bond because the work was going well. But she got annoyed when Becca came to Diane's defense. Jo was grooming Becca for the great things the girl had talent enough to do. Diane was no role model.

Diane approached, saying "They'll take the abaya back, we'll only have to pay the shipping. Surface mail."

"Never mind. Call it a souvenir." Jo felt her button being pushed again and turned her head away. It was the little stuff that bugged her. She could handle the big things: Diane's having had a baby too young, and out of wedlock; having arrived in Oakland in desperate need of a job. Big things could be managed. But little things made anger well up inside her before she could control it. She knew she should be nicer to Diane. Perhaps in another life.

She grasped her mouse and clicked on email. A batch of

notices came up on the screen: there, in the middle of the column, a message from Owen Associates. She held her breath while she read. She forwarded the email to her lawyer and went out to the studio to tell Ev. He had resumed working on his whirligig, and plastic blades in different shapes and sizes lay scattered on the workbench. She stood in the doorway, watching him stoop over his work. A jazzy trumpet emanated from the radio.

"Owen sent his demands. He wants to pay us sixty days after he gets paid, and he wants editorial control. He's a bully. I forwarded the email to Helen."

Ev lay down the tin snips. "Is there light at the end of this tunnel?"

"What do you think?" She meant to ask a question but it came out shrill.

Ev turned down the music and leaned against the drill press. He looked up at the ceiling. He thought for a beat. "Do you think he would stiff us? I mean, if the Saudis paid him, wouldn't he pay us? We know a lot of the same people."

"Yeah. So?"

"So ask to be paid simultaneously."

She thought about it. "You're saying share the risk?"

"That would be fair."

She felt her hackles lower. "But we can't give him the final word on design."

Ev came over and took her by the shoulders. "Work on it, woman."

"I'm dead serious."

"So am I." He slid one hand down her back and squeezed a butt cheek.

"You are impossible!" She pushed him away. "Go play with your toys." She blew him an exasperated kiss and turned to leave.

He called after her, "I have faith . . ."

Faith in her tenacity as a negotiator, as he had said before when deals looked dicey. And she had delivered. But you have to know your line in the sand before you negotiate. She might agree to share the risk of being stiffed by the Saudis, but she would never give Owen control of their product. Invention was their hallmark; she would not let Owen attach his name to their work or force them to adapt to his chrome-plated style. She would guard their reputation at all costs.

The office was quiet. Carlos was on assignment at another client's place of business, Andy was at school, and Becca sat engaged with her computer, occasionally hitting the keys. Jo went to the kitchen and put on the kettle, hoping for inspiration while the water heated. She could smell the ramps Ev had cooked for dinner the night before, foul things he had developed a taste for in his West Virginia youth. Diane appeared at her elbow.

"I can drop off the abaya on my way home tonight."

"Don't bother."

"I thought you'd want me to encourage Becca." Diane held palms together in front of her chest, as if praying. Or begging, even more irritating.

"Forget it. Can I see the revised budget?"

Diane bustled to her desk, returning with a pad and a spread sheet. "I adjusted the contingency and profit a little lower, but we can't pay international shipping and keep it under a hundred grand. Can we deliver in the US? It's a small load. Carlos could handle it."

"Maybe." Jo inspected the page. She felt Diane hovering, begging for an "attagirl" for simply doing her job. "I can work with this." She turned off the kettle and returned to her desk, leaving Diane empty-handed in the kitchen.

The landline rang. Becca picked it up. She said a few words, then beckoned Jo vigorously. Jo mouthed, "Who?" Becca mouthed something Jo couldn't read. The girl pointed to the calligraphy scrolling across her screen, installed while she was working on the Saudi pamphlet. Jo thought it must be Owen. She took the receiver from Becca. It was Myriam, calling from Riyadh, saying the director would be coming on the line. Jo shot out her arm toward the studio, and Becca darted out of the room. In the three seconds it took Myriam to transfer the call, Jo zoomed into high alert.

Madam Deputy Director said, "Good evening. Thank you for the brochures. They are beautiful, and the tone is right. Did you show them to the committee in Dubai?"

"No, we didn't. We were so surprised by their decision."

"The timing was unfortunate. I was attending a family function."

Jo held her tongue.

The director said, "I want you to know that I want you to develop the exhibits for my museum. You interpret my intention properly."

"Thank you. But the committee has selected Owen Associates as the lead."

"Please do not misunderstand. That is administration. I am urging you to accept the conditions. If you encounter difficulties, call Myriam. I have complete confidence in her."

"I will discuss your request with my husband. He will be very glad to hear how much you liked our proposal."

The director said, "Good. I will say good-bye. Myriam wishes to speak."

Jo heard a snatch of Arabic and Myriam came on the line.

"I want to help you. Please tell me what I can do."

Jo decided to test the director's candor. "May I ask you a question?"

"Of course."

"If this is the director's project, why is there another layer of administration? I am concerned that too many people will interfere."

"The director is not from Qassim. The government is loyal to her husband's family, not to her. She must work carefully. She understands the value of your design. She will approve."

"But Owen will set goals and define procedures. Our work will come second."

"The director and I will watch. There is no payment unless she approves. You will see that we control, in our way. Please. We want to work with you."

"Thank you. This helps."

"You must call me when you have questions. I accept no one else."

"Understood."

Jo replaced the handset. Ev and Becca popped into the room and gathered around her. Diane joined them.

"The director wants us to build her exhibits. She said the deal with Owen is bureaucracy. She said we can back-channel to her through Myriam." Jo scanned Ev's face.

Becca said, "Myriam's the woman I spoke to. She's cool."

"But why did the director call?" Jo asked. "Why does she need a back-channel? Maybe she's powerless. Maybe she's window dressing to make the project look better to Westerners."

"If they cared what Westerners thought, they wouldn't push us around," Ev said.

Diane said, "Maybe it's hard for a woman there. Shouldn't you support her?"

"It should be the other way around," Jo said.

Diane looked away.

Ev said, "Well, I'm glad the lady likes our stuff." He pointed to the studio. "Got some plastic in the heater." He loped away.

Jo rose, saying she needed that cup of tea after all, and went to the kitchen. Diane had provoked her. Of course she sympathized with women seeking equality in a man's world, but she did not feel compelled to act on their behalf. She was no feminist. She expected to compete on an equal footing with every other design firm, to win projects because of D-Three's excellence, not because a client could check off the "woman-owned business" box on a government procurement form. No one in the business had ever accused her of playing the woman card. She wasn't about to play it now.

She turned on her heel and went to her desk to email a provocative reply.

TO: phil.owen@owenandassociates.com
FROM: joanna@dunhilldanadesign.com
SUBJ: counter offer

We will forego being paid for the demonstration displays until you receive payment from the Saudis, but we expect to be fully reimbursed within 48 hours. And we'll ship to any US location of your choice. Your team can handle the demo from there. Thanks for your consideration.

The reply came immediately.

TO: joanna@dunhilldanadesign.com
FROM: marc.andreesen@owenandassociates.com
SUBJ: "you've got to be kidding"
Phil had to leave the office. He told me to send you his reply, above. He will communicate with you himself tomorrow.

Good, Jo thought. He's riled.

Owen phoned the next afternoon, and Jo put the call on speaker so the others could witness. Diane and Becca gathered round. Jo texted Ev to come in from the studio.

"You are doing your best to sabotage our relationship," Owen began.

Jo said, "What are you talking about?"

"I suppose you've heard from the committee?"

"No, nothing since the RFP."

"Well, now they want every drawing to show three signatures. Yours, mine, and the deputy director's."

Jo gave her team the high sign.

Owen got louder, "Why did you go to the deputy director behind my back? Where is your sense of fair play?"

"She called me. I didn't initiate."

"How am I supposed to work with a bunch of whining women?"

"You can back out of the project." She stared at the hostile speakerphone, feeling heat spread across her face.

"You have added unnecessary steps to this thing. You are stealing my time. I should have listened to my friend Roberto. He said you were capable but you showed bad judgment back then. Clearly you still do."

Jo could not talk. Images of Robbo flashed through her mind's eye.

Owen continued, "I don't want my team touching the demo, it's all yours, installation as well. If you get the director out of this, I'll consider simultaneous payment. That's my offer."

Jo could not talk.

Diane looked questioningly at Jo, then across the table to Becca, then back to Jo. She said, "Mr. Owen, this is Diane Dunhill.

I'm sorry that Mr. Dana was not able to be here. May we call back after we talk with him?"

"You can call back until the cows come home." He hung up.

Becca said, "He's nasty."

Jo nodded. Her throat would not unclench.

Diane said, "I'll type it up for Ev."

Jo whispered, "Excuse me" and pushed away from the table. She climbed the stairs.

In the spare room, she sat on the floor, back to the wall, to steady herself. How had Owen known about Robbo? Could they really be friends? Perhaps Owen had done the interiors for one of Robbo's buildings. He did that kind of thing between museum jobs. Owen probably thought he could shock her into submission. He'd shocked her all right, but not the way he'd anticipated. At the sound of Robbo's name bursting from the phone in a male voice, her heart had contracted, not with shame but with something like love. Perhaps because she'd dreamed about him and dispensed with her sorrow in the dreaming, she'd felt a tiny surge of joy at hearing him invoked. Somewhere deep inside, her body remembered the happiness she had found in his embrace all those years ago, and the memory now radiated through her. She hugged her knees into her chest in wonder at her pleasure. She hoped it would last.

She rose and straddled the exercise bike. She pedaled hard because it helped her think. She recalled the way Robbo had laughed, head thrown back, at her tentative jokes, and how his hands had skimmed her skin. Of course she had fallen for him, the elegant sonofabitch. She'd been a kid. For the first time since college, Jo felt compassion, not blame, for that awkward girl dazzled by a commanding man.

That was it, wasn't it? She didn't miss Robbo, she missed following a strong man's lead. Ev never led her anywhere, except in design. She was always the one in charge, monitoring his appearance as well as his activities. Sometimes she felt more mother than mistress. Evidently, part of her wanted to surrender control. Of course, she wouldn't tell Ev about this little longing. They were better off maintaining things as is, in the business and the bedroom.

She pedaled a while longer, feeling the burn in her thighs, until she realized the others might be waiting for her. She dismounted and went downstairs. Sitting at her desk, keeping a neutral face, she made order: she checked her calendar; she checked the weather. And when she felt perfectly calm, she emailed Owen, copy to Ev and Becca and Diane, saying they accepted his offer with the proviso that they could not influence the director.

In a minute, Becca loomed over Jo's desk. She crossed her arms and said, "Will it work?"

"I think so. Owen's getting a good deal. He doesn't have to touch the demo, and he keeps the overhead. He knows no one can control the client."

"Why wouldn't he sign?"

Jo shrugged her shoulders. "Pride? Ego? Maybe delay is a tactic?"

"Why do you want to work with him?"

"I don't. The client imposed him on us."

"Ev says we could back out anytime. Ev doesn't like this job."

Jo wondered where Becca got her information. "Have you been talking to him about it?"

"No, but I see how he acts. He's usually so happy when he's designing something. He's been . . . I don't know, somber?"

True enough, Jo thought. Becca must be watching Ev closely, like a colleague rather than a junior employee. Or, it suddenly occurred to her, like a crush. Becca never talked about boyfriends or dating. Jo had thought she liked her privacy, but perhaps there were no boyfriends, and she had a thing for the boss. After all, she went for a beer with him now and then, and she made coffee for the two of them every morning. In staff discussions, she usually endorsed his opinions. But not inappropriately, and Ev had never mentioned her flirting. Perhaps he had missed the cues. Perhaps there were no cues, and Becca bore her crush with perfect composure. Perhaps there was no crush.

Jo said, "You know Ev. Allergic to bureaucracy. He'll be fine once the job starts."

"I hope you're right." Becca's face clouded over. She pursed her lips in a gesture that looked to Jo like concern.

"We'll see soon enough." She suppressed a smile.

Becca turned on her heel and went back to her desk.

If she is in love with Ev, Jo thought, it wouldn't affect the business. Ev wouldn't exploit her. But Becca would suffer in the end. Jo felt a wave of sympathy for the girl, pining away for an inaccessible man, just as she now felt sympathy for her younger self.

Two days passed without word from Owen. Ev stayed focused on his whirligig, and none of the others seemed to notice that Jo took more walks than usual. She forced herself to think about how hard it had been to recover from the blow Robbo had delivered, and her nostalgia gradually subsided. She welcomed its retreat; it wasn't fair to Ev, and it got in the way.

Then on Friday, Owen wrote to accept the deal, and the team decided to party.

Diane threw a cloth over Carlos's drafting table and laid out cheese and crackers. Becca brought beer, a dark, local brew she and Ev liked. Carlos contributed the home-made tamales he kept in Tupperware in the fridge, and Andy cut school to join them. They gathered around the table, nibbling, waiting for Ev to return.

Jo said, "I feel like we're on *Star Trek*. Full speed ahead into the unknown! But this team can handle anything. Within reason."

Becca asked, "Do you think the Saudis will be reasonable?"

Jo said, "Some will, some won't. They're just people."

Becca's lips tightened. "They're religious fanatics whose government bombed the hell out of Yemen. And our government looked the other way."

Andy said, "Yeah. Like Syria, only the media ignored it."

Diane said, "Becca, you promised."

Becca faced her. "I'm sorry, I don't mean to spoil the party, but we need to keep our eyes open."

Diane said, "Of course."

Jo thought Diane was the last person to promise open eyes. Diane had stumbled through most of life blinded by sentiment.

Ev appeared in the doorway carrying a carton. Diane made room in the center of the party table and he deposited the box. He reached into it and pulled out a book with a shiny, laminated jacket.

"Been to the library. Got everything about Saudi Arabia. I'll give these out and we'll do book reports." He turned to Becca. "This one's for you. About the political system." He pulled out another book. "I think Carlos will go for this one, about the Bin Laden dynasty." He took out two more. "For Jo, story of Gertrude Bell, the British woman who divvied up the Arabian Peninsula after World War I. For Diane, true life interviews with Arab women. Andy, you're excused. You have school."

Andy said, "I want to do my part. I'll monitor Reddit and a couple other sites."

Jo asked Ev, "What do you get?"

"Poetry." He picked up the carton and slid it under the table. "Pass me a beer, please."

Diane frowned. "When do you want the book reports? I won't be able to do mine right away. I need to get Joey ready for his check-up in San Francisco."

"Whenever you're ready," Ev said. He took a long swig.

Jo turned her book over to read the blurb on the back. She said, "How will you report on the poetry? In a slam?"

"Nope. You'll see it in my work." He took another swig. "That's good." He tipped the bottle toward Becca, who returned the gesture. He turned to Carlos, "Which are the veggies?"

"You have to eat chicken. My *abuela* ran out of green chilies," Carlos said.

Ev looked shocked and everyone laughed. Carlos told him to relax because the chicken tamales were just as delicious as the veggie. He toasted his abuela, and the others raised their glasses. Jo felt a surge of gratitude toward her unpredictable husband. The staff would not have reacted as well to book reports if she had assigned them. Together, she and Ev could pilot this starship anywhere, in any universe.

After the others left, Ev bundled Jo into his pickup truck to drive into the hills to watch the sun set from under his favorite live oak. He often disappeared for hours into the hills at the eastern edge of the city. He called them "salad hills" because in the dry summers, the ground cover smelled like oregano. He would drive up, saying he needed quiet to listen to the trees, and return refreshed, with a new approach to whatever lay on his workbench. So Jo let him be. Now, it tickled her to be invited to go along.

Ev drove far more slowly than she would on streets that wound steeply upward. She assumed he was preoccupied with the surroundings, processing everything in the peculiar light of his mind. Last week, for instance, while taking a walk they had come across a mound of feathers on a strip of grass. She had speculated that a cat had gotten a bird. He had replied that feathers and fur were the same item, skin cover made of keratin. Then he calculated how many crow feathers could be converted into a square inch of cat fur, if evolution so demanded. No one else would make such a connection. Ev lived in a singular wonderland that she glimpsed every once in a while, but never for long. In her opinion, the best place to watch the sun set over the Bay was the deck of the Claremont Hotel, but she was content to be driven in companionable silence to the ridge above.

They wound upward to Redwood Park. He parked on the shoulder, and they walked a couple hundred yards along a faint trail to a gap in the trees. Behind them a gnarled live oak stood among the tall redwoods. A boulder lay near the oak tree, and Ev invited her to sit. They perched beside one another and looked west, past the flatlands, across the glittering Bay to the distant San Francisco skyline and the hunched hills of the peninsula. An orange sun hung momentarily between two layers of cloud, and a light breeze brought bird sounds and muted road noise. Jo felt at peace.

"I see why you come here. You own the world."

Ev put hands on knees and leaned forward. "Actually, I come for the tree. More accurately, for the bark. I thought you'd like the view."

Jo turned behind her to observe the gray trunk, which seemed to be shedding an outer layer, like an insect molting its shell.

Ev said, "There's a system to the way the bark peels off, but there's no pattern. I never know what it will look like the next time."

"Don't you know in general?"

"Yes, but I want detail."

"What's the difference between knowing in general and detail?"

Ev thought for a moment. "It's the difference between having a recipe and tasting the food."

Only Ev would make that comment. She wanted to thank him for being Ev. "I do like the view."

"I like to see you happy."

"I am happy. I love sticking it to Owen."

Ev sat up. "I thought it was the view."

"That, too."

He began to root around in the ground at the base of the rock. He picked up a shard of grayish bark. "I got a vibe from the staff. Everyone's uptight. Me, too." He waited a beat. "I'm having second thoughts."

"We've been over this. You agreed it's good for the company." She didn't want to break the mood, and she wanted to pretend he had no grounds for concern.

"Yeah, but this is going to be a tough one. I've been rethinking it. If we're lucky, we'll struggle to produce something in Saudi Arabia that we already know how to produce. It won't advance our work. I'm more interested in developing something new."

"Fine, but who's going to pay for it? Develop something new for the Saudis."

He shook his head. "I don't see it happening. They're hung up on formality. I won't be free to invent."

She pleaded with him. "This job is the bird in the hand. You've already excited the staff about spinning. Let's run with it!"

He shook his head and stood. He took a few steps toward the slope and shaded his eyes with his hand to watch the sun disappear behind the hills. He turned back to Jo. "I need more time."

"So do I." She stifled the rest of her words, tallying the hours she spent caring for house and business so he could watch a tree shed bark.

He must have read her change in tone. He spoke softly, "Let's go down before it gets dark." He led her back along the ridge to the truck. She followed in silence.

As they headed downhill, she resented his spoiling the sunset. Yeah, he had a point about struggle, but there was so much he didn't understand about the business. About how hard she worked to keep them afloat. About how important this job was to their future. That it was now or never for her. He didn't get it. Other couples had trouble communicating here and there, but she and Ev had a mountain to climb. It made her weary. She hugged herself and breathed deeply. By the time the truck pulled into their driveway, she had managed to reconcile with the status quo. She opened the passenger door and said, in what she hoped was a neutral tone, "Salmon or chicken for dinner?"


On Monday, Becca came late to the staff meeting. The others had pulled their chairs up to the whiteboard, where Jo wielded a marker. Becca slipped behind Diane and stood, head lowered. She swayed from foot to foot as Jo walked the team through a best-case timeline for the Saudi job: one week for Owen to mobilize, two weeks for coordination, and then the clock would start ticking. The staff had no questions, and Carlos gave huzzahs. They went back to their places.

Becca approached Jo with hunched shoulders, looking smaller than her five-foot-eleven. Jo gestured for Becca to follow her into the kitchen where they'd have a degree of privacy to discuss whatever was weighing on her mind. Jo rinsed the teapot, waiting for Becca to unload. She had never been reticent.

Becca folded hands in front of her chest. "I don't think I can work on this project. I hope you don't fire me because I love working for D-Three. But I can't commit myself to propping up an oppressive regime when I could be doing positive things."

Jo paused, expecting her to continue. Becca remained silent. Jo said, "What sort of things?"

"Things that are unambiguously good. Like, maybe a playroom for a clinic in the flatlands. Maybe we could build one pro bono."

Jo shook her head. "And you'd forfeit your salary? What happened this weekend?"

"The Saudis used a billion dollars of US equipment to smash a hospital in Saana. Don't you know?"

"Not a single Saudi four-year-old was to blame. What happened to *you* this weekend?"

Becca looked like she wanted to cry. "I met somebody I used to know online. She came to San Francisco for a conference. She's an American but she lives in India and teaches children whose moms are in a microloan club. She talked about the mothers standing up to their families for the first time in their lives after they made independent money. I want to do work like that. Everything else is a waste of time." She paused, took a deep breath. "When my parents ask me what I'm doing, I want to be proud of the answer. I don't want to tell them I'm helping hypocrites."

"Don't you think your folks are proud of how successful you are? A senior designer at your age."

'My family doesn't care about titles."

"I forget you come from Puritan stock."

"This has nothing to do with religion. It's ethics. I want my work to feel as good and clean as my friend's."

"Did your friend say your work was dirty?"

"Of course not. It's me saying I should do better." Becca's shoulders hunched tighter. "I'm sorry, but I can't pretend the Saudis are innocents. I hope you don't fire me."

"Not now I won't." Jo abandoned the effort to sympathize. "Take some time to think about it. I expect you to realize that Saudi four-year-olds deserve the same break as any other four-year-olds."

Jo replaced the teapot in the cabinet, more concerned than she had shown. She took pride in mentoring Becca—she'd not had a mentor in her own early days—and the girl responded as well as Jo could wish. She didn't want to lose Becca, especially for the wrong reason.

"Why don't you invite your friend to come over and see the kind of work we do?"

Becca frowned.

"I'd like to meet her."

"I'll ask if she has the time." Becca left the kitchen.

Fingers crossed, Jo thought. Now, maybe they could all get to work.

At four o'clock Becca ushered a pregnant young woman into the office and seated her on the couch in the cubby D-Three used for meetings. She hung up two jackets and stepped over to Jo.

"You told me to bring my friend. I'm driving her to the airport at five. I'm going to show her our museum portfolio, if that's okay."

"Of course. May I join you?"

Becca gestured to the cubby. Jo followed her there and took a seat opposite the young woman, who smiled, really smiled, eyes crinkling in the corners.

"You must be Ms. Dunhill. I'm so happy to meet you. I've heard a lot about your work." She wore bangles on both wrists and filigree earrings but no makeup. A pleasant, plump face. A cotton dress tied loosely over the swell of her belly.

Becca said, "Jenn lives in India and runs a school for poor children. I told you she came to San Francisco for a conference." She pulled one of their portfolios off a shelf and spread it open on the coffee table. She began to turn the pages.

Jo said, "Now, *that* sounds like interesting work. How did

you come by it?" She wanted to draw Jenn out a bit, see why Becca had befriended her.

"My husband was originally from India. We both wanted to give service, and somehow we wound up doing what we do." She readjusted herself on the seat. "My husband and I partner with a microloan organization, but we are educators. He helps the adults and I tend to the children."

"Working with children is the best part of our design practice. You can have such an impact." Jo turned to Becca, "I think you agree?"

Becca squirmed and withdrew her hand from the portfolio. The page she'd been about to turn fell back in place.

Jenn said, "Actually, I came to here go to a workshop on 'kitchen science.' One of our donors thought it would be useful." She shook her head. "Kitchens in the deep countryside where we work are not equipped like American kitchens. I was hoping to learn about simple apparatus, like the ones Becca says you make."

Becca said, "Maybe we should go to the studio and see what's on Ev's workbench?"

"In a minute," Jo said, not ready to let go. "If you see something you like, we'd be happy to ship drawings to India for you, pro bono."

"Thank you! But I'm not going back to India for a while. I'll be staying with my mother in New Jersey until the baby is born."

Becca frowned. "I didn't know that. Why?"

"My husband wants me to deliver our baby in the world's best hospital." She waved jazz hands. "But he'll have to settle for Englewood, near my mom. I'll go home as soon as the baby can travel."

Becca's brow furrowed. "That doesn't seem right. Like it's a slap in the face to your clients. You're putting your baby into a different class." Her voice sounded tight, as if her throat were constricted.

"I wish every one of our babies and moms could get the world's best health care. But they can't, and I have a first duty to my child. Arun will keep our promises to everyone back home."

"They may never trust you again. You're acting like a colonial."

Jenn leaned back. "I understand your concern." She folded her hands. "I think it will come out right. We've earned their respect."

"You're healthy, aren't you? Why risk losing ground?"

"Becca, I'll only be gone six months, max."

"This time. And then you'll come back to put the kid in a better school." Becca spoke with a flat voice, no teasing in her tone.

Jo stood. She didn't want them to argue. Something had made prickly Becca even more prickly this afternoon. Poor kid. "Let's go check in with Ev."

Jenn rose heavily and the three of them walked to the studio. Jo opened the door, and Ev looked up from the workbench, a question on his face.

Becca said, "This is my friend Jenn. She's interested in science exhibits you can make with simple materials and tools. She lives in the backwoods in India."

Ev looked back and forth between them. Jo followed his gaze: Becca tall, blonde and exigent; Jenn short, dark, and pregnant. Ev said, "Come on in. How do you know each other?"

"We met in an online class on situational ethics a couple of years ago," Becca said. We read each other's submissions and decided we needed to talk. This is the first time we've been in the same place physically."

Ev motioned Jenn to come closer to the workbench. "I've been playing with a zoetrope today. You can make things spin without fancy equipment."

As Jenn stepped into Ev's orbit, Jo pulled Becca aside. She spoke softly.

"You seem a little testy toward your friend."

"I'm fine. I always tell her what I think. She expects it. She likes it. I'm surprised at her decision is all."

Jo didn't buy it. "Are you still upset over Saudi Arabia?"

Becca hesitated. "Yes and no. I know you don't think it's wrong to take their money. But it's ignoble. I need more from my work." She turned away to join her friend at the workbench.

Jo stood in the doorway, contemplating. She remembered Becca's once telling her, in another context, that when she was little, she used to rub salt into the cuts and scrapes she got on knees and elbows. She thought the pain would make them heal better, and she always wanted to be better. At the time, Jo had wondered what kind of mother let her kid develop a relationship with pain. Perhaps a mother who was herself a martyr. Jo didn't pretend to understand the source of Becca's overweening morality, but she felt its force. She hoped Jenn's visit would end on a happy note. Becca needed friends.

Did it make sense for people to seek nobility in their work? Pride, yes. Reward and recognition, certainly. But a job was a job, not a higher calling. She expected to reap a spectacular reward from the Saudi job down the line, but not to earn a place in heaven. Something weird was going on in Becca's head. Jo sighed. She'd wait until Jenn left before broaching the subject again. She stepped toward the workbench to join the conversation.

The staff stood around Andy's table, watching his photos from Calgary unroll in a PowerPoint. Andy stopped the slide show at a picture of a little girl looking at herself in a mirror. She wore three pair of outsized eye glasses, dreadlocks made of wool in her hair, and a metal collar around her neck. Behind her, sepia photos of nineteenth-century men sporting mustaches and sideburns were mounted on the wall, with a sign, "Re-design Your Face."

Carlos said, "Where did she get the gear?"

Andy said, "From bins on the table in front of the mirror.

Becca said, "Sure makes the point."

"What's the point?" Diane asked.

"That we construct our identities with props."

"Will kids get that?"

"Yes, if they play around with the stuff."

Jo addressed Andy. "Did you find anything about careers we can use?"

Andy said, "Nada. But they have some good classroom programs. I'll type up my notes for Becca." He ended the slide show.

Jo said, "Nice job." She turned to the others. "Anybody have anything else?"

Carlos said, "I didn't finish the book Ev gave me, but I discovered something. The author, he's a reporter. You know how he figured out how much money the Saudi big shots make? They get divorced in the US and their wives tell the lawyers."

The others laughed. Carlos said, "Wouldn't happen in my house!"

Andy closed his computer. Except for Jo, people returned to their work stations. In the few days since Becca's friend, Jenn, had visited, she and Becca had hardly talked. She decided to take advantage of the light-hearted moment and stepped to Becca's desk.

"Ev told me he sent a packet of sketches to your friend in New Jersey. Have you heard back from her?"

Becca sighed. "She said thanks."

Jo leaned over the desk to look into Becca's eyes. "You don't seem happy. What's going on?"

"Not much."

"Come on. Talk to me."

Becca leaned back in her chair and folded her arms across her chest. "I'm disappointed. All the time Jenn and I messaged each other, I was excited. Another woman my age who cared about what I cared about. And she was so smart, and humble, and thoughtful. And rigorous. I thought we'd be tight."

Jo waited.

"She's screwing up, and she's subordinating herself to her husband." Becca's face contorted.

"What did she say about her husband?"

"Nothing specific, but I could tell. She glowed every time she said his name."

"Becca, you can't know what the deal is between them. You could be reading your own biases into their situation."

"So could you. You like it when one person is the boss."

I do and I don't, Jo thought. Becca was still so green.

"The men I date say they want equality in relationships. But they really don't." She paused. "I have standards."

And they're getting in your way, Jo thought.

Across the room the landline rang and Carlos answered. He called over to Jo, saying Phil Owen was on the phone. Jo braced herself to hear Owen renege about something or other. She nodded to Becca and crossed the room to Carlos. She took the handset from him and put the call on speaker; Carlos hovered beside her.

"I have had a mild heart attack, or so my doctor says. An early Christmas present. Now my doctor is forbidding travel. So I propose to trade roles with you on the ground in Saudi. You supervise the market research as well as the demonstration, and I'll write the entire strategic plan. We'll bid jointly on the next phase, assuming there is one."

Stunned, Jo said nothing.

"I'll make it worth your while, say a ten percent bump on your fee."

"I'm sorry you're ill." Jo tried to collect her racing thoughts. "I'm surprised to hear your proposition. I don't think you and I are interchangeable."

"Unusual circumstances require unusual solutions. Can you work with me?"

"Let me talk to Ev. When do you need an answer?"

"ASAP. The research is scheduled to begin February first. You can fly to London and join my staff for the rest of the trip."

As Jo hung up, electricity surged through her, not because Owen had suffered but because she spied opportunity. D-Three could hook up with a research team and run the whole shebang. Surely the director would be pleased. Her heart beat faster; her prospects suddenly looked smashingly good. She turned to Carlos, whose face was screwed into a question mark. She gestured toward the studio and he followed, Diane on his heels. They found Ev sitting on the concrete floor, fitting erector set pieces together. He stopped, hands mid-air, when the three of them tumbled through his door. Jo repeated the conversation word for word. Ev slowly got up and put the metal slats he had been holding into a cereal box.

"We don't do research," he said.

"What if we get Jeff's crew to do the research? Their research, our demo, we write the strategic plan. No more Phil Owen. Period."

"If we farm out the research piece we won't make a dime."

"Yeah, but we'll get the implementation contract later."

"Can we talk in private?" Ev asked.

Jo nodded to Carlos and Diane, who backed away.

When the studio door had closed completely, Ev said, "Are you sure you want to do the whole thing? It may never go to implementation. Or they could gin up a lower bidder."

"Hey, business means risk."

"You're asking for a load of misery. Strategic plans are bullshit."

"I'm asking you to agree to a challenge. We can shape *this* plan so it works."

"Is this about revenge on Owen?"

She was miffed. "Of course not. This is about autonomy."

"Is this about paying off the bank? We could get another extension."

"Probably not." She felt a surge of impatience.

Ev wedged the cereal box into a crowded shelf above the drill press and spoke over his shoulder. "You are overreaching. The Saudis want to import a children's museum but they don't want the behavior that goes with it." He turned to face her. "I don't want to spend the next two years explaining open-ended play to bureaucrats. I don't want more heartache, for either of us."

Now she was angry. "Don't talk to me about heartache. I'm the one who cleans up messes around here. We need the business."

She spun on her heel and left him behind. He could be so obstinate, and he sucked at strategy. She felt one hundred percent justified. Instead of entering the house, she walked around outside to cool down.

Ev took his dinner plate to the sink and offered to do the dishes. They'd eaten a tuna salad again, about which he hadn't complained, again, although he had complained about her perseverating about Owen. She'd tried, again, to convince him they should take over the whole shebang. And he'd resisted, changed the subject to how much he'd enjoyed talking with Becca's friend the other day. Jo had had to stop listening.

She told Ev no, she'd do the washing up because she wanted to collect her thoughts. He left the kitchen, and she carried the rest of the dishes to the sink. She squirted detergent into the basin as it filled with hot water and picked up a sponge. Ev had accused her of hubris. He'd been wrong. She could run the whole project better than Phil Owen could. Authentically, without phony hand waving. But they had signed an agreement, and the lawyers would object to breaking it. And it would cost thousands and take months. He'd been right on that score.

She reached for the glasses, soaping and rinsing them under the faucet one at a time. When she moved on to the big wooden salad bowl, submerging its lower half into the suds, an idea occurred to her. Perhaps the two firms could share both halves of the job. What if she took Phil Owen's place on the research team and collaborated with him on the plan? D-Three might be able to achieve a degree of independence as well as make a profit.

She picked up the oily Pyrex cup in which she'd whisked Ev's favorite salad dressing. If Owen agreed, she and Becca could get in gear right away. Damn. Becca, who now wished only to serve some exalted purpose. She needed Becca to make the deal work. No one else in the office would be as accurate yet imaginative. Getting her to want the Saudi job was the problem. Getting her to open her mind! Becca needed to learn that building a museum for a Junior Leaguer was no holier than building one for a woman shrouded in a veil. Becca needed to learn that, in the real world, "good" and "bad" were sometimes indistinguishable.

Could she keep Becca on the project? Ev would know. Ev could share a beer with her. Or, Diane might be able to help persuade the girl. The thought of depending on Diane made her shudder.

She lifted a spatula from the soapy water and used a scratchy to remove the cheese encrusted at its tip. Something rankled the pit of her stomach. What if Becca's objections were valid? What if the Saudis tried to manipulate her into violating first principles? She shook her head. A strong-minded person could stick to her values no matter what. She had a plan, a good one. If the director would still back her.

She dried her hands and found her phone. It would be morning in Riyadh. She dialed Myriam.

Jo said, "Owen and I have been talking about exchanging some of our roles. The proposed work will still get done, and Ev will still be creative director. Will that affect you?"

"If you are happy, we are happy."

"What if I accompany the research team instead of Phil Owen?"

"Excellent! The sooner you come, the sooner you learn how we do things. I want you to meet the leaders of the Riyadh school district."

Jo took a deep breath. "I think Owen has already planned the visit."

"Then you must change the plan. I want you to meet the school district."

"Will you come with me to translate?"

"I will go to the female division, Inshallah. They will tell you the truth. You will have a male interpreter for the male division. They will be formal."

Jo thanked Myriam and hung up, heart swelling in anticipation. This new arrangement had possibilities. She wanted to meet the female leaders of the school district and hear "the truth." She was bound to learn a thing or two, regardless of what Phil Owen said and did. She turned off the kitchen light and went upstairs to find Ev.

At eight o'clock on New Year's Eve, Jo and Ev stood on the threshold of Diane's apartment. Diane opened the door before Jo could knock a second time. She had asked Jo to fill in for her regular babysitters, who were all partying. Jo hadn't planned anything special for New Year's and Ev had said he'd help, so they'd agreed to sit. Joey could be fun.

Diane wore tight black pants, four-inch red heels, and a white blouse that slipped off one shoulder. Over forty and still a looker, Jo thought. The living room smelled faintly of dog. Diane's new mutt raced past and jumped up to sniff the box in Ev's arms. Joey emerged from his bedroom and lunged after the dog. He beamed at his uncle and aunt, shouting, "Hell-o, hell-o" in his man's voice with its childish inflections. Ev had brought a box of homemade blocks, expecting to build forts and bridges with his nephew. Jo had brought her laptop, expecting to work while the guys played. Both men could concentrate on towers and bridges for hours.

Diane said, "Hairy needs to go out back before bedtime. The landlord wouldn't let me put in a doggy door, but the yard is fenced. Sorry for the inconvenience."

Ev said, "No problem," and laid the box on the coffee table. Jo saw him survey the room looking for the best construction site.

"Any other instructions?" Jo asked.

"Joey usually goes to sleep at ten, but he can stay up later tonight. He's excited to see you."

"Does he go to sleep by himself?"

"He knows what to do. Ev should watch him in the bathroom, though. And it would be great if you read to him. There are some books beside the bed. He sleeps with a nightlight."

She bustled around the room, straightening throw pillows and gathering purse and shawl. "I'll be back around one. Thank you so much. I really appreciate this." She hugged her son. "Listen to Aunt Jo, okay? I'll see you in the morning." She kissed him and stepped to the door. "Happy New Year, all." She closed the door behind her.

Diane's living room looked a lot like her childhood home: threadbare furniture, an old-fashioned TV, nothing on the walls except for a poster of redwoods from AAA. The kitchenette was festive in comparison: Joey's artwork festooned the fridge and cabinets; flyers covered a bulletin board; an oversized calendar bore color-coded notations and stars for good behavior. On the wall above the Formica table, Diane's associate's diploma hung in a cheap frame. Jo unloaded her laptop on the table, popped a bottle of bubbly into the fridge, and stepped into the hall. It had been a while since she'd visited, so she intended to snoop.

The master bedroom where Joey slept was impeccably outfitted. On one wall, shelves full of books and toys and electronic apparatus; on another wall, a desk with reading lamp, computer, and colorful notebooks from which papers protruded. Near the bed, a cabinet for medicine bottles, jars of herbal remedies, and a humidifier. On the floor, a spotless area rug and a doggie cushion in the corner.

Across the hall, in Diane's bedroom, which was barely big enough for her bed and bureau, piles of clothes lay on the floor in front of the closet, as if they had had toppled there when she last opened the door. A basket on top of the bureau held too many lipsticks and vials of makeup and hair gunk. Pictures of Joey were taped haphazardly to the wall beside the window. Jo thought, if Diane can keep house for Joey, why can't she keep house for herself? The chaos made her shudder.

Noise came from the living room: the clatter of wooden blocks spilling onto the floor and Joey whooping. Jo returned to see Ev carefully positioning blocks on top of the coffee table. Joey sat next to him, running his fingers over the shapes and grunting in obvious pleasure. The dog cruised the table top, nudging things askew with his snout.

Jo asked, "Do you want me to take Hairy into the kitchen so he doesn't bother you?"

Ev said, "Nah, he's fine here."

"He's playing, too," Joey said.

Jo nodded. Ev had a soft spot for dogs as well as kids. He sometimes put dog food out behind the studio in a metal dish scrounged from one of his projects and played with the creatures that came to eat it. She was indifferent to animals.

She went into the kitchen to plug in her computer. Glancing around for an outlet, she noticed a mess of dirty dishes and pots in the sink. She whispered "shit" and turned on the hot water. Cleaning up after her sister—what a way to ring in the New Year! But this new year promised better, and the thought of all D-Three might accomplish in Saudi Arabia gave her heart.

They let Joey stay up with them to sip champagne and watch the New Year Ball descend. Ev offered to read him to sleep and escorted him to his bedroom. Ev soon emerged and sat down beside Jo to share the rest of the bottle.

"Joey's a sweet kid," Ev said. "I've been thinking. If Diane ever needed it, we could take him in."

"What are you talking about?"

"He needs to be cared for by people who understand him."

"Did Diane say anything to you?"

"I could take good care of him. In her absence, I mean."

"We don't have time to care for a handicapped child."

"I would find the time, if you were agreeable."

She was not, and he knew it.

Ev stood and stretched. "I'm going to snooze a while. Join me?"

She shook her head. They'd settled the children issue years ago. The champagne must have got to him. She did not relish ignoring his desire to nurture. It pained her to deny him. But she had no choice. She had other priorities. She took another sip.


Jo woke, shivering on the couch, as Diane slipped into the living room at four in the morning. Jo turned on the lamp, thinking she must have fallen asleep over the last of the wine. Her throat hurt and she had to pee.

Diane said, "Sorry I'm late. I met a guy and I had a great, great time." She sounded drunk.

"You're in bad shape. How did you get home?"

"Nooooo, I'm in goood shape. My handsome prince drove me." She kicked off her shoes and sank into the chair opposite Jo. "If I hadn't promised to come home, I'd still be in his bed." She closed her eyes. "It . . . felt . . . so . . . good. Not just the sex."

"Will you ever see Prince Charming again?"

"Does it matter? An adult male danced with me, drank with me, and fucked me. This doesn't happen every day."

"You're asking for trouble."

"I'm asking for a break. I need a break." She sat up. "Where's Joey?"

"Asleep. Ev gave him two sips of champagne at midnight. He didn't like it."

"Great." She leaned back and covered her eyes with her hand. "So tell me about Prince Charming."

Diane shook her head. "He's the kind of guy you meet at a party. Not the kind of guy you bring home to Mama."

"Are you going to see him again?"

"It's none of your business!"

Jo felt insulted. "Don't ask me to babysit if you're just going to screw around." She heard the righteousness in her tone, but didn't care.

"There's nothing wrong with screwing around once in two years! You always suspect me of god knows what." She sat up again. "I bet you inspected the bathroom for drugs."

"Should I have?"

"Oh, lord. Get the poker out of your ass!"

Jo had heard those words before, sometimes said with affection, sometimes with scorn. She stiffened.

Diane rose. "I have to lie down. I'll see you in the morning. Thanks for everything." She tottered into her bedroom and closed the door.

Jo got up to pee, stifling the protest in her throat. She had every right to ask about Diane's business. Diane had dragged her in. Diane always dragged her in sooner or later. She stepped out of the bathroom and saw Ev standing in front of Joey's door, the dog at his feet. He shushed her with his finger across his lips. They tiptoed into the living room.

Ev said, "Do you want to stay here or go home?"

"Home. I don't want to see Diane's hangover in the morning."

He let Hairy out the back door. "Joey can take care of himself, and he'll take care of his mom, too." He chuckled.

Jo did not find it funny.

Ev picked up a few straggling blocks, tucked them in the box, and shoved it under the coffee table. Jo retrieved her laptop from the kitchen. They exited quietly and got into the truck. Ev turned the heat to full blast and backed away. He drove more carefully than usual, "watching out for drunken revelers," he said with a grin. Jo did not reply, her louche baby sister's words echoing in her ears. If not for her fight with Diane, the New Year would have started off perfectly well. She kept her mouth shut all the way home.

Jo sat at her desk reviewing the plan for the coming research trip to Riyadh. Owen had sent an outline, and Diane had annotated it, interweaving Jo's travel schedule and documentation with precision, with the same level of care with which she organized Joey's room. Jo thought about what things were like at D-Three before Diane joined the staff, before Diane became adept at Gant charts and everything else she did behind the scenes. The business ran better because of Diane. She depended on Diane, although she didn't like to. And why not? Because Diane would make another, thoughtless life mistake, and it would be so damn frustrating to watch.

Jo got up and went to the kitchen, mechanically putting on the kettle while New Year's Eve replayed in her head. She disapproved of casual sex with a stranger who could be a mass murderer for all Diane knew. It could lead to an STD, or abuse, or at the very least, heartache, and Big Sister would be left cleaning up. But something else festered.

The poker up her ass.

The accusation hurt. She considered herself a risk taker, an adventurer of the mind if not the body. She did not consider herself crabby or prudish or rigid in any way that counted. Determined, yes, but not rigid. Yes, some people reacted badly to her drive. But until now, never Diane.

Her phoned buzzed. Ev texted, "Come to the studio." She turned off the kettle and put on the jacket hanging by the back door. When she nudged the studio door open, Ev was standing on a stepladder on top of the workbench, working on something suspended from the ceiling. Too wobbly and too high!

"Will you please come down? I can't talk to you up there."

He grasped the top of the stepladder with both hands before looking down at her. "I'm done." He climbed down the stepladder to the workbench and jumped from the bench to the floor, looking pink and proud of himself. "New Year's resolution: install that pulley. Now Carlos and I can lift with the winch instead of our backs. Want to see it work?"

She nodded. He was going to show her anyway. She took a step back. He attached the rope that hung from the pulley to a crate and pressed a remote control. The machine on other side of the workbench growled, and the crate slowly rose from the floor.

"Cool, huh?" He pressed another button and the crate lowered back down.

She gave him a weak smile.

He approached her. "I thought you'd be pleased."

"I am."

"So? What's up?"

She might as well spit it out. "Diane said I have a poker up my ass."

"Ouch."

"She was drunk and angry because I criticized her one-night stand."

"Kiss and make up."

"Easy for you to say."

He pulled her toward him. She rested her head on his shoulder. He whispered in her ear, "You and Diane just have different styles. Poker versus gin rummy."

She pushed him away. "It's not funny. I have to be the taskmaster around here. No one else is going to make things happen."

"You do it well. I'm grateful, and so is Diane."

"That's not what she said."

"She is. She's different from you, but she loves you."

Yeah, Jo thought, and she harbors resentments that come out with booze. She would have to be careful around Diane going forward. And she would watch her own behavior in the office. Because sometimes she did feel a poker in her spine. Sometimes it saved D-Three's collective ass.

She turned to leave. "Thanks for listening. Don't climb that ladder alone."

"Right."

As she crossed the studio threshold, she visualized the time he had tried to erect a scaffold by himself, and she'd found him unconscious and bleeding on the studio floor. She'd panicked, called 911, howled at the thought of losing him. He'd turned out to have suffered a concussion, from which he recovered, but she'd spent two weeks in hell until he'd come back to himself completely.

He *was* himself.

She went back to her desk and powered up the computer, feeling better able to concentrate. Ev had that effect on her, and it had nothing to do with his words. His oblique approach to the world, so different from hers, refreshed her.

She pulled up the file of questions for which she would seek answers from teachers, school administrators, leaders of extracurricular programs, and, of course, the client's representatives. It would be up to her to gather qualitative information while Owen's team ferreted out hard data. The travel itself didn't excite her, but getting a better feel for possibilities in Riyadh did. Diane would see that she captained the ship with a steady hand and all necessary flexibility.

On this February morning in Riyadh, the sky was a cloudless blue. Jo stood outside the hotel, waiting in the mild sunshine for Myriam to collect her. A group of women stepped out the lobby door, chattering and stealing a glance at her in passing. Amazing how quickly you got used to seeing women in abayas. Even more amazing, how quickly you got used to wrapping yourself up in black. The head scarf sitting uneasily on Jo's curls occasionally slipped backwards, and she hoped a foreign woman's inadvertent breach of etiquette would be excused. She looked across the street to the pale stucco walls of a building complex. Not much color on these streets except for the occasional commercial sign. She wondered if she could get used to a city made of sand.

She had not asked Peter to join her because Myriam would translate. Ev had stayed home to design a skeleton structure on which to mount the demonstration exhibits. He'd been sulking since they finalized the subcontract. He didn't think she should assume responsibility for any part of the research, and certainly not for the "bullshit" strategic plan. She reminded him that she had not assumed control of anything, just taken over Owen's plane ticket. Owen's two-man team would do the legwork—visit the zoo, collect demographic data, etc.—and she would conduct one-on-one interviews. She'd asked him to trust her and prepared to proceed alone.

A gray SUV pulled up. The driver, a young man in Western dress, got out and opened a backseat door, gesturing for her to enter. He said good morning in English. Inside the car, Myriam beckoned. A wide woman, she occupied half the leather banquette. Jo swished in beside her.

"Your driver speaks English?"

Myriam laughed in a low rumble. "That is my son, Ahmed. The one who studies physics. I want him to meet you and Doctor Everett. For inspiration."

"I'm afraid I can't inspire anyone in physics." Jo addressed the back of the young man's head, "You'll have to meet my husband when he brings over the displays."

"It will be my pleasure. I look forward to seeing them."

"Where did you learn your English? You sound almost like a native."

"A native of which country? I went to American high school in London for a few years. It was my mother's idea, so of course my father agreed. She was an English teacher, you know. It was good for me in many ways."

Myriam asked, "Do you have children, Mrs. Joanna?"

"Just 'Jo,' please. No, I don't. But I work with children in museums." With those kids, and her clients, and the staff, she did plenty of mothering.

Myriam nodded, with a slight pursing of the lips. Jo chose to interpret her reaction as sympathy for her childlessness rather than disapproval. Yesterday at the research team briefing, she had learned this was a nation of families, with a huge population under eighteen in need of education. The five Saudi men present—they always seemed to flock in fours or fives—had addressed all their comments to the older of Owen's young, male research associates. She'd had to ask her questions through him. She hadn't taken it personally, but felt frustrated nonetheless.

She addressed Ahmed. "Do your siblings speak English as well?"

"No, I went to the UK alone. I don't mind the cold."

Myriam clucked her tongue. "My other sons are lazy."

Jo wondered if Myriam had daughters but didn't know if she should ask. She returned her attention to Ahmed. "Are you working on the children's museum project with your mother?"

"No, but I am interested. My mother does interesting things. You are going to the school district office today. Why?"

"I want to find out about the field trips elementary school kids take, and what support the teachers might need. In the US, we help teachers prepare for the field trip, to make the most of the day."

"You will see that our schools are more structured than in the West. Our teachers work very hard. I think they will want to hear your ideas."

"I hope so. Thanks for the encouragement. And the ride." She leaned back into the seat. Myriam pressed her hand to her chest and smiled with obvious maternal pride. Jo thought, wherever you are in the world, mothers are mothers.


Jo called Ev from the hotel just after dinner—morning for him—to debrief the day. She could hear him moving around the kitchen making his coffee as he listened. She hurried because there was so much to tell.

"Myriam's son dropped us off at the school district office. Only it wasn't the main office, it was the female division office. Everybody inside the building was female, even the janitor. As soon as Myriam introduced me, they said "Take it off, take it off!" in English and I took off the abaya. Theirs were already off. Most of the women were hefty. They wore makeup, and fancy blouses over long skirts, and some pretty amazing jewelry. Myriam translated. Bottom line: the administrators say teachers will bring the little ones if the principals tell them to. But they warned me that it will be hard to convince parents to bring their girls on weekends. They *might* bring their boys. The administrators say *they* have a hard time communicating with the traditionalists. We brainstormed a little. It was really good that I came."

Ev grunted.

"We had this really lively discussion about teacher preparation. I showed them a reference on my phone, and instantly each of them whipped out her phone, snapped a picture, and forwarded it. They discussed it for a while in Arabic. It was clear they had a lot of respect for Myriam. Then she asked them to join us for a late lunch. These confident, professional women put veils over their faces to walk across the street to a restaurant! Can you imagine!"

Ev said no, he couldn't.

Jo hurried on. "There were fifty items on the menu, from all over the world, but no Saudi dishes because, Myriam told me, there are no Saudi chefs. Cooking is women's work. I ordered paella and two others did, too. They tried to include me, but Myriam couldn't keep up with the chatter. It didn't matter. My mind was already blown."

Ev asked, "Why?"

She stopped to think. "I guess I expected them to be aloof, maybe even a little hostile to the foreigner coming in to tell them what to do. But they were warm and welcoming. So different from the men. I wanted to take a picture, but Myriam said photos are verboten because they could be seen by a strange man. But here's the kicker: when we left, Myriam's driver came to pick us up, not her son, her regular driver. And she put a veil over her face! When we were in the back seat I asked her why she covered. She said, 'I have a right to feel comfortable outside my home.' Then she looked at me as if I were a child and patted my hand."

She waited for Ev's reaction.

He said, "And?"

"I don't get it. One of the women at lunch kept her face veil on during the meal, even though we were in a private room. She slipped bites of food underneath. I thought okay, she's from the provinces. But Myriam is a sophisticate. She sends her son to study in England. She's helping her boss make social change. Why hide from her own driver?"

There was a loud noise on Ev's end. She could hear Carlos swearing in Spanish. Ev said, "Gotta go. Text me your flight info again."

She ended the call, unsatisfied. She wanted to talk. She thought about going out for a walk to replay the day in her mind, but she could not without an escort. Stuck in the hotel, with no place to sip a nightcap, she stepped to the window to watch lights come on as the sky darkened over a modern city with medieval customs. Before the internet era, she would never have been invited here. She would never have met Myriam, an intelligent woman who liked being repressed. As a girl, Jo used to wonder what she would have done if she had lived centuries ago when only the nobility had privileges. Would she have been a faithful servant, or would she have put on boy's clothes and caused trouble? It would have been a short, hard life in either case. And Myriam wanted to lead a twenty-first-century version of that life. A bad taste filled her mouth.

She turned away from the window and went to the desk where her computer sat open. Owen's team had set up a series of

Google Docs in which to collect field notes. She did not want to insert flat, antiseptic data into the matrix labeled "schools." She picked up her phone and dialed Phil Owen direct.

"I've been talking with the supervisors at the school district's female division. They advise us to focus on school groups because parents won't bring their girls on weekends. *Maybe* they'll bring their boys. The supervisors say it'll be really hard to buck tradition. I think we should take their advice seriously."

Owen's voice was muffled. "You can set up the demo in a school, but it's too soon to change the business model."

"What business model? Aren't we about to invent one?"

"My dear girl, the committee already has ideas on how they expect their museums to operate. They like the American format, half state funded, half earned income. They *expect* us to market to the parents, and they expect to attract weekend visitors by the thousands. I tried to sell them on a five-year audience development plan. They pushed me back to a maximum of three."

"That's crazy."

"I must agree."

"Why didn't you tell them what you really think?"

"Because they wouldn't hear it. Governments are the worst listeners."

"I'm putting the school supervisors' advice in my notes."

"Please do. My team will want to know everything you've learned."

Jo ended the call, disgusted. Clearly, Owen's instructions from the committee didn't match hers from the director. She needed clarification. Urgently.

Myriam called as Jo was covering her head to go down to the lobby for breakfast. Myriam apologized for being unable to accompany Jo that morning, but Ahmed would drive and translate. He would be good to her. She could ask him anything. Myriam would meet them for lunch after prayers.

She took the elevator down to the lobby without wearing her abaya. Last night she had seen another woman dining in Western dress with only a scarf over her hair, and she'd decided to follow suit. In the dining room, she put her purse down on a table and walked over to the omelet station. The mustachioed chef watched her point to peppers and tomatoes. Moving slowly, he prepared her omelet and placed the plate on a tray. When she said thank you, he did not acknowledge her, even with a flick of the eye. So much ado about so little, she thought. The omelet was delicious.

She returned to her room to brush her teeth and collect her notebook. As she prepared to leave again, she glimpsed the abaya spread across a chair. She realized she needed to wear it for young Ahmed's sake, because she wanted to be able to talk to him without offending the men they would meet. Or him. Myriam had said "ask him anything." Myriam's absence might be opportune. She slipped the abaya over her clothes, considering it like a disguise.

Ahmed was standing near the door in the lobby. He nodded politely and ushered her into the gray SUV parked in the driveway. He started the engine and asked which museum she wanted to see first. She replied the renewable energy center—yes, there was one!—and sat back to plot her bit of intrigue. Outside the window, sand-colored walls gave way to modern congestion: flat, glass-clad buildings, a Starbucks on a corner, a few scraggly palm trees planted in the median in front of the tallest structures. The sky was almost too blue.

"Thanks for taking the time away from your studies," Jo began.

"It is my pleasure. I want to help. I know it is hard to under-stand a country different from your own."

"If you come to America, it will be my turn to escort you."

"I would like that very much. But I have no plans." He turned the side of his face toward her. "Except completing my degree."

"Come afterwards." She leaned toward him. "If my husband were here, he would ask you where the trees are. I don't see many."

"This part of my country is desert. It is too dry for European trees. I can show you a date plantation to the north if you want to see trees."

"I wonder if date palms are actually trees. They look like giant dandelions gone to seed. I'll have to ask Ev."

"There are many different kinds of palm. We have grown them for centuries. Dates are very nutritious."

"Speaking of history, Ahmed, can you explain why your mother and the school district leaders worry about convincing the 'traditionalists' to visit the museum? I thought education was part of your tradition."

"It is. But there are different interpretations, and my mother respects them."

"What about you?"

"I have less patience." He paused. "More than two hundred years ago, our king and our religious leader made a compact. Reli-gion showed us how to live, and government kept us safe. It is a powerful tradition, and people fear to change it. Because their family does something, they think God wants it. They do not sep-arate what is custom from what is holy." He paused. "My mother is distressed when I speak like this."

"Don't worry, I won't tell." She waited a beat. "It seemed like your mother and the others are afraid to even *start* a conversation with the traditionalists."

"Mrs. Joanna, if you want to talk about change with a traditional person, you do it in private. We are not like Europeans. Except for online."

"Yeah, I noticed everyone has a smart phone. But I still don't understand."

"Because you are American. You do not have a long history. Change takes time." He smiled, looking more like Myriam as his cheeks widened.

This kid had something going for him. Maybe Becca could come on the next trip and meet him. She might like to talk to a thoughtful young physicist who had unconventional opinions about convention. They might get along, that is, if Becca didn't first jump down his throat.

"Do your siblings think like you? And your half siblings?"

He laughed. "I do not have half siblings. The Quran tells us a man may marry four wives if he treats them equally. My father says it is impossible to treat women equally and so he married only once. Really, I think he knows my mother would kill him."

Jo thought, your mother is woman enough for any man. "I see."

Ahmed nodded and drove on. She sat back in her seat, content to wait for another opportunity to interrogate him. She had spotted a fissure in the façade of perfect Saudi obedience.

Ahmed led Jo and his mother into a booth in the "family" floor of a Lebanese restaurant. They settled around a table behind a privacy screen, and Myriam suggested they order a local fish much loved by her family, even by Ahmed with his English tastes. She ordered for them and then asked Jo's permission to talk to her son in Arabic to make sure he had been a good guide. Jo said he had.

As they waited for the meal to arrive, mother and son conversed and Jo reflected on her morning. She had been struck by the contrast between the two places Ahmed had taken her, the brash, high-tech energy center and the old-fashioned National Museum. Both were based on Western museum practice, but, clearly, different standards had been at play. Which standards would the director prefer? At the first break in the Arabic conversation, Jo pressed ahead.

"May I ask you something, Myriam? I spoke to Owen yesterday. He said the committee expects the museum to earn half its income in three years. The director has said nothing about charging admission. I am concerned about making premature assumptions."

Myriam stopped eating the carrot stick she had taken from the crudités plate in the center of the table. "Mr. Phil made many promises to the committee. We will see if he can keep them."

"Are you saying that earned income was Owen's idea?"

"It was discussed. The committee liked Mr. Phil's proposal for the budget. The director wants to understand it. You will help her."

The waiter brought three plates of fish and a pile of flatbread. Ahmed broke one of the slabs of bread and offered Jo a piece. She took it in silence. This project was like an onion, layer beneath layer. She'd never get to the bottom of who said what to whom about earned income, and it didn't matter. The work would unroll anyway, or it wouldn't. She watched Myriam cut into her fish with the side of her soupspoon and maneuver a bite into her mouth. The waiter had left knives and forks at their places as well as spoons. Jo picked up her knife and fork. The fish was delicious.

Myriam said between spoonfuls, "I went to the school district this morning. The women like you very much. They say to come again. Is that possible?"

"Not this trip. The next few days are spoken for. Please thank them for the invitation, though."

"You have touched their hearts. You treated them as colleagues. With respect. I hope you will visit longer with me the next time you come. As a friend." Myriam reached into her handbag and removed a small package tied with a gauzy bow. "A little souvenir."

"Thank you." Jo tucked the box into her briefcase, wondering what had impressed the school district leaders. She had done nothing unusual. That is, nothing unusual in an American context. She took another bite of fish.


Ev answered his phone on the first ring. "Sorry I cut you off yesterday. Carlos dropped an I-beam. No damage."

"I'm fit to be tied. Last night I found out Owen promised the museum would earn fifty percent of the operating budget by year three. Myriam says the committee will press him to deliver. And today Myriam's son took me to the renewable energy museum. It's actually a visitor center with a few artifacts and one slick audio-visual display after another. And the logo is a lantern from the Quran, sort of like Aladdin's lamp, lighting the way into the future!"

"Huh. Clever."

"They spent a fortune on video. No evaluation to speak of. They're too enamored of the place to check if it really delivers the message."

Ev said, "Slow down. What's got you buzzed?"

Jo took a breath. "It's propaganda. Propaganda full of gizmos."

"So? You've seen that before."

"I'm worried they will want us to produce the same drivel."

"Don't jump to conclusions. The director wants us. Anyone who wants *us* doesn't want whizz-bang."

"But they're so proud of the place. Even Myriam's son liked it, and he's a thinker."

"Come home and we'll talk about it."

She ended the call, calmed a bit by the sound of Ev's voice, but worried that the committee might demand all sort of unexpected things. She remembered the time a former government client had come up with an ultimatum: D-Three had created a show about food for a state convention and visitors' bureau. Just before installation, the client threatened to withhold payment unless the show featured products from every region in the state. So they added an extra section on grapes, at no additional cost to the client. They lost money on the deal. Something similar could very well happen here, with a much higher price tag.

She undressed and stepped into the tiled bathroom. She turned the shower lever to hot. When it began to steam, she stepped in. Needles of heat hit her back and shoulders. She urged herself to relax. In twenty-four hours she would be on her way home.

In response to Jo's impromptu request for a meeting, the director had cleared a slot in her schedule. At nine in the morning, Myriam escorted Jo to the director's door and withdrew. Jo entered an ordinary bureaucratic office containing a metal desk and one hard chair for a guest. Sitting behind the desk, the director looked anything but ordinary: cashmere shawl wrapped around her shoulders, earrings rimmed with diamonds, perfectly polished fingernails, perfectly sculpted eyebrows. Jo felt her own appearance lacking and pulled her sweater lower on her hips. The director signaled her to sit and reached for a bronze pot on the credenza behind her. She poured steaming tea into two glass cups and offered Jo a plate of sweets.

Jo took a sticky date. "Thank you for making time for me. I hope you can clarify something for me before I go home."

The director nodded.

Jo took a breath. "I believe one of the purposes of the strategic plan we are developing is to estimate how people will react to the central museum as well as the regional branches."

"Yes, that is ideal."

"I gather that the committee already has some assumptions. They expect large enough audiences by year three so that half the museum's operating budget comes from admission fees."

"Yes, that is correct."

"With respect ma'am, what I've seen so far tells me we don't know how parents will react. I doubt the American business model can be transplanted here wholesale. You don't have a history of museum-going or private philanthropy."

"The committee hopes that life is simple, but they know better. You will show us the American model and then the alternatives. I will be guided by *your* plan." The director sipped her tea. "Is there another issue to discuss?"

Jo shook her head.

"Myriam tells me that you met her son. His English is quite good."

"He was a terrific guide. So was Myriam. I learned a lot."

"Excellent. I will be happy to read your report." She leaned back in her chair. Jo understood she was dismissed. She rose and thanked the director for the meeting.

In the elevator descending from the female floor, Jo felt her gorge rise. The American model *and* the alternatives. Not one strategic plan but several. Scope creep: you sign a contract for a fixed fee and then something gets redefined and then something else, and the scope gets bigger and bigger, and you lose your shirt. Ev's skepticism had been justified. She felt stupid and vulnerable. It wasn't the money—Owen would share the cost of scope creep—it was the whole, stupefying deal. She couldn't wait to get home.

Carlos beamed at Jo, pleased with the folding frame he had constructed while she was in Riyadh. He had used double hinges, the kind that let you fold a door flat against a wall, attached to aluminum struts into which he'd inserted power cords for mounting spotlights. He told Jo to collapse the thing and pick it up with one hand. She could carry it on a flight herself, he said, worse comes to worst. Not that she would need to, because he was on schedule. He boasted that when the frame came out of its shipping crates in Saudi Arabia, anyone anywhere with a level floor and electricity would be able to set it up. No instructions necessary, like an Apple product. Jo folded two of the aluminum panels together. Truly tight and light. She said she'd had plenty of trouble getting Apple stuff going, and his design was better. Carlos went back to his drafting table, all smiles.

Jo went to Diane's desk to deposit her travel receipts in the inbox. Dumping the bookkeeping chore on someone else was a minor luxury. She could record the expenses herself, but Diane would do it more quickly, and Diane had the time. She often left early or came late—always doing something with Joey or the dog—but she worked more than twenty hours some weeks to balance it out. Jo had something more important to do: write a report that would satisfy both Owen and the director.

Last night Ev had picked her up at the airport, and, as they drove across the ghetto and up the hill, she'd explained the scope creep. He'd not said a word, not a hint of "I told you so." She was grateful for whatever it was in his character that kept him from being petty. They climbed the stairs to their bedroom, Ev hefting her luggage, and despite the hour and the jetlag, when they lay in bed, she reached for his body under the covers and they made love. This morning he was gone when she opened her eyes. She dressed and went downstairs. She peered out the back window and spotted him behind the glass wall of the studio, bent over the workbench. She decided to wait for him to call her. First, she had a trip to debrief.

As she walked into the kitchen to get breakfast, Becca opened the front door. Without removing her jacket, Becca made straight for Jo.

"Did you get the news?" Becca crossed arms in front of her chest.

"I just got up."

"There was another bombing at a bazaar in Baghdad. Fifty-two people killed or injured. ISIS is claiming victory."

"Sorry." Jo turned her back to open the fridge.

"Don't you care?"

Jo spun around. "I didn't do it."

"It's no joke!" Becca averted her eyes. "I hate worrying about whether you'll make it back alive. You don't understand what you're getting into."

"Nothing happened while I was in Riyadh. Riyadh is safe. Saudi Arabia is safe."

"The 9/11 radicals were Saudis! It's the breeding ground!"

"Calm down. Please." She closed the fridge and took Becca's hands, uncrossing her arms. "If you met the people I'm dealing with you would think differently. They're special people who want to do better for their kids."

Becca opened her mouth and closed it. She looked into Jo's eyes. "Special people on the verge of war."

"That's not how it feels there."

"You see what you want to see."

"I'm tempted to take you with me next time so you can see for yourself."

Becca blanched. "Do I have to go with you?"

"No, but you have to get to work. We have a lot to do."

Jo dropped Becca's hands and watched her leave the kitchen. Becca had been placid as an undergraduate, but somewhere along the way she'd turned militant without Jo's marking the transition. Maybe it was over Trump. Jo stayed away from politics for the sake of the business, and Ev stayed away by temperament. It seemed Becca couldn't stay away. With a sigh, Jo realized Becca might never want to converse with Myriam's son. But the girl's concern for her own safety touched her.

Diane pushed the front door open with her hip, her arms laden with packages. She tucked her burdens under her desk, and as she straightened up she noticed the jumble in her inbox. She leaned over to retrieve the receipts. Jo approached.

"The director's assistant paid for lunch a couple of times. Everything else is there."

"I'm so glad you're back. We were all worried. The news is so awful."

"Nothing happened in Saudi Arabia. Have you been talking to Becca? Something's spooked her."

Diane looked hurt. "I wouldn't want to spook her. Ev has been holed up in the studio, and we've hardly seen him. Carlos is spending money, but you had authorized it. We missed you."

"Carlos is making progress. I'll go check in with Ev." She

didn't like the sound of "holed up in the studio." He should have been directing the team.

She stepped out of the office into the cool, damp morning and knocked on the studio door. She opened it without waiting for a reply. She expected to see a cardboard mock-up or two on the workbench, but there was only an open notebook. Ev turned down the music and faced her.

"I changed my mind. Can't do spinning. Too clinical. We need to connect to daily life."

Uh, oh. Her pulse quickened.

"I really want water play."

"We're not building a filtration system for a two-week venue!"

"I know. So I'm thinking . . . dirt. What's under my feet. Not solid ground. Dirt vs. soil. Microscopic creatures. Roots. Seeds."

"Two thousand square feet, Ev. One month. Must we start over again?"

"I started." He had the grace to look sheepish. "Becca's done some research. Carlos's stuff will be fine. We may need to ship express, though. You want to tell Owen? You want me to?"

"Jesus Christ, Ev! This job is screwy enough!"

He looked away. "Gotta make it right."

Lord, what a homecoming! Becca talking about bombs and Ev's head in the clouds! And there was no point arguing with him. His mind moved only in one direction. If past was prologue, he'd work his new idea night and day and *almost* finish in time. She'd have to do all the explaining. He was so damn stubborn. She turned on her heel and flounced out of the studio.

The office smelled like coffee. Becca was waiting for her with a cup in one hand, a folder in the other. "When Ev switched to soil, I called your person at Cal. Here's what he sent." She handed over the folder. "There's not much research on children's ideas about the underground. Ev wants to use plastic granules or seed hulls to make clean dirt. I think it will work." She hovered.

Jo collected herself. "I'm going to need you. Finish up whatever you're doing for Ev and come find me."

Becca nodded and carried her cup to her corner.

Jo took a breath. He'd been too chicken to tell her last night. But he had a point. "Underground" was the better topic, and if Ev felt inspired, they'd make something wonderful. If she let him loose, she'd be able to stare down those misogynistic, supercilious Saudis, come home proud and intact, whatever the committee ultimately decided to do. Tension began to diffuse from her body. She realized she'd been holding her breath all week in Riyadh. The very air in Oakland felt so much gentler.

At Jo's request, Becca refrigerated her brown bag lunch and climbed into the truck. Jo drove them to Berkeley, to her favorite deli near the Cal campus, and they took a table near the window. They sat catty-corner, and Jo set a notebook and pen on the table beside her. After a skinny thing with a ring in her eyebrow took their order, Jo began.

"I'm going to need you to concentrate on programs for the next little while."

"It's only a two-week venue."

"I'd like you to collect ideas for programs. You know, making collages with seeds. Worms under glass. Cooperative play with a front-end loader. They don't do exploratory activity in school, and we have to show them what it means."

Becca pursed her lips. "I really don't want to go to Saudi Arabia."

"Just figure out the programs. I'll get someone over there to present them. Or I'll do it myself."

The waitress laid a salad in front of Jo and an overflowing corned beef sandwich in front of Becca. The girl dug in with both hands. Jo continued. "I'm toying with an idea, and I want your help."

Becca used a napkin to wipe mustard off the corners of her mouth. "I have a couple of newsletters to finish."

"The teachers in Riyadh said parents might not bring their girls. Those women fight for equity, and they don't often win. I'm on their side."

Becca looked puzzled.

"If we want girls to come, we need to get to the moms. The women all have smart phones. The internet is the only place they roam free." She took a forkful of lettuce.

"And so?" Becca took another colossal bite.

Jo said, "We need to make the moms want to bring their girls. I'm thinking of some sort of online club, with incentives, like Avon, or Mary Kay. Say we give the school kids seeds and two cups of different soils and ask the moms to report what sprouts, and when. Get them talking to one another, so they'll pull each other. Are you ready to tackle it?"

"Sounds out of my league."

"Well, *online* is out of mine. You start, and we'll show whatever you come up with to Myriam."

"Is two weeks long enough to launch a club?"

"It's long enough to test the concept."

Becca stopped eating. "Are you sure the moms will want to join a club?"

"No. It might not work. In which case, we'll know we need to try something else."

"D-Three doesn't do apps."

Jo leaned back. "Time to start. Saudi girls need a leg up. If there had been any sort of encouragement in the town where I grew up, Diane might not have gone off the rails."

"She went off the rails?"

"Ask her about it." She pointed a finger at Becca. "Are you ready to design a moms' club?"

"I have to say, when you dream up stuff like this, I remember how lucky I am to work for D-Three."

"Thanks." Jo picked up the pen and notebook. "Any idea on where you'll start?"

Becca shook her head. "I haven't had much time to think about soil. I was working on spinning." She paused, sandwich in hand. "I don't know anything about Mary Kay. Maybe someone in computer science at Cal would be better."

"Nerds don't know anything about moms of four-year-olds. You can do this."

"I don't think I can channel a Saudi mom."

"You can. Summon your courage and go for it."

Becca stared at her sandwich. "That's what Ev said. Courage builds confidence. He said it's the secret of your success."

So, Jo thought, she's been talking to Ev. "Tell me more."

Becca began to blush. "We were talking about the state of the nation. I was feeling desperate and Ev told me to follow your example."

"My example? Or D-Three's."

Becca flushed red against her pale hair. "Yours. He said you're not the paragon of confidence I assumed you were. You're just gutsy. He said I should take heart."

Jo reflected a moment. She didn't think herself particularly brave, but she also didn't shy away from challenges. Ev had a point.

Becca lowered the sandwich to her plate. "I'm trying to ignore all the crap out there and just do my thing. Like Ev said."

Got to be one hell of a crush to make this one put aside her politics. "Sound advice. Are you taking it?"

Becca's face contracted. "I have to." She looked down. "This is home."

"What about your family back East?"

Becca shook her head. "I won't go back. They wouldn't take me in."

"Why do you say that?"

"Because it's true." Becca looked away, as if unwilling to say more.

"Well, finish up. We have a lot to do."

Becca nodded and resumed eating. Jo took a mouthful of salad. She had not suspected that beneath the feistiness, Becca harbored such vulnerability. All that tough-girl talk, just a front. She felt responsible for Becca's professional life, but not her psyche. She would have to talk to Ev about giving advice. He'd already done too much. She signaled the waitress for the check.

Outside the sun had sunk behind the coastal range. Jo sat alone at her desk in the twilight, waiting for Ev to close up the studio. Despite the office distractions—Diane's phone calls to doctors' offices, Carlos's mariachis, her computer chiming notifications at every turn—she'd managed to write her report, except for the section on the business model. She couldn't figure out how to finesse scope creep, and she had run out of gas. With a sigh, she clicked "save" and left the office to go find Ev.

Light from the studio windows illuminated the way. She

saw Ev behind the glass holding the whirligig mechanism in both hands. She burst through the door.

"What are you doing? Changing your mind again?" Her chest contracted.

Ev looked up. "Finishing this off. Becca wants it for a friend of hers."

"So you're jeopardizing the schedule to make Becca happy?"

"This is a twenty-minute favor for a friend. I like doing it."

"She's not a friend. She's a heartsick girl who's in love with you, and she works for you! Haven't you noticed? You drink coffee with her every morning."

"She's lonely. That's all." Ev lowered the mechanism to the workbench. He picked up a notebook and beckoned her to look at the open pages. "This is what I'm going to build for you."

Jo forced herself to look. The whole deal depended on his idea. He had drawn a tree sliced in half vertically, from crown to roots. Kids crawled beneath the roots and coiled around the trunk. Next to the tree, adults and kids sat in a circle, playing with stuff. In the background, a conveyor belt ran between two big bins into which children were digging.

Ev said, "The set is a little heavy, but it ships in pieces. Everyone on staff has an assignment for filling in the pieces."

The vision charmed her, thank goodness. She pointed to the slice of tree. "Shouldn't you use a date palm?"

"There are deciduous trees in the Saudi mountains. I need to use a tree with a deep root base so kids will feel immersed in the ground beneath it."

"Why so elaborate? We could get away with less."

"Like you always say, kids deserve magic."

She felt her chest release a notch. "Carlos says anyone anywhere can install this."

Ev shook his head. "I'm going to do it myself. With you." He reached out to her shoulder.

She felt her guard lowering. "One month, Ev. One month to get it done."

He grinned and pulled her toward him. He held her carefully for a beat, as if asking forgiveness for alarming her. She let him hold her. She wanted to believe he had thought it all through. She wanted to believe the pieces would fall into place in time. She also wanted a bath, and a glass of wine, and to lay her head on her own pillow.

"Okay, okay." She pushed out of his arms and turned to leave. She turned back: "You'd better be careful with Becca."

"I'm always careful."

"Right." She'd have to manage Becca closely, for her own good.

She walked through the dark office to the foot of the stairs and switched on the overhead light. The cantilevered steps cast slabs of shadow on the office floor. She climbed heavily, her resolve forming. Yes, she would pick up the burdens Ev's about-face had created. She would make the necessary excuses and sell the plan to the skeptical. D-Three would work nonstop for a month, and then, after the crates arrived in Saudi Arabia, for another month without hope of profit. Ev had stolen whatever joy she might have found in besting Phil Owen. But they were still in the game.

The challenge: build fifteen displays in thirty days. Carlos constructed the stage set and fabricated cabinets, Ev built the mechanisms, Andy did the wiring, Becca sourced materials and programs, and Diane planned the crating and shipping. Jo supervised and wrote copy, designing and printing the labels herself. Every minute counted. It felt as if they were cramming for a final together: intense, but also fun. Andy filled Carlos's boots with "clean dirt," to break the tension, he said. In return, Carlos spread "soil fungi"—actually mushroom paste—on Andy's lunch. Andy and Carlos rigged the conveyor belt between their two desks for the crate guy to measure. They conveyed pencils and markers back and forth just to needle Jo. She played her part, scolding them like naughty children. At the end of each day, Jo charted D-Three's progress. Two weeks in, pieces of displays had accumulated in the corners of the office, and the job looked doable.

Then on Wednesday afternoon, Ev disappeared. Jo tried not to worry. At six she closed her computer—he had still not returned or turned on his phone—and busied herself filing. Then she did the laundry. Then she ate dinner, growing more concerned. It was not like him to abandon a project; it was like him to lose track of time. She heard him at the door around nine o'clock, and went to meet him. He sauntered into the office and laid the portfolio he'd been carrying on top of the flat file. He then went into the kitchen and opened the fridge.

"Got any leftovers?"

"Where have you been?" She kept her voice low because Diane had returned with Joey, who sat hunched under her desk playing video games while his mother punched her adding machine.

"Across the Bay, at an art gallery. They want to give me a show." He rummaged behind the fridge door and emerged with a foil packet. "Is this the lamb from Sunday?"

"A show of what?"

"They think my models deserve to be on pedestals." He opened the foil and sniffed. He sprinkled salt into the packet and nibbled a bit of meat. "Becca showed the whirligig to a friend of hers, who showed it to her cousin who runs the gallery. They asked to see my other pieces, so I brought them photos of my exhibits, the more artsy ones. They liked them. Is there any beer?"

"You can't do a show. There's no time to spare. None." Her body tensed.

"I don't have to do anything now except give them my stuff. Maybe a little polishing."

"Absolutely not!" She didn't care if Diane heard. "The job comes first. The whole thing depends on you."

He raised his chin. "I can do my stuff and still drive over the bridge once or twice before we ship."

"Why are you even thinking about it?"

"Opportunity. I want to see how grown men and women react to my work. I'll learn something about it, and about me."

She spoke through clenched teeth. "You changed the topic at the last minute, and then you promised you'd make it work. You had better."

He stopped chewing. "Wow. I'll ask the gallery to wait if you want me to. But you're wrong. I can walk and chew gum at the same time." He put the foil on the counter and turned back to the fridge. "I need a beer."

Diane stepped into the kitchen. "Sorry, but I overheard you mention San Francisco? I'm taking Joey for his exam next week. Can I do anything for you while we're there?"

Ev said, "Sure. Deliver some models."

"No!" Jo faced Diane. "Why are you going now? Can't it wait?"

Diane's brow furrowed. "It's been scheduled for six months. There are four doctors involved. I can't change it."

On the verge of tears, Jo said nothing.

Ev closed the fridge and leaned against the door. "Diane has to do what Joey needs done. We'll be fine."

"I can take calls while I'm there. Everything's lined up except for crating the pieces we haven't finished," Diane said.

"Exactly. We're not ready. If we're late this time, we can't pop everything into a van and drive all night. It could take six weeks to clear customs, for chrissake." Jo felt her face grow hot with frustration. Then strong arms wrapped around her from behind. Joey, out from under the desk.

Diane said, "Joey honey, Aunt Jo is okay. She doesn't need a hug now, but I do. Come here." She opened her arms. Joey released Jo and lumbered to his mother. She hugged him and said, "Thank you for caring." She addressed Jo over his shoulder. "I worked out a backup plan with Phil Owen."

"And you expect me to rely on a plan you and Owen cobbled together?"

Ev said, "Jo, the backup plan is not your problem. And we will finish in time."

"Not with both of you running off to San Francisco." She blinked back tears.

Diane released her son and said, "It can't be helped. I'm sorry."

Jo turned her back and climbed the stairs. Ev and Diane, the two people closest to her in the world, were ignoring her when they should be helping. Ev knew she was counting on this job, but it didn't penetrate his cloud. As for Diane, the old frustration thickened her tongue. She went to the bathroom to brush her teeth.

She stood at the sink and saw herself in the mirror. Of course she looked tired, propelling this project forward by force of her will alone. She turned on the faucet and scooped water to rinse her face. The shipping schedule came to mind; they might possibly complete on time, even with Ev absent for an afternoon or two. Maybe she had overreacted. She wanted to think she'd overreacted. But the deadline loomed.

As she reached for a towel, she spotted the package Myriam had given her in Riyadh, lodged in the corner of the shelf where she'd stashed it. She dried her face and hands and picked it up. Unwrapping it, she found a lipstick-sized bottle of perfume inscribed in Arabic, and a note: "Made from roses in Taif. To my American sister." Sister, yes, sister in spirit. How ironic that Myriam, who covered her face in public, seemed more like a sister than Diane, who had no shame. She replaced the bottle on the shelf and turned off the bathroom light.

When she woke in the morning, the clock read 9:50 and Ev was gone. She'd been unable to sleep, alternately angry and contrite, until nearly dawn. She dressed quickly and went downstairs to find him. She wanted to apologize for not discussing the gallery offer calmly. He was not in the office, nor in the kitchen. She grabbed the sweatshirt hanging from a peg at the back door and went out to the studio.

No one there. Ev sometimes left notes on the workbench. No note in sight. She peered around the corner at the driveway. No truck. She shivered in the early morning fog and returned to the house.

Carlos sailed into the office smelling like cinnamon. He went to the kitchen and laid churros out on a platter along with a box of coffee.

"Hazelnut this time. They did not have any special tea, sorry."

"Are you meeting Ev somewhere?"

"No. I'm almost finished with the bases. I want to prime them today so they dry over the weekend. You want to help me pick a color?"

"Do you have any idea where Ev went?"

"No, no. Don't worry, he's cool."

Carlos poured himself a cup of coffee and wrapped two churros in a napkin. He carried them to his drafting table and sat to eat. "This is really good, Josita." He waved a churro at her.

Jo ignored him. She found Diane at the copy machine. "Do you know where Ev went?"

Diane looked up. "I haven't seen him this morning. I revised the schedule again. Crates will arrive in April. Can I show you the revision after I finish copying?"

She glanced over to Becca's desk. "Where's Becca?"

"Working from home. She's going to Cal later to talk to somebody."

Oh, jeez, Jo thought, she's making it too complicated. "Andy?"

"He has a test this morning." Diane spread papers on top of the copy machine and began to collate them. "He should be back before I have to leave."

"You're leaving, too?"

"Joey's aide has to go home early."

Jo turned away and sat down at her desk. Her heart began to pound. She felt drained, not enough energy in her arms to reach her computer. She managed to pick up her phone to text Ev. No reply.

Her heart beat faster. She could hear her pulse in her ears. Heat flashed through her, and her head filled with cotton wool. She tasted bile. She swallowed and tried to ease the pressure enveloping her chest. It gripped her harder and she began to fear something awful was happening. She put her head down on her desk and closed her eyes, but it didn't ease the pain. I need to go to the hospital, she thought. How am I going to get to the ER? She opened her eyes but the world turned black. Her hands felt clammy. She must be having a heart attack. She moaned.

Diane materialized at her side, offering a glass of water, wrapping an arm around her shoulders. Diane said something she couldn't hear. Fear ripped through her. She clutched Diane's arm. Diane rubbed her back. She couldn't get enough air. She thought she was about to die. She felt her forehead hot on the desk and tried to sit up, but Diane shushed her and said wait a few minutes. The pressure in her chest mounted. Diane stroked her back. Jo raised her head.

"I don't know what's happening."

"I think you're having a panic attack. They run in the family."

"This happens to you?"

"It used to. When I didn't know if I could handle Joey by myself." Diane paused. "I haven't had one in years."

Jo dropped her head. She tried not to cry.

"Do you want to tell me what you're worried about?" Diane asked.

"You already know."

"If it's the schedule, we'll be fine. You'll be fine." Diane patted Jo's arm.

"Please don't tell anyone about this."

Diane nodded. "Maybe you should lie down. Let's go upstairs."

Blood throbbed in her ears. She rose slowly to test her legs. Steady enough. She let Diane walk her upstairs and ease her onto the bed.

Diane said, "Rest. You'll be fine in fifteen minutes."

Her heart shuddered but breathing was a little easier lying down. She closed her eyes.

"I'll be downstairs if you need anything. Or if you just want to talk." Diane shut the bedroom door behind her.

Jo tried to doze. Impossible, but she felt her terror ease a bit. She wasn't dying. According to Diane, she wasn't even sick. So what was wrong? Somehow she knew. It wasn't Ev's disappearance that panicked her: it was the thought that the Saudi deal could implode. God, how she craved a win. Paying off their debt was the least of it. She wanted to show the world what she could really do. What D-Three could do.

Jo sat up testily. She stood slowly and then went to the bathroom to wash her face and stare down the fear. She returned to the bedroom feeling calmer. She lay down and placed her hand on her chest; she felt her heartbeat gradually slow. She breathed deeply; she wasn't going to die. The business would survive. Relief began to edge out fear.

There was a scratch at the door. Ev poked his head in. She beckoned him, and he hovered over her.

"Diane said you're not feeling well."

"What else did she say?"

"That you were looking for me."

Thank you, she thought. She wouldn't tell him what had happened until she understood it completely. "I'm better. Where were you?"

"Looking for a tree to slice. I went to a couple of nurseries, no luck. The trees were too green. Then I canvassed the flats. I saw a hunk of driftwood with the remains of a terrific root ball. Roots are like brains, you know. They use the fungus that lives on them to send messages across the forest floor to other trees." He grinned at her. "I'm going to get Carlos to help me salvage the root ball tonight. Unless I find something better across the bridge." He stopped short.

"While you're in San Francisco, don't promise to polish any of your pieces until we get back from Saudi Arabia."

Ev leaned down to peck her cheek. "I won't."

Jo raised her arms toward him. "Let's go down. Carlos needs to pick a color."

He helped her up. She felt steady. Amazing to lose control so quickly and then get it back so soon. The whole episode took maybe ten, fifteen minutes. She didn't want to think about whether she might panic again. They walked down the stairs, Ev holding her elbow.

Carlos said, "Hola" as they approached. Ev ran his hands over the tops of the bases and grunted approval. Carlos dug into a drawer and brought out a color sampler.

"I'm thinking lime green. Goes good with soil." He fanned open the green section.

Ev fingered the samples and made a suggestion. Carlos disagreed and countered. Jo withheld comment—they could pick any green they wanted—and walked toward Diane's desk. She felt strong again, ready to do business. She wanted to see Diane's revised schedule. If they could ship the bulk items in two weeks' time, they could carry the little stuff with them on the next flight. Maybe they were still in the game.

Jo said, "Can I see the schedule?"

Diane shuffled folders on her desktop and handed over three sheets of paper. Jo scanned them.

"This is great. Let's do it." She handed back the papers, meeting Diane's eyes. "Thanks for not saying anything to Ev."

"Don't mention it." Diane smiled and lowered her gaze. There was a different set to her jaw.

A slippery something spread inside Jo's chest. The rules of engagement between them had altered. She didn't know how.

# DEMONSTRATION

Ev and Jo walked along the Al Khobar corniche, stopping here and there to throw pebbles into the Persian Gulf. The road snaked along a narrow beach lining the shore along the eastern end of the Saudi coastline; ships on the blue-gray horizon steamed toward Qatar. Wearing the abaya over her jeans and t-shirt, Jo felt warm in the April sun. Ev had removed his jacket and swung it from the crook of a finger. They walked into a steady, salty breeze on a well-paved sidewalk, past men in Western dress, past several families whose children played near the water. The women held their headscarves in place with one hand, while the wind pressed their abayas closer to their bodies. On a spit of ground extending into the Gulf, a large building stood under construction. A minaret in the distance rose taller than the rest.

The houses bordering the corniche looked swanky to their foreign eyes. Two stories, multiple window bays, stucco perimeter walls with elaborate front gates. Ev stopped to take a photo of one of the gates: a metal arch framing panels of opaque glass with silhouettes of vines and love birds. He said he had rarely seen such delicate ironwork. Jo thought the owner must have spent a pretty penny. As far as she was concerned, he'd won the competition for most impressive gate. She wondered who he was; probably not a date farmer refusing to educate his girls.

They turned their backs to the wind and walked away from the water, toward the hotel where they would spend the next two weeks shuttling back and forth to the demonstration venue. The hotel belonged to an international brand but had Middle Eastern decor. They sat in armchairs in the marble-floored lobby, hearing the fountain that trickled into a bed of rose petals floating in a pool at its base. Jo scanned an English-language newspaper on the coffee table beside her; Ev paged through the photos in his camera. A torso appeared in front of Jo and she looked up. Peter, from Cairo. She had called him weeks ago to ask for help negotiating with the venue, getting permissions and an installation crew, and translating for the demo. Her last trip to Riyadh had convinced her they needed their own man. And there he stood, looking as she remembered: tall and portly, rumpled jacket, mirthless smile.

Peter sank heavily into a chair near Jo's. "How do you like the hotel?"

"Very comfortable. I notice they have perfume dispensers in the hallways."

"Ah, yes. Sometimes they have trouble with the sewage system. The area has grown so fast. You will like the dining room. The chef is very good. Lebanese."

"When can we begin setting up?"

"Tomorrow morning the crew will come. First, we must pay

our respects to the management. The museum is closed today but the director wants to meet you."

"Tell me again why we are here and not in Riyadh."

"The committee wants your demonstration here because this is a liberal city. Near Aramco headquarters. You can do things here you cannot do in Riyadh."

Ev said, "Such as?"

"I received special permission for Mrs. Joanna to participate in all the activities. She must be covered, of course. Not her face, the abaya and head scarf."

Jo said, "Does that include the installation?"

"Yes, yes. The crew are friends of friends. No problem."

Jo rose. "Let's go pay our respects."

Ev rose. "I need to work on the piece I brought with me."

Jo said to Peter, "I guess I'm your man."

Peter called a taxi and escorted Jo to the Islamic Heritage Museum, to which D-Three's crates had been delivered early that morning. Jo had paid a surcharge to expedite shipment because, as predicted, Ev hadn't quite finished in time. The surcharge plus Peter's fees meant there was no possibility of profit, but they were still in the game. She was determined to show the world how well they played.

A uniformed guard met their taxi and led them to the museum lobby, where a white-haired man in Western dress waited. Peter bowed slightly as he introduced the director to Jo. They followed him to an office that looked like any other museum director's office: schedules and posters tacked up on the walls, curios crowding a credenza. The director motioned them to sit and addressed Peter in Arabic. Peter turned to Jo.

"The director is honored to meet you. He wants to know what you will put in the lobby."

"Please thank him for his courtesy. Tell him we are going to set up fifteen exhibits of a kind people here may have never seen before. For children."

The men exchanged words. Peter said, "He wants to help you. What can he do?"

"Ask him if he has any data about his visitors. Where they live, if they are repeaters, anything he knows."

Peter translated, "He says he has no budget for research and so he has no data."

"I will be more than happy to share whatever we find."

Peter translated, "He's pleased. He wants to know what you expect to discover."

"Well, we have a picture in our minds of what people will do at our displays, but we have never worked in the Kingdom before. Museum audiences can be unpredictable."

Peter translated. The director held a hand up to his cheek and shook his head. Peter laughed and turned back to Jo.

"He says he wished someone had told him about museum audiences before he took this job. He says you are most welcome here."

Jo said, "Thank you. Can you tell me how many visitors we should expect?"

Peter did not relay the question. "It has been arranged. You will have two classes of six-year-olds from the male school and one group of their teachers this week. The same from the female school next week."

"What about families?"

"They will come on the weekend."

"How many people will that be?"

Peter shrugged. "It has not been arranged. Whoever comes, comes. The plan was made by the committee. It must do." He spoke to the director and both men stood. Jo rose as well, glad to have connected with the director however lightly, concerned that the sample of family visitors might be too small. Ev had warned her not to expect American-style conditions.

Peter asked, "Shall we visit the exhibition? They have opened it for you. It is polite."

She followed him down a corridor into a large room in which six hexagonal kiosks formed a circle. Each contained illuminated panels with faceted geometric designs as borders. Some panels featured ancient manuscripts; others included drawings of odd-looking apparatus. Peter pointed to a panel that displayed the digits one through nine in diamond-shaped windows, with zero at the top. He said the exhibition was about inventions by Muslims that had ushered in the modern world, such as algebra, for example. In the Islamic tradition, he said, the Dark Ages were not so dark.

Jo turned to inspect the two displays in the middle of the room. A mannequin hung from the ceiling, dressed in a shift and turban, with wood-and-cloth wings strapped to his back, evidently intending to fly. Another mannequin sat on top of a full-sized elephant with a six-foot cage behind him; a serpent, a bird, and bells adorned the cage. Peter explained that the elephant was a clock with a water-based timing mechanism. It had been built by an Arab polymath in the thirteenth century AD to advance Chinese and Greek clockwork. Peter surveyed the elephant clock with obvious pride. Jo thought, if only visitors could get their hands on a clock mechanism or two, then the exhibition might appeal to everyone in the family. That is, if she could predict the behavior of Saudi families.

In the taxi back to the hotel, Peter chewed gum and hummed to himself. Jo took two sheets of paper from her briefcase and handed them to him.

"This is the questionnaire for the weekend. Please have it translated and make a hundred copies."

Peter ran his eyes over the papers. "A hundred copies?"

"We probably won't need to interview that many people. This isn't a random-controlled study."

"How many do you actually need?"

"Beats me. Enough to show a pattern." She didn't mean to flaunt her worry, but the words escaped her.

"I will translate right away."

"Shouldn't you have a Saudi do it? You're Egyptian."

"All Arabs share the language of the Quran. We are united in its beauty. It is the same in every place." He swiveled his wrist with a flourish, as if to excuse her ignorance. "It has not changed for centuries. It will not change."

Jo turned away, unable to respond. Neither of them spoke for the rest of the ride.


In the golden hour before sunset, Ev and Jo decided to take a stroll. Ev had solved the mechanical problem that had been bugging him, and Jo had finished responding to emails. She'd also sent the interview schedule to Myriam and Owen. The latter had replied he didn't give a shit about sample size, "Just hold a focus group and be done with it." Pity she couldn't forward his petulance to Myriam without appearing unprofessional. As she pocketed their room key, she decided to chance leaving the abaya behind. In this "liberal" city, perhaps a foreigner might walk with only her head covered. She put on a duly modest, long-sleeved shirt over her jeans.

The sky remained clear, but the wind had died down, and they could smell the sea. They walked in the direction of the Heritage

Museum, turning onto a broad commercial avenue, and stopped at a light. Jo thought they could be walking in Las Vegas: in front of them lay a newish concrete sidewalk and utilitarian mid-rise buildings housing a rhyme-less mix of cafes and furniture outlets, with bare, sandy lots interspersed among them. A Porsche pulled up to a restaurant frontage; a youngish man in Western dress got out and disappeared into the restaurant. He did not glance their way. There were no other pedestrians.

The light changed and they stepped into the street to cross. Two cars drove through the intersection alongside them, horns honking. They walked on. A string of cars approached in the lane facing them; the last two drivers honked. Jo felt her chest tighten. Could the drivers be protesting no abaya? She took hold of Ev's arm. They walked two blocks farther; a motorist sounded his horn for such a long time they heard the Doppler shift as he streamed past. She grew frightened. Ev halted mid-block.

"Maybe we should turn back?"

"Yeah. I wouldn't want you to get shot." Gallows humor. Her chest did not loosen.

They returned to the hotel and made their way to the courtyard behind the lobby. They sat on an outdoor sofa beside a blue-tiled reflecting pool in the mild evening air. Jo took Ev's hand in hers. No more experimenting with dress, even in Al Khobar. She feared they'd never understand Saudi taboos well enough to design something that reached into parents' hearts. She felt defeated although it was stupid to do so. Nothing here should be taken personally.

Ev said, "When you're ready, I want to go up."

She gripped his hand harder.

Her phone buzzed: Peter, in the lobby.

"Will you stay until Peter comes?"

Ev nodded.

Peter appeared in the courtyard carrying a manila envelope. "I am early!" A big grin. "Here are the questionnaires in Arabic. I made fifty because I had to do them one by one. The feeder was broken." He placed the envelope on the coffee table in front of them. "I will do the manual later." He surveyed them. "Are you ready for tomorrow?"

"We'll start as soon as you can get us into the building" said Ev. "How about seven thirty?"

"I will send a car."

Jo grasped Peter's arm. "Before you go, can I ask a question? We were walking on the boulevard, I was dressed like this, and drivers kept honking. They didn't slow down, just honked. Were we in any danger?"

Peter laughed. "Danger? No. I think it was the opposite. They were admiring your Levi's."

"So the honking was like a wolf whistle?"

"I do not know that word. But you were not in danger. Not here." He raised his hand in a salute. "Seven thirty." He turned to leave.

Relief flowed through her. And embarrassment for having been wrong. She stood when Ev did and waved good-bye to Peter as he disappeared into the building.

They took the elevator up to their room. Ev said he felt grubby and went to the bathroom to shave and shower. She took off the long-sleeved shirt and sat at the desk. She did not power up her laptop. No, they had not provoked an attack in the street, but there was still the problem of the wolf whistle.

Back in Atlanta at her first job, she took the bus downtown and walked past a construction site to her company's office tower.

Every morning for the three months it took to complete the steel work, some hard hat or other whistled at her. The shrill chirp rose above the noise of machinery, penetrating her ears and stabbing her consciousness. She felt dirty, somehow. She pretended she didn't notice and strode purposefully, keeping her eyes focused straight ahead. When she left the building in the evening, the hard hats were already gone for the day, to her relief.

One day at lunch, one of the copywriters mentioned that she liked being whistled at; she felt flattered. She was a big, pretty woman; Jo was short and plain. In a flash Jo had realized the construction workers whistled at women indiscriminately. It hurt to be treated as a commodity. It hurt to be probed sexually, albeit by sound, when you had no power to escape. She told the copywriter she dreaded the whistling. An older woman at the table gave her a remedy. She told Jo to say to herself, "Buddy, I have more degrees and make more money than you ever will, so eat your heart out." Jo took the advice, and it helped, on the days when she believed in her own success. When the steel work ended, her problem went away but not the revulsion it had engendered.

Was there a difference, Jo wondered, between an American construction worker's whistle and a Saudi driver's honk? They both felt threatening, although the perpetrators intended no physical harm. Yet, hadn't she risked provoking the drivers just now by leaving the abaya behind? They couldn't have known she was a foreigner with a different understanding of female modesty. Perhaps today's honkers were less culpable than the whistlers had been. It seemed wrong to think so, though, given the mess the Saudis made of gender issues. A mess she knew she didn't—and probably wouldn't—understand or condone.

She heard Ev's electric razor whine behind the bathroom

door. Being married to Ev had changed her feelings about sexual predation. Ev would never pull a power play, of any kind. He didn't expect her to assume a traditional role. He had dulled her edges without trying to, just by being Ev. She was grateful. She rose and knocked softly on the bathroom door. She wanted to touch him and thank him, just for being Ev.

At seven thirty in the morning they exited the lobby and got into the promised car. Jo wore her abaya this time. Peter didn't show. At seven fifty he phoned to say go ahead without him and please pass the phone to the driver. The driver took them to the rear of the museum, where three laborers in work clothes relaxed on the steps. He said something to them, and they opened the door for Ev. Jo followed him in. They walked through internal corridors and emerged in the lobby, where D-Three's shipping crates and a pile of extension cords had been stacked against a wall. Ev motioned for the laborers to follow him and pointed to a crate marked TOOLS. The men helped him wrangle it. They began to unpack.

Jo took inventory: all crates present. She set out to look for the museum's forklift. She could operate a forklift in an emergency, and this might turn into one if Peter didn't appear. One of the men ran up behind her shouting, "Mrs.! Mrs.!" shaking his head and waving his arm in the direction of the lobby. She turned back; she would have to wait until the men had done the heavy work before she could be useful. They had two days to complete the installation, and then the museum would reopen. They might need to work into the night.

Ev and the crew seemed to understand each other, speaking the language of crowbars, wrenches, and cables. They pushed crates up against the far wall after they'd emptied them. Under Ev's direction, the crew laid out parts of displays on the floor where the finished exhibits would stand. They made good progress; Jo cleaned up behind them with broom and dustpan. Peter arrived shortly before noon, bringing lunch for the crew and a box of sweets for the solitary museum guard observing them. The crew hailed Peter and crowded around the containers of food he placed on top of a crate. Ev rubbed his stomach to signal his intention to eat. Jo hung back and confronted Peter.

"Where were you this morning?"

"Ah, Mrs. Joanna. I was doing your business. I went to the university to get words. 'Fungi.' 'Substrate.' Words from your manual that I have not seen before. You will use these words with children?"

"No, with teachers. And parents, if they want to know more." For some reason, she didn't believe his excuse. She remembered him disappearing in Dubai. He might have had something extra going on there, and perhaps he moonlighted here. But the installation appeared to be on track now, and she could afford to be generous. "Have some lunch. I have work for you afterwards."

Like a good Saudi woman, she leaned against one of the crates and waited for the men to eat first. She watched Peter take a generous helping from each of the containers, and she thought about the rest of the installation. In only a matter of days they'd know how Saudi families reacted to their style of displays. They'd see the true dimensions of the challenge. She felt nervous and excited in equal measure.

On Sunday, after the first week's visitors had been through the demo, the Heritage Museum closed and Ev went there to prepare for the next round. Jo gave Peter the day off and called Myriam at her office, thinking they might meet, but she was tied up. The hotel concierge suggested Jo use her free time to go shopping in Bahrain. He said you drive on a sixteen-mile causeway over the Persian Gulf and you come to another country, an island Arab state with fewer social restrictions than the Kingdom and European haute couture on sale. You could have English tea in a hotel. Or a glass of wine. Jo asked him to find her a car and driver. She had a multiple-entry visa, and she intended to use it.

Promptly at ten, a dark-skinned man with long hair shellacked to his head picked her up in a clean Ford Fusion. She got into the backseat, smelling a heavy perfume that may have wafted from his hair or perhaps from the upholstery. She cracked the window open and the breeze fluttered her head scarf and abaya. She couldn't wait to make it through the border so she could strip and travel like the American she was. Cars clogged the causeway, and it took an hour to cross over the calm, shining sea into Bahrain.

His name, he said, was Hassan, and didn't she like his hair, so much better than the Saudis? He faced forward as he drove, talking nonstop over his shoulder. He said he was Pakistani and complained about his boss, and especially about his boss's boss, who was Saudi. He'd been driving for eleven years and hated every minute, but the money, ah, it should be better, they could afford it. Nevertheless, he intended to stay in Saudi Arabia if he could get himself a better job. But the deck was stacked against him because, he said, they were all racists. Even though his Arabic was pretty good, if he said so himself.

Jo did not encourage his talk, nor did she squelch it. Something about the way he'd instantly unloaded his opinions made her wary. She hoped his discontent did not extend to foreign women because then she'd have to shut him up, and the ride would get ugly. She pressed her lips closed and looked out the window. Too bad Ev hadn't come.

They drove along the Bahraini side of the causeway, which looked the same as the Saudi side, and she asked to be taken to a historic house she'd read about online. He asked if she wanted a ladies' room. She said, yes, when convenient. He pulled into a parking lot surrounding a glass-and-steel building where, he told her, she'd find a bathroom and could visit the shops. He would wait at the car. She walked into the marble-floored shopping arcade, past the glittering windows of luxury boutiques, to a marble-walled bathroom where a uniformed attendant in a *hijab* handed her a soft towel. On the way back, a suit in one of the windows caught her eye. A four-thousand-dollar price tag was attached to the skirt and a tag she couldn't read hung from the jacket. She wondered who would spend ten grand on a suit only to cover it with an abaya. Talk about conspicuous consumption.

When she returned to the car, Hassan said he was surprised to see her so soon, and didn't she like the mall? He offered to take her to another, or to a club where she could buy a day pass to enjoy the entertainments. He smirked and rotated his wrist in what she took as a sign for hanky-panky. He offered to show her the sights. She said she wanted to see the historic house. He frowned and confessed he'd never heard of it. His customers had other desires.

Hassan pulled out his phone and called his office for directions. They told him to find a policeman, who would be Pakistani and so would help him. He turned left, then right, left again, right again until they came to a police station. Two officers stepped up to the car, one talked to Hassan in Urdu, the other tried to chat with Jo, but she couldn't follow his English. Hassan saluted them and proceeded to drive around several corners, telling her the police weren't really sure where to find the house, but he would find it. She began to doubt it.

The streets began to narrow. Stucco houses with a shop window carved into the ground floor leaned into each other; dark-looking men hung around doorways, smoking and shooing skinny dogs. Hassan stopped the car abruptly. He got out and scratched the back of his head with one finger—he didn't muss his hair—and hailed an older man sitting in front of a shop at the corner. They argued, gesturing right and left. Hassan got back behind the wheel and the old man got into the front seat. Jo wanted to yell "Hassan, what are you doing?" but she couldn't get the words out quickly enough. She clutched her purse. The car took off. They turned several more corners. Hassan stopped, backed up half a block. The old man got out, walked away. Hassan turned to her.

"It is there." He pointed down an alleyway to a white house with a wooden balcony suspended outside the second story windows, as if clinging to the wall. "I picked the oldest man because he must know."

Jo got out of the car, feeling sheepish for having feared a kidnap, and walked to the house. It bore a plaque in Arabic and, below, an English sign stating the museum's hours. It should have been open, but it wasn't. So much for Bahraini historic preservation. She got back into the car, deflated, and told Hassan, "Now you can show me the sights."

He drove to a mosque where, he said, women can enter at certain times. Jo saw three domed buildings, a minaret, a tower, and walls penetrated by rows of archways. Hassan drove to the entrance to read a sign and then told her she couldn't enter now, so he would take her to the sea. On the corniche, he drove past entrances to villas with speedboats moored at the docks just visible behind them. He did not stop, and Jo began to feel trapped. She told him she wanted to go to a hotel for tea. He said he refused to let her be "ripped off" at a hotel, and there was a better place. He drove into a downtown-looking area and parked. She scurried behind him for four blocks to the restaurant of his choosing.

At the entrance to the restaurant, he passed her along to the maître d', who grinned and seated her at a table at the back. On the menu he handed her, she saw pictures of bottles of booze and fried food. Not a hint of tea. She asked him, as he leaned over her, for a soft drink. He placed his hand on hers.

"I will be soft. American women, they like me." He leaned closer, smelling like cooking grease, and sweat, and something raw.

She recoiled and pushed her chair away. She said she'd changed her mind and hustled to the door. The maître d' followed. Hassan stood outside, blocking her path.

"Why don't you eat? The food is good." he said.

"I'm not hungry. I wanted tea. Please take me home."

The maître d' scowled at Hassan, and Jo realized he must be paying a kickback.

"But you have all day." Hassan spread his hands apart, as if confused.

"I'll pay you for a full day and rate you five stars. I want to go home."

Hassan shrugged and stepped aside. She pushed past him, eyes forward. They got in the car. She sat on the cool leather feeling angry and alien. If Ev had accompanied her, she thought, that creep wouldn't have fooled with her. She'd been victimized by a lecher and a bully out to make an extra buck, just because she was female. The concierge who recommended Hassan must have been told by Saudi businessmen that he delivered the goods. Not her kind of goods. She had learned nothing about Bahrain except that it catered to Saudi vices.

Hassan must have sensed her antagonism because he drove silently toward the causeway. They passed through the Bahraini gate and into Saudi passport control. He turned off the engine to wait their turn, asking her for her passport to present to the officials. She gave it to him, because she had no choice, and watched the cars ahead. Uniformed officers made travelers get out of their cars. They opened doors and trunks and packages and thumbed through passports, seeming to berate people. Jo put on the abaya and head scarf she had left on the seat as one of the officers approached. Hassan got out of the car and handed over both passports; he kept his eyes lowered. The officer walked around the car and peered through the window at her; he sneered and her pulse quickened. She sat still while the officer talked to Hassan, feeling helpless. After a beat, the officer handed back the passports and waved them clear. As they drove away, she spread the abaya carefully across her lap, feeling secure for the first time that afternoon.

My god, she thought with a catch in her breath, I actually want to be covered. She remembered Myriam's remark the last time they talked in Riyadh. Now she understood.

Myriam sat across the table from Jo at a seafood restaurant over-looking the Gulf. They were alone; Ev was fiddling with the exhibits once again. Jo looked at the water lapping peacefully at the pier on which the restaurant stood. Myriam had said Al Khobar was proud of this establishment, on a par with the latest in the West. Jo sipped her "Saudi cocktail," a minted, fruity, fizzy soft drink in a champagne glass, and silently begged to differ.

Myriam looked flushed as she ordered their lunch, pointing to items on the menu and grilling the Philippine waiter. She ordered lobster from the Gulf, caught that morning, for both of them. The waiter bowed away, and she settled back in her chair.

"You must think I eat in restaurants all the time. No, I am too busy. But you are my guest."

"Thank you."

"Tell me, how do you like Bahrain? You went yesterday?" Myriam folded her hands on top of the table.

"I didn't see much of Bahrain except for a shopping mall and a police station manned by Pakistanis. On the way home, the passport control officers were stripping cars looking for contraband, and they were nasty. So I put on my abaya and I felt protected, and I said to myself, 'Now I understand what Myriam meant when she said she had a right to feel comfortable.' It's about privacy. If you follow the rules, even if you don't like the rules, you keep your privacy."

Myriam unfolded her hands and smiled into Jo's eyes. "I am sorry you did not enjoy Bahrain. I took my family there when the IMAX cinema opened. It was very educational. My daughter went there to learn to drive, before it was permitted here."

First time Myriam had mentioned a daughter. "Does your daughter drive?"

"My daughter, yes. It is not important for me. I am earlier generation."

"You are just as important as your daughter."

"A mother knows her children belong to the future. I am content in my time."

Myriam looked into Jo's eyes. She spoke gently. "Mrs. Joanna, I do not cover for privacy. I cover because it is who I am as a Muslim and a woman. I cover out of respect for a way of life based on faith. It is my joy."

Jo could not suppress a loaded question. "Did your faith stop you from driving, or was it the religious police?"

"Good people who live the Quran believe we need the *mutaween*, and I honor those people." She paused. "First is my faith. Then my family. Then my country. I hope you can understand."

Jo said nothing. The religious police revolted her.

Myriam adjusted her perch on the chair and removed a notebook and pen from her purse. "Now, tell me your plan for the girls. I am excited for this."

"That's the other thing I wanted to talk about. Right now, we don't have anything special in mind. They'll explore just like the boys. But I always root for the underdog."

Myriam smiled.

"What else should we do?"

"I am a feminist. It is excellent to treat the girls just like the boys. I will make sure they know it. And the teachers, too."

The waiter brought two plates, half a pink-shelled lobster on each. Myriam put down her pen. The waiter laid the plates on the table. Myriam said, "Shall we eat?"

Jo picked up her knife and fork, glad for a gap in the conversation. She needed time to reorganize her thinking about this woman whom she was coming to trust as a leader, yet who accepted the unacceptable. She took a bite of lobster: tender and sweet, best she'd tasted in years.

Jo sat on the floor of the museum lobby next to Ev, who had taken apart the conveyor belt and spread the pieces on the ground. She watched him pry food out of the gears of the hand crank. A kid must have smuggled in a snack. Most of the exhibits had held up well. Ev's tree section had suffered the most. The boys had ignored the tree's interior behind its clear plastic wall and tugged away at the exposed bark and roots. They'd crawled beneath the root structure as anticipated, but, Peter said, they had not imagined themselves to be underground. Ev's *piece de resistance* was the only flop in the demo. Yet Ev was happy about the whole. She knew so because she'd found a doodad next to her pillow this morning after he had gone down to breakfast. Doodads were always a positive sign.

The thing was a hand mirror with a plastic flap over the top. The flap contained a hole situated so that when you looked at yourself, you saw only your eyes, forehead, and the bridge of your nose. In other words, Ev had made a method for boys and girls to put on—and take off—a woman's facial veil. He might have wanted her to test the idea on kids and parents over the weekend, but she had feared the committee wouldn't want boys to imagine themselves female or girls to imagine themselves unrestrained. She'd tucked the doodad away in her suitcase. Maybe she'd bring it out in the next phase of the project, if there were one. She'd thanked Ev mentally, though, for siding with the girls.

She watched him tend to machinery in his familiar, steady way. Absorbed by the exhibits, he hadn't said anything about the doodad. He often abandoned ideas, perhaps because he had so many to choose from. He blew hot and cold about many things. He'd blown hot and cold about the entire Saudi deal over the course of the past year. She'd discounted his vacillation and steadied him along. It amused her to think they defied gender stereotypes: Ev was the one fueled by emotion while she worked on logic. At least most of the time. This particular job, she admitted to herself, affected her illogically.

"I asked Myriam if we should do something extra for the girls. She said no. Being treated equal to boys would be enough. It must not happen often."

"Huh." He slid the handle and gears together and got up. He picked up one end of the belt. "Want to hold the other end?"

She rose and grasped her end of the belt. They carried it in tandem across the room. She fastened her end to the table and waited for Ev to secure his end in place. He would be finished tinkering soon, and a janitor would come to clean. No American museum ever looked as spotless as this place. Perhaps hyper-cleanliness was a Saudi tradition. A benign tradition compared to arresting a woman because her sleeves were too short. She leaned against the wall to wait for Ev to make the rounds of the displays one final time.

Her thoughts meandered to the war she had long been waging against tradition. The first skirmish took place when she was fifteen, and Diane wanted to play Pinocchio in the third grade recital. Diane had come home from school crying because the teacher wouldn't let her audition. Jo cut first period the next day to talk to the teacher, arguing a wooden puppet could turn into a girl as easily as a boy. Miss Lucy offered to star one of her brothers, knowing they were much too old. Jo smelled hypocrisy masquerading as tradition and she hated it.

The next skirmish happened freshman year at college, when Jo's roommate, a self-described "traditional girl," suggested Jo would make more friends if she lost her down-home accent. Jo cleaned up her speech all right, and swore never to act like her roommate. She'd tasted snobbery and recoiled in disgust. Skirmish number three lasted all senior year when she felt snubbed by the design department over Robbo. Although they claimed they'd followed the rules, they'd abused their authority, and it sickened her. She came to associate tradition with rigidity; she came to expect that people who vaunted tradition really wanted to squelch innovation. She came to doubt conventional wisdom and to seek a fresh angle in her work. Ev always saw fresh angles. She loved him for it.

Now, Myriam confused her. A traditionalist—no, a fundamentalist who puts her faith first—but also an activist for women and girls. Jo felt attracted and repelled at the same time.

"Ev, do you think we'd understand these people better if we were Mormons, or some other fundamentalists?"

He placed the wrench he had been using in the toolbox and tucked the box into the janitor's closet. "Nah. It's not about religion, it's about tribe. Some anthropologist discovered that people only relate to about a hundred fifty other people, the ones closest to them. People don't naturally tolerate everyone else. You'll always be on the outside here."

"That's not very encouraging."

She'd heard his rant on tribalism before. He'd say the trees would outlast us because they never made war on their own species. She usually countered by saying democracy required people to transcend the tribe. Not a good argument to make in a country content to be ruled by an absolute monarch.

Ev said, "I don't mean to discourage you. You'll get close enough to do your job. But don't expect more."

Did she expect more? She felt drawn to the female teachers who were so warm and welcoming. And to Myriam, who defended civil rights she did not personally enjoy.

The janitor appeared, and Ev gestured to indicate they were about to leave. Jo re-fastened her abaya and wrapped the scarf around her head. They stepped into the street and Ev waved for a taxi. Apparently, he was ready for the girls to arrive at the demo tomorrow. Myriam would translate for the teachers. Jo would be happy to see her and grateful for her help. Understanding would have to wait.

They'd been home for two days, most of which Jo had spent at her computer going over the data and composing a draft of the report she would send to Phil Owen. It had to be a work of art, a politically astute narrative that communicated clearly to the committee yet preserved D-Three's ability to flex. She decided to read through one more time before sending it on.

## DRAFT

Dunhill + Dana + Design
**Children's Museum Project**
**Demonstration Study**
Al Khobar, February 2017

The demonstration was hosted by The Islamic Heritage Museum, which opens to the public four days a week. On Wednesdays and Thursdays, the museum's visitors are predominantly school groups; families come on the weekend, Fridays and Saturdays. Admission is free, with the exception of special features and occasional films presented by local clubs.

Our crates were delivered to the museum on Sunday. Our crew of four people completed installation in two days as planned: the twelve demonstration exhibits plus stage set were mounted in the museum's lobby, where they were accessible to all visitors for two weeks. A principal of Dunhill + Dana + Design was present at all times to observe visitors and maintain the exhibits in good working order. A representative of the museum was also present.

With the help of male and female interpreters, we administered a short survey to those family visitors who agreed to be interviewed. In addition, the museum had arranged for four classes of six-year-olds from two nearby schools to visit, along with their teachers, specifically to test our displays. The interpreters helped us converse with the teachers after they had watched their pupils use the displays.

Preliminary results of the demonstration study are summarized below, followed by specific recommendations for the next phase of the project. Detailed descriptions of the displays and activities may be found in Appendix A. Detailed observations, protocols, and survey responses may be found in Appendix B.

We wish to thank the Islamic Heritage Museum, our skillful interpreters, and the Ministry for enabling us to mount this demonstration. We and our partner, Owen and Associates, are grateful for their generosity and support. The findings of this study, along with the market research Owen and Associates has undertaken in parallel with this work, will be invaluable for informing the design of the eventual Children's Museum Project. It has been an honor for us to assist the Ministry in furthering its important objectives for enhancing early childhood education, thus helping to ensure a productive future for Saudi youth.

The committee led off every meeting, every document, every oration with its ultimate agenda, so Jo paid homage, too. The tone seemed right.

## SUMMARY OF FINDINGS

**Audience segment: six-year-olds**
***Research goal:*** *to look for barriers to engagement with the displays*

Two classes of six-year-old boys totaling twenty-nine children visited in the first week. Two classes of girls, totaling twenty-five children, visited the second week. Essentially, boys and girls behaved the same at the exhibits, with the exceptions noted below. We found that:

- Children were shy at first, not knowing what was permissible. When urged to touch the apparatus by a teacher, one or two children led the way. Almost immediately the others followed. Girls required a bit more urging initially than boys.
- Children had no trouble understanding what to do at the displays. The exhibit controls are designed to be self-evident, and the children were comfortable

working with the mechanical and technical inter-faces. The children stayed engaged throughout the forty-five minute session. Girls talked more to their teachers than boys did.

- At the facilitated display, a workbench where chil-dren sit and an adult leads them through a series of hands-on experiments (e.g., look at different soils under a microscope—see Appendix A), children were quite willing to go along with the facilitator. (In this case, it was one of the teachers whom we had coached for fifteen minutes at the start of the visit.) Many children asked questions and made original observations. No child refused to cooperate.

Note: several children asked about creatures that live underground. We recommend including live animals in any permanent installation.

She nodded to herself; how could anyone take umbrage at moles?

**Audience segment:**
**elementary grade teachers**
*Research goal: to understand teachers' attitudes to this style of display; to discover what can be done by the museum to help teachers use such displays to advance their curriculum*

We were able to converse with four male teachers for twenty minutes; Joanna Dunhill met with five female teachers for twenty minutes. The same protocol was used in both sets of conversations (see Appendix B). We urged the teachers to be candid in their comments, and the interpreters assured us that they were. We found that:

- Teachers expressed enthusiasm for the style of the displays, saying they liked seeing the level of engagement their pupils showed.
- Teachers say they would bring their classes to the Children's Museum, resources permitting. The schools that participated in the demonstration allow two field trips per year; teachers warned that many other schools are not as generous. Female teachers were more concerned about lack of resources; they urge the museum to provide busing since transportation is often not available for girls.
- Teachers would prefer that the topic of the demonstration relate explicitly to their curriculum, which is primarily Islamic studies and Arabic language arts in first grade.
- Teachers asked for help in utilizing the field trip. They suggest that we provide a manual stating the standards to be used in evaluating both pupils' cognitive gains and their own performance as facilitators. Female teachers in particular thought benchmarks would be important for their professional standing.

Note: standards for evaluating teacher and pupil performance, as opposed to aligning curriculum, are not generally provided in US children's museums. We recommend that they be developed for Saudi teachers' use.

The committee might see this as a pitch for more resources—and so it was. Bus money for teachers, an additional deliverable for the contractors. She hoped none of the teachers got in trouble for telling the truth.

### Audience segment: parents of younger children

*Research goal: to understand visitor demographics and prior experience with museums or similar institutions such as zoos; to understand parents' perceptions of the demonstration; to inquire about what they wish their children to learn.*

Most of the family visitors declined to participate in the survey, but we were able to interview eighteen sets of parents of children younger than ten after they and their children had used the exhibits for an average of thirty-five minutes. (None of our interviewees had brought toddlers, unfortunately.) Couples were not willing to separate to talk with same-gender interviewers, and mothers spoke up far less often than fathers. A consensus emerged among them, however. We found that:

• Parents allowed their children to use the displays and sat with them for the facilitated activities, which were led by one of the interpreters. Several of the fathers wanted to direct their children's experience, but when the children split up to use different displays, the fathers let them.

- Parents handled the displays themselves, although not as eagerly as their children in the case of mothers. Some parents expressed confusion about the purpose of the displays (e.g., "Why are my children playing with rocks?"—see Appendix B). They had no experience with interactive pedagogy, although they were interested in learning more about it.
- In contrast to teachers, parents want their children to learn practical content and skills. They appreciated the natural history subject matter of the exhibits and found them readily accessible.

Note: we suspect that many parents would not have engaged with the displays without the tacit encouragement of the museum. We recommend that the Ministry undertake a consumer education program well in advance of opening a children's museum to prepare its community. Special emphasis should be placed on communicating to mothers.

The payload. If the committee agreed to reach out to parents, and if they took parents' desires into consideration, D-Three could design a spectacular children's museum, complete with extra opportunities for mothers. Maybe they'd get to create Becca's phone club. What a happy thought! Jo couldn't help smiling.

## SPECIFIC RECOMMENDATIONS

*[Phil—This is a long, detailed section. Should I put it here or combine it with your marketing recommendations? I will complete after hearing back from you.]*

Okay. The draft was good enough. She had downplayed the differences between the boys and girls so as not to discourage the client. Yeah, they'd have to work around the girls' evident fear of disobedience, but they'd figure it out. Jo hit "send" and the draft flew over the ether to Owen, copy to Becca, blind copy to Myriam. It was evening in London, night in Riyadh; she expected replies the next morning. She wanted Myriam's feedback on the format. Owen would have his say, of course, but he'd be easier to accommodate than the Saudis. She closed her laptop and went to the kitchen to scrounge a lunch.

She had not included one word about the best part of the research because it had occurred outside the official agenda.

After the second weekend of family visits, Myriam had invited Jo to meet the members of her entrepreneurs' club. Myriam believed the key to women's independence was having an income, and she'd founded a club to introduce educated women to home-business opportunities and teach them the necessary skills. For the sake of the research, she had asked club members to bring their daughters to the demonstration, and several had come all the way from Riyadh to participate—and to meet the American female CEO they'd heard about. Myriam brought Jo to a restaurant for a mother–daughter tea.

A dozen women and preteen girls sat with Jo and, after Myriam's introduction, began to ask questions. Myriam translated. At first, the mothers were shy and pushed their daughters forward. The smallest girls giggled and said they had enjoyed cranking the conveyor belt at the demonstration because it was something new. An older girl, who looked to be about ten, wrapped her abaya around herself and turned away from the conversation. Too old for the demo, Jo thought, but she had an opinion. Jo pointed discretely, and Myriam said her name was Faten.

"What did you notice?" she asked Faten through Myriam.

The girl cast her eyes down and said something so quietly Myriam had to bend closer to listen. Faten glanced at her mother, who nodded, and then she spoke up.

"I learned about roots in school, so it wasn't new. Except for the picture on the round table."

Jo had not observed children reading the table-top labels. "Yes?"

"I saw a girl in a laboratory wearing a white coat and holding instruments. I wanted to wear that coat."

She looked down, blushing. Her mother clapped her hands together and unleashed a torrent of Arabic that made the others smile.

Myriam whispered to Jo, "There are no pictures of working women in their schoolbooks. They are old-fashioned."

Faten's mother addressed Jo through Myriam.

"Do you wear a white coat in your work?"

"No. I wear a business suit when I talk to clients and jeans when I'm crawling around on the floor plugging things in."

They laughed and their faces opened.

"How did you come to be the CEO of your company?"

"My husband and I formed our company ten years ago. He's good at making things, and I am good at organization and money matters, and so it was natural for me to become the boss."

The mothers buzzed among themselves. Faten's mother asked, "How does your husband react when you give him orders?"

Jo laughed. "I try not to give orders."

Another mother said, "I cannot imagine what my husband would say if I wanted to control the family money. What is your secret?"

Jo thought for a beat and decided to tell these earnest women the truth, even if it defied their imagination. "Many women in America believe their husbands should be older, and smarter, and richer than they are. I believe one's husband should be supportive, and little else matters." She would not mention sex in front of children.

There was a silence.

Then one of the women asked Jo how she balanced the demands of career and family. Jo explained she and Ev had no kids, but their staff was like family.

Another silence.

Questions came in a steady stream then, about Ev and the staff and the house-cum-office in Oakland. Then the mothers and girls talked among themselves for ten minutes as the tea grew cold.

They stood to leave. One of the women, evidently the spokeswoman, cleared her throat.

"We must leave because the drive is long. We want to say that although the exhibits are nice and the idea of the museum is good, we are most grateful to you for telling our girls about your experiences. Thank you for being an inspiration, and for helping us picture a different future."

Jo had been touched. She'd embraced each of them as they left the restaurant. Myriam had beamed all the while. In the taxi back to the hotel, Jo had thought that even if the job imploded, she'd achieved something worthwhile. She'd reached into the hearts of a few women, and their daughters, despite the barriers of culture. She'd responded in kind to their generosity of spirit. She'd felt satisfied in a way she would not soon forget.

But she hadn't told Ev. It hadn't seem fair to tell him she'd admired the mothers when she'd precluded him from being the father he wanted to be. A flicker of guilt had silenced her.

Diane stepped into the kitchen, mug in hand. She poured herself a cup of now stale coffee and placed it in the microwave. As the coffee heated, she leaned against the counter and pointed to her sister.

"It's a relief to have you back."

"You didn't need to worry about terrorists in Al Khobar."

Diane laughed. "I wasn't thinking about terrorists. It was just really quiet around here. I got a head start on this year's taxes."

"Are the newsletters up to date?"

"Yes. I sent them. Andy was in school, Carlos was replanting his backyard, and Becca was working at that gallery on a catalog for Ev's sculptures."

Jo sighed. "Do we have a contract with the gallery?"

"No. Becca's doing it pro bono. She'll be in this afternoon." The microwave dinged. Diane removed her mug and headed for her desk. "Almost done with the bank reconciliation. You're going to like the results."

Jo reached into the cabinet for a foil packet of tuna. As she ripped the top off, she wondered if Ev had asked Becca to write a catalog or if it was her idea, a kind of welcome home present. Perhaps she'd been pining for him. Jo hadn't seen much of him since they got back except in the bedroom. She'd been immersed in data and he'd been preoccupied fixing the demo displays even though the demo wouldn't be used again. He seemed hung up on perfecting his craftsmanship. A dog with a bone. She took the tuna, a fork, and a napkin to her desk.

At the top of her email, a reply from Phil Owen.

TO: Joanna@dunhilldanadesign.com
FROM: phil.owen@owenandassociates.com
SUBJ: aren't you speedy

Not sure the demonstration was worth it, given what you learned. Go ahead and list your recommendations. Marc is still working on ours. I'll finalize the format after I see the lot.

Hot dog, she thought, he'll buy our conclusions. She pushed the laptop closed with her elbow and sat down to eat the tuna straight out of the packet. She couldn't be bothered to make a sandwich; too much sailed through her head. In a matter of weeks, this phase of the project would end. Would the Saudis offer D-Three a contract for the next phase or make them bid again? Would they tie them to Owen or somebody else? Or nobody else? The prize, the chance to design, was verging into sight.

Her phone rang. Myriam.

Jo said, "I'm surprised to hear from you. It's late there, isn't it?"

"Yes, it is late. I just read your email and I must tell you how much I like it. Normally when there are male and female parts to a report, they are separate. It is because the men and women write their parts separately. But you have joined them. It is a benefit."

"I'm glad you like the format."

"I am going to talk to the director tomorrow. I will call you."

"Do you want to see our recommendations?"

"Later. After you and Dr. Phil complete the report. Now I will say goodnight."

Jo ended the call. Holy cow, they even separate men's and women's comments. How could Saudi men ever learn to treat women as equals without being able to fraternize with them? You fear people whose faces you never see up close and whose formative experiences you do not share. The committee asked for "separate but equal" facilities for boys and girls. She worried that even in a children's museum, in Riyadh "separate but equal" was a lie.

Years before, she had seen the lie enacted. Sophomore year in college, a friend who roomed down the hall had urged her to take a new women's studies course that a controversial poli-sci prof was organizing. Curious about the politics, she had joined her friend Penny in the class. The teacher assigned Simone de Beauvoir at the start. Jo found the teacher irritating—because she pounded on the podium—but the discussion fascinated her. She'd never heard the social order critiqued like that before. None of her high school teachers had thought to deconstruct the system that paid them. Sitting in the classroom among the other questioners, Jo felt like a pioneer in a wagon train crossing into new territory.

As the weeks passed, some students stopped coming to class. By mid-terms, only half showed up. Believing herself to be more strong-minded than most, Jo determined to stick it out. Then Penny stopped coming. Jo confronted her friend.

"I had to drop," Penny said. "They're mocking me."

"Isn't that the problem we're addressing?"

"My dad says no employer will believe a major in women's studies is equal to one in engineering."

"So? You're not interested in engineering."

"Yeah, but he's right. No one will think us equal."

"What happened to 'be the change you wish to see'?"

Penny grimaced. "I wish I could."

She was deeply disappointed in Penny. She completed the semester—the prof gave her an A for perseverance—and, disillusioned, withdrew from the course.

Now, Myriam, who called herself a feminist, appeared to believe that, in the Kingdom's segregated social order, "separate but equal" meant something good. She said a children's museum could help girls see themselves as boys' equals. Myriam implied that giving girls freedom to explore and the opportunity to do precisely as boys do would help them dream big. Jo wondered if the rest of Saudi society would let the girls realize their dreams, as some of their mothers wished. She hoped Myriam would eventually be proven right.

Becca sailed in the office door, interrupting Jo's woolgathering. She deposited her sweater and laptop on her desk and trotted over to Diane. They chatted. Jo took one last bite of tuna and went to join them. They grew quiet as she approached.

"Tell me about the catalog you're writing." Jo leaned against Diane's desk and tried to sound casual.

Becca flushed. "I set up the dummy while you and Ev were away. The gallery can fill in the content after they curate the show. It didn't take long."

"Did Ev ask you to help?"

Becca looked down. "Not with the catalog. That was my friend's idea." She paused. "He asked me to help with the tree, which is where I was this morning."

"What do you mean?"

Becca looked into Jo's eyes, as if challenging her. "The vertical section he made for the Saudi demo. He's been rebuilding it to put in the show. I've been sourcing things for him."

And he didn't think to mention it, Jo thought. "Where are you two doing this?"

"At the gallery. They have a warehouse behind the showroom." She glanced out the window.

Why is she being so unusually close-mouthed? "So you're done?"

Becca lowered the pitch of her voice. "I'm ready for whatever you assign me."

"Okay. Start formatting the demo report, with plenty of illustrations. You have a thousand photos to pick through. I emailed you the draft."

Becca nodded and went to her desk.

Jo turned to her sister. "Did you know about the tree?"

"No. Sounds like our Ev is full of surprises." Diane remained seated and sipped her coffee.

"What do you mean by that?"

"Only that he often changes things. Like the demo."

So he does, Jo thought, but he should tell her about it before assigning staff. Especially Becca. "Thanks."

Jo went back to the kitchen to dispose of the empty tuna packet. She'd *told* Ev to be careful with Becca, and he hadn't listened. Or he'd forgotten the conversation because it didn't make an impression. If something didn't resonate with Ev's peculiar logic, it flew out of his mind in a nanosecond. She washed her hands at the kitchen sink and went back to her computer. Ev would get a talking-to whenever he showed up.

It had been ten days since Owen submitted the report and an
invoice for payment, but who knew when the committee would
reply to him, and he to her? Restless, Jo checked her calendar: nothing imminent. She opened her tickler file and clicked on a newsletter Becca had prepped for a car dealer. They'd promised him a
steerable toy car to use at a sales event this weekend, and Ev was
finishing it up. She scanned the newsletter: nothing to edit. She felt
tension load her arms and legs. She got up and wrapped her shawl
around her shoulders to go out to the studio. It was chilly for May.

Ev stood bent over the workbench; the toy car sat on top of
the table saw across the room.

"What are you working on?"

"Remember that sound machine I made for the Canadians?
I've got an idea how to rework it."

"Why do you want to? Have they asked?"

"I'm going to take it to the gallery. They're calling my show
'Give It a Whirl,' after the whirligig. The sound piece will fit in."
He showed her his notebook, beaming like a kid with a treasure.

Something about his glee made her uncomfortable. Naïve.
Ripe for exploitation. "I don't understand how the show is supposed to work."

"I'm going over on Saturday. Come with me." He straightened and looked at her, eager.

She had the time and she saw the need. "Saturday's okay."

He nodded and again bent over the sound machine. She touched the middle of his back and turned to leave. She'd go check the Saudi files one more time. Never before had she felt so uncomfortable waiting to hear about the fate of a report.

The cars on either side of Ev's truck seemed close enough for the occupants to shake their hands, not that anyone merging onto the Bay Bridge would want to. They'd been creeping for nearly an hour in a funnel formation, eight lanes merging into two, those two leading into another eight that merged into two. Why, Jo wondered, did so many people need to go to San Francisco on a Saturday? If she and Ev could have taken the train, they would have, but the sound machine was too big and awkward, and the gallery, in the densest part of town, had a loading dock where they could park.

The owner had flown in from wherever he'd been skiing to discuss Ev's show. He was a short, florid man who spoke loudly, wore cowboy boots, and said "Call me Jack." Hardly the aesthete Jo had been expecting, and she liked him the better for it. He helped Ev unload the sound machine and led them through the gallery to an office at the rear. The present show comprised realistic paintings of redwoods and the Bay. Jo wondered if the sort of people who bought scenery would appreciate Ev's oddities. She didn't think of his pieces as sculpture, really, because they had more vital functions in the hands of children.

Jack motioned for them to sit on the spindly chairs across from the gallery manager's antique desk and offered a drink. They declined. He picked up a manila folder from the desktop and took out some papers.

"Here's the media plan we discussed, Ev." He passed the papers to Ev, who turned them over to Jo. "Basically, Mrs. Dana, I want to select twelve pieces from the twenty-five your husband will show me and then I want exclusive rights to price and sell them for a year. He gets forty percent of the base price."

"It's Ms. Dunhill, but call me Jo. Why only forty percent?"

"I do all the work. Your husband has nothing to lose."

"It's *his* work, and he has a reputation to lose."

"Not in the art world. Not until I make him. Are you his manager? Do I go through you?"

"I'm his partner." She felt slammed. Yes, she managed their affairs, and she sometimes managed Ev's time, but they collaborated as equals. She was so much more than an impresario, and she would not let Jack diminish her. She straightened her back.

"Look, Jo, Ev's new at this, and he needs my smarts. Are we doing this deal or not?"

Ev said, "It sounds good to me."

Not to me, she thought, but he'd cut her off her ability to negotiate.

Ev said, "One thing, I want you to use the catalog my staff designed."

"Yeah, sure. Can't say how many I'll print, but you'll get ten. Okay?"

Score one for Becca, Jo thought.

"As far as I'm concerned, the only thing unsettled is the delivery date. For a fall opening, I'll need to see the twenty-five pieces by the end of the month. Two months the latest. Okay?"

Jo felt herself pale. If Ev committed to Jack's schedule, he'd have no bandwidth for the next step in the Saudi job, if it came through. He knew the Saudi deal was her priority. "That's too tight. How about opening next spring?"

"I'm aiming at Christmas. People buy whimsy. Grandparents buy presents. Your husband's sculpture will see some play."

Ah, the "s" word, she thought. Jack's trump card.

As if reading her thoughts, Ev turned to her. "I can make it work. I'll work weekends. This is important to me."

She shrugged. Without word from Riyadh she had no ammunition. She felt pulled under the tide of Ev's desires. She'd have to nurse his genius once again, and this time the thought of doing so repelled her. And whose fault was that?

Jack rose and moved toward the door. "Now that we've eyeballed each other, we can finish this remotely."

He took them back through the gallery and left them at the door with a "Nice meeting you, Jo." They walked around the side of the building and climbed into Ev's truck. He drove toward the freeway. She opened the passenger window, hoping the breeze would refresh her. She felt too depleted to argue. The two feet separating them yawned like a mile. Neither of them said a word about Jack as they crossed the bridge back into Oakland.


Jo sat at her computer crafting cash flow projections for the next Saudi job with three different start dates. Ev was in the studio refurbishing an old display he'd retrieved from storage to add to his portfolio. She'd written off the time he would dedicate to his dream show in all three projections, and cash was tight. She thought about calling Myriam for a scoop on the committee's timeline but decided against bugging her. She closed Excel and went to the printer to gather the spreadsheets. She decided to show Ev the numbers, although they wouldn't likely affect his thinking. She stepped out of the office and across to the studio. She opened the studio door carefully. She stared. She saw Becca in Ev's arms, the girl clinging tight as they kissed.

Jo banged the door wide and the two pulled apart.

Becca gasped. Ev stared. Jo turned on her heel and stomped out.

Blood surged into her legs and she strode up the hill. All her years catering to his desires, desires he didn't bother to control. It hurt to the quick.

And Becca, in whom she'd placed such hope. She'd been a fool, a sentimental fool to expect loyalty from a moonstruck kid.

But Ev! He shouldn't have talked to Becca, let alone kissed her.

How far had it gone?

She couldn't believe he'd had an affair with an employee.

The thought stopped her cold. Hot anger inflamed every cell of her being. She turned back downhill. They'd both have to leave. She would not give an inch.


Diane brought the teapot and a mug to Jo's desk. No one else was in the office. Ev was in the studio where he'd spent the night. He had tried to explain how the kiss came about, but Jo would not hear him, and so he'd withdrawn. Jo had spent the night alone, sedated, and this morning sat at her desk, pretending to work. She wanted to believe that Ev had not betrayed her, but he and Becca had had something going for months. When he'd gone for the gallery, maybe he'd gone for her.

She should have kicked him in the groin. She should have smacked Becca across the Bay instead of running out of the studio.

Diane poured tea into the mug and passed it to her sister. "Would you like milk or lemon?"

Jo's mouth filled with straw. She could not answer.

"Becca told me you found them in a clinch. Can we talk about it?"

"I have never been this angry before." She spat out the words.

"I expect so. But maybe you don't have to be."

Jo grunted.

Diane took a breath. "Did you know how Becca wound up at college in Virginia? She's a Yankee, so first she went to the Rhode Island School of Design. But she got in trouble and had an abortion and her father disowned her."

"How do you know this?"

"You once told Becca that I'd gone off the rails. She asked me about it. We shared stories. Found out neither one of us went off the rails. Our families deserted us." She paused. "Except for you."

"So?"

"The abortion and the rejection left a hole she hasn't been able to fill. She's passionate and mouthy, but she's still a wounded, fatherless girl."

"Don't tell me she thinks of Ev as a father."

"No. But he treats her like a daughter."

"He was *kissing* her."

"Maybe he was just returning her kiss."

"If you say so."

"Listen." Diane shook her head. "Last week Becca's sister wrote that she'd had her baby, the first grandchild in the family, and Becca's not invited to the christening. It knocked her back. She went to Ev for reassurance."

"Hardly. She's been mooning over him for months."

"This was different. I think it was innocent."

"Diane, he encouraged her." She'd warned him about Becca's crush and he'd ignored her. He'd liked being the object of the girl's affection. Clearly, he prized flattery more than fidelity. It turned her stomach.

"The rules are looser for Becca's generation. She needed a shoulder to cry on."

"She should have come to *me*."

"She's been wary of you because of the Saudi job. It goes against her conscience to work with those people. She's been trying to overcome her scruples. For you."

"She has scruples?"

"Please, Jo. It's no big deal to fall in love with your boss. Becca's a great girl, and she's a good worker. She admires you. Yes, she kissed him. But it's not important."

"Why are you defending her?"

"I'm defending you. You have a wonderful marriage to protect." Diane stroked her forearm. Jo did not respond. After a beat Diane got up and left. The tea cooled, untouched.

Was it a marriage or a business she needed to protect? She had never anticipated a conflict between the two. Ev should not have put her in this position. She did not know what to do. She would not talk to him until she did.

She turned to her screen, but the thought she'd been avoiding for twenty-four hours burst into mind. Had Ev been attracted to the girl because she *was* a girl, more supple and needy than she herself? Maybe he wanted a different kind of mate, a soft heart rather than a managing partner. The idea of being insufficiently female for him dismayed her. She had to shut it down.

In the afternoon, Becca entered the office and marched stiffly to Jo's desk. Her face was pale and puffed. She did not remove her sweater. She stood, hands clasped at her breast. "I'm so sorry I behaved stupidly. I got some bad news from home and I just lost it."

"You could have told me."

"I didn't think you'd listen. You don't lose it. You can ignore things that blow my mind." She looked away. "You are tough."

"I'm not tough, I'm tolerant. But there are limits."

"I never meant to hurt you. I just needed a hug."

Jo sat silent.

Becca looked at Jo with something flinty in her eyes. "If you want, I'll quit."

Jo did not bristle back. To her slight surprise, she felt neutral toward the girl. Becca's Puritanical conscience would punish her enough. She did not feel neutral toward Ev. She would not enable his fraternizing with a lovesick assistant. She spoke gently. "I think that's for the best. You can go today. Debrief with Diane before you leave."

Becca's eyes widened. Surprise? Fear? She pulled herself taller. "Thank you for everything you've taught me." Her face tightened, as if she were stifling tears.

"You're welcome."

"I'll go collect my things." She extended her hand. They shook. Becca stepped to Diane's desk and the two of them talked quietly.

It occurred to Jo that Ev would not approve. Too bad. He did not deserve to be consulted, and in her present mood, she might say something she'd later regret. She opened the cash flow spreadsheet to transfer Becca's salary to the contractor line. Someone would have to pick up Becca's hours when the Saudi deal started cranking. She began to compile a list of potential replacements, feeling preternaturally calm.

Becca went into the storage closet; they heard her rummaging inside. She emerged with a cardboard carton and carried it to her desk. She opened drawers and fiddled with the computer. Diane sat down next to her and took notes as they talked. Jo looked away.

She did not text Ev. If he came in now, they would fight over her letting Becca go. She did not want to fight, not until her thinking cleared. She began to feel uneasy, aware that she may have been hasty. But something about Ev had propelled her. The idea of losing Ev—to a smart young woman like Becca, or to a showman like Jack—made her catch her breath. She wanted him beside her. She couldn't stand him beside her. The contradiction crushed her.

Her phone pinged. She glanced at it: Phil Owen. She opened his message. He wrote "We need to talk. There's a problem with your demo. When can I call?"

Oh, lord, what now? Her heart began to flutter.

# CONTINGENCY

22

They sat around the table, Jo, Ev, Carlos, and Diane, listening to Phil Owen snarl through the speakerphone. "I don't know why you had to prod the Saudis, but now we're stuck.'

No one said a word. Jo braced for another blow.

"The chairman called me to say they consider the demonstration to be incomplete. Evidently you promised them some kind of online deal? He wants to see it before he will pay us."

Jo shook her head. Ev looked puzzled. Diane whispered, "Could he be talking about the mom's club?"

Jo roused herself, pulling on her psychic armor. "Phil, we didn't make any promises. We asked some of the mothers if they would join an online club to help their children do take-home activities, and we showed them a storyboard. That's all."

"You introduced a new idea, and now the chairman is convinced an app would improve the kids' experience. Jesus, Jo, the man wants to *lead* the world in innovation."

Ev said, "An app would ruin the kids' experience."

"Right. The Saudis don't need us to design an *app*, they need us to design a *museum*. I have a plan." He paused; they heard the metaphorical drum roll. "I've been cleared to travel short distances. I invited the chairman to meet me at La Villette. He knows the French reputation. My colleague at La Villette will turn him off technology, rest assured."

Ev leaned back and cupped his hands around the back of his head. Carlos made the A-OK sign.

"So you need to meet us there. Bring the author of the storyboard."

"Can't. She quit. I'll cover it." Jo stretched out her arm to block objections from the others at the table.

"Cover the cost of your travel, too. I'm saving the contingency money for whatever extras the chairman wants."

"Do we have to give him anything?"

"We don't have a choice. You opened Pandora's box."

Goddamn, she thought, another trip on our nickel. All because she had wanted to reach out to the moms to get to the girls. The client had misunderstood her; she'd done a rotten job communicating.

"Evidently the chairman likes Paris. He scheduled the meeting for this weekend. My assistant will send you the details." Owen cut off the call.

Ev sat up and turned to Jo. "Do you need me to go with you?" His voice was flat, perfunctory. His mind must have moved on, into the studio where another old exhibit awaited refurbishing. She squelched a twinge of . . . what? Jealousy of his new obsession?

"I'll take care of it."

She found it hard to look at him. He didn't acknowledge her anger. He didn't believe she had cause. Of course she did. She

wasn't angry at Becca, or the pain-in-the-ass Saudis, or even Phil
Owen. She burned against *him*. He'd left her out. He shouldn't
have schemed with Becca about the whirligig. He shouldn't have
let Jack's voice override hers. "I'd better check on flights." She went
to her desk, eyes averted. Ev got up and headed for the back door.

Diane came over. "Would you like help? I've got some free time."

"No. Yes. Can you go through the data and pull out any comments about the moms' club? I'll try to re-spin it. Find out if I need
an interpreter or if Owen's got that covered."

Diane nodded and disappeared behind her computer. Jo
forced herself to concentrate on the next task; she had no choice
but to click into gear. Thank goodness for the poker in her spine.
She pushed her ire at Ev to the back of her mind. She opened her
email to look for Owen's latest.


Inside the immense science museum at Parc de la Villette, Jo stood
at the entrance to the children's division. It had changed since her
visit years ago: now there were two museums, one for two- to seven-
year-olds, and one for five- to twelve-year-olds. She showed her pass
to the attendant on the little kids' side and followed a young family
in. The exhibits looked the same as she remembered, but beefed up,
naturally, after so many visitors. She watched kids scramble into a
suite of ramps where they navigated mazes and hopped on stepping
stones, challenging their baby minds to locate themselves in space.
She parted from the family and whipped through the rest of the
exhibition. Not a computer screen in sight.

She stepped over to the older kids' museum and trotted
through. She saw sections labeled "the factory," "the garden," and
"the TV studio" where kids were handling artifacts and engaging

in costumed role-play. Quite a few of the displays included technology that enabled kids to manipulate a variable. Surely the chairman, a cultivated man, would see that the museum didn't include technology for technology's sake, but only to help ten-year-olds ask good questions. She tipped her hat to Phil Owen; meeting here might be the master stroke.

She descended to the central lobby to meet Owen in advance of their rendezvous with the chairman. He appeared on time, dressed in a business suit instead of his usual dapper duds. His complexion was sallow, with dark smudges under the eyes. He did not offer a handshake.

"Do you know Roger Coutant?"

She shook her head.

"Didn't think so. He's my secret weapon. He'll ooze compliments in French, charm them, and sell them his approach to technology the while. The man is a magician. I am advising you, let him take over the meeting. Just shut up and look pretty."

She stiffened.

"That's what I intend to do." He raised his hand to his heart.

"You can't. You look like shit." She could tolerate him in his reduced circumstances.

"My dear, the show must go on. We are going to pull this one out of the fire even if I have to call for an ambulance." He gestured toward the elevator. "Shall we?"

They made their way to the administrative offices, Owen boasting about his long collaboration with Coutant. Owen's sidekick, the patient Marc, had already arrived, along with a short man with thick glasses who had to be the magician in question. As they shook hands all around, the conference room door opened and the chairman walked in, followed by a Saudi man Jo did not recognize and, blessing of blessings, Myriam, wearing a head scarf but no abaya. She bustled into the room in a jacket and long skirt, looking like a dumpy matron rather than a political operative. Jo took heart; at least one reasonable Saudi voice would be raised. After another round of handshakes, they settled into chairs. Myriam sat across the table, beside the chairman.

Owen cleared his throat and said, "Mr. Chairman, my colleague here, Roger Coutant," gesturing to him, "led the redesign of the *Cite des enfants* some years ago. He will give us a tour, and then we can return to this room to discuss matters."

Jo piped up, "Monsieur Coutant, has Phil told you that we are looking at a very young population? Perhaps we should see the two-year-old side first?"

The chairman looked at Jo. "Why should we begin there, Mrs. Joanna?"

"Because we want to get into the mind of the child."

"I wish to get into the mind of the older child, as well as the younger." The chairman raised his eyebrows with what might be displeasure.

Coutant waved his arm and said in a thick accent, "I generally start to tour with the little ones because the parents bring them when they are small and they grow up with us. There is a sequence to their experience. First, we opened the museum for the little ones, and when it was an enormous success, we added the museum for older children."

Jo could kiss him.

The chairman nodded, apparently accepting the notion of a sequence. Jo glanced at Myriam, who smiled broadly as if to cheer her on. They all rose, and Coutant opened the door to lead them out.

Jo waited in Myriam's ornate hotel lobby, her umbrella folded at her feet. It was late, hours after the dinner at which the group had continued their unresolved discussion of educational psychology and the use of information technology to support learning. Jo had walked to Myriam's place through a cold drizzle to talk privately. She wanted Myriam's help getting paid. She needed reassurance.

Myriam stepped out of the elevator's brass doors and waved at Jo. They sat together on a couch in a corner, Myriam tucking her head scarf tighter and smoothing her skirt. They were safely alone.

"Thank you for meeting me," Jo said. She hesitated, temporizing. "I see you don't need an abaya here. But you still need to cover your head?"

"I do not need to, I choose to. It gives me an advantage."

"Isn't the veil illegal in France?"

"Yes, but not the head scarf unless your employer forbids it. When Europeans look at me, they see I maintain my integrity. They see my power." She raised her chin and locked onto Jo's eyes.

Jo felt Myriam's power, but not because of her head scarf. How odd to consider it an asset rather than an encumbrance. Every time they met, Myriam forced her to rethink something. She admired the woman's strength of character and her acumen.

"In the plane coming over I watched a Japanese film. In the end, the hero sacrificed himself for his buddies. At the end of American films, the hero gets the girl. The Saudi film I once saw ended with a woman giving her daughter a bicycle despite social disapproval. Is that the Saudi ideal?"

"Saudi people like tradition. Because we share a culture, we trust one another. We can be generous. We can give a girl a bicycle if that is her way of loving God."

"You're making an argument against democracy. At least the kind we have in America with people from many cultures."

"Is it successful?"

Jo had to think again. "Yes. Not entirely."

Myriam crossed her arms in front of her chest. "It is late. You have something to ask me?"

Jo took a breath. "I don't want to put you in a difficult position, but can you tell me what's going to happen? Will the chairman insist on getting an app?" Jo felt tension in her chest and took another breath to clear it.

"Yes, I think so. He is a proud man. But I agree with you and Mr. Phil that children should not carry smart phones in their hands at our museum. I will tell the director, and she will discuss with the chairman. You must have patience."

Jo felt a glimmer of relief. "Thank you. I am grateful for your support."

"You do not need my support. Your ideas are good." She waited a beat. "I have something to tell you, privately. I want to tell you I am retiring next month, Inshallah. The director has nominated someone to take my place. I cannot say her name because it is not official yet, but she is like you. She is dedicated to the children."

Jo felt stabbed in the belly. "I'm sorry to hear that. Not for you, for me. I don't know how to communicate without you."

"The director understands. Do not worry about the others. I do not."

But I do, Jo thought. I have to. "The chairman doesn't want me around."

Myriam clicked her tongue, *tsk, tsk*. "You must not listen to the words. You must follow the meaning behind the words."

"He wants to eject us. He does not value me." She felt panic begin to rise,

"He does not think about you. He thinks about his own position. You must understand your position better." She readjusted herself on the chair and took Jo's hand. "This is our last meeting, my friend."

Jo nodded, breathing deeply, trying to keep the fear down.

"It has been a pleasure. You are brave and you do your best for our girls." Myriam squeezed her hand and stood. "Please give my regards to Mr. Everett. I always remember his bird made from chain."

"Myriam, can I call you sometimes? Or write?"

Myriam let go her hand. "Of course. I will link with you on the internet. You will see I am modern."

Jo nodded, feeling hot and hoping Myriam wouldn't notice. "Thank you."

"Good night."

Myriam rose and trundled into the old-fashioned elevator. The uniformed operator closed the shiny doors behind her.

Outside on the boulevard, Jo let the rain cool her bare head. As she walked, her heartbeat gradually slowed and the threat of panic faded. She followed the wide street to a brightly lit intersection. She stood in front of a cafe where people sat outside, crowded under an awning, conversing and drinking at this late hour. The metallic stink of Gauloises accosted her despite the damp. She stepped to the curb to hail a taxi. It splashed by without slowing down. She was disheartened by everything Paris. She anticipated another sleepless night before her morning flight home.

Jo sat at the departure gate, waiting for the delay to end and her head to clear. The sleeping pill she had taken had left her feeling dislocated in space. The arched walls of the terminal seemed to press on her from overhead. She'd traveled through vaulted corridors and tube-like passageways to arrive at this uncomfortable chair, feeling like an ant crawling unconsciously through the colony, subject to the order an unfeeling nature imposed. In her case, the architects of the airport and the Paris city fathers who had hired them. And the Saudi establishment that would not reckon with her. She folded the magazine she had been trying to read and closed her eyes. She rued the time and money she'd spent on this latest episode in the Saudi saga, but she'd had no choice. If only Myriam could have been more reassuring.

Myriam. Her one reliable collaborator. A fully developed woman who thrived in circumstances Jo could never have tolerated. She wanted to know the secret to Myriam's equanimity. She craved her respect. What had Myriam meant by "you should know your position better"? Her position was clear: the Saudis should hire them to design their children's museum because they could do it best. Ev could light a fire, and she'd manage the burn. Was that her "position," packaging Ev for public consumption? No, no, she did more. She taught clients how to think, and they admired her for it. She earned more than a fee, she earned admiration. She'd thought the Saudi job would earn her the world's admiration. Instead it tortured her with stops and starts and unanswerable questions.

A gate agent appeared at the podium and fussed with the microphone. He announced in French and English that the flight had been cleared to board. Jo slipped the magazine into her suitcase and collected her purse and raincoat. She stood behind a fat man with two overflowing bags and braced to spend the coming eleven hours crammed into an economy seat. The line began to creep forward. She felt alone and friendless. The pit of her stomach contracted: perhaps the job wasn't worth it after all. She'd insisted that D-Three take a big, fat chance, and they had less than nothing to show for it.

Ev had been right about the job. She bowed her head in contrition. She should have listened better. He understood things she didn't. Perhaps he understood Becca in a way she didn't. She should forget about the kiss. She needed him just as he was.

The fat man could not find his boarding pass. While he fumbled through his second bag, Jo slipped around him and into the Jetway. She wanted to lay her burdens down for the next little while. She wanted to watch movie after movie to distract herself until she could rest at home.

Jo searched the kitchen cabinet for zinc or vitamin C or anything else that might kill the germs clogging her sinuses. If she could get a little physical relief, she thought, maybe her spirits would improve. She'd been home for two days, in bed with a cold thanks to her late night walk in the rain, laid low by vertigo. For the last couple of years, every time she got sick she got dizzy. She hadn't been able to sit at her desk for more than five minutes, and she hadn't really wanted to. She could not troll for a new project in case the Saudi job imploded, not while feeling so low. Instead, she had lain down and let the sounds of the office drift up to her sickbed. Ev had noticed her sneezing, of course. Each morning he asked if she needed anything, and when she said no, he disappeared into the studio to refurbish another of his old pieces. Jack had set him on a course from which he would not deviate. She'd had no energy to protest.

It was early; no one else had arrived yet. Diane, Carlos, the friend of Andy's who had taken over some of Becca's work—any one of them might walk into the office and see her disorder: uncombed hair, ratty T-shirt, eye bags unconcealed. You could tell she was pushing fifty. She groped along the upper shelf beyond her line of sight. Her hand brushed against a cylinder in a back corner and she pulled it forward. An ancient canister of bouillon cubes. Might help, couldn't hurt. She removed a cube and returned the canister to the shelf. She put on the kettle and took a mug from the dishwasher. She needed three more minutes of privacy to make a lousy cup of broth. Who said having your business in your home was a good idea?

The kettle whistled. She poured water over the bouillon cube and, moving slowly, steadying herself with one hand on the wall, took the mug upstairs to the bedroom. She set it down on the night table beside her phone. Next to the phone lay the Shenandoah River rock Ev had given her a million years ago. A poor substitute for the man himself, she thought. She sat on the bed, and as she slid her legs under the quilt, the phone chimed. Owen, so soon. She reached for the phone and knocked the broth onto the floor. A moan burst from her throat. She unlocked the phone.

"I've had a call from the chairman's office. The director wants to move the app into the next phase of the project. The chairman has agreed to sign off on this phase, and we'll see our money within a month."

She sat up straight. Hooray for Myriam and the director!

Owen gloated, "La Villette did the trick. You can thank me now, and then again, after you get your check."

She didn't bother to correct him. "Thanks for the good news."

"I trust you're satisfied with our little collaboration?"

She'd be damned if she would ever share a project with Owen again. "That's putting it mildly."

He mumbled good-bye and ended the call.

She pulled back the quilt and went to the bathroom to get a towel to clean up the spill. She could feel a grin widening her cheeks. Her heart rose from the depths to its rightful place in the center of her chest. She had to spread the news. She texted Ev to come see her. She sent a cryptic message to Diane, asking her to pick up Vitamin C on her way in to work. She wanted to tell them face-to-face that the Saudi project lived on. She felt vindicated for having pushed so hard. She felt happier than she had in weeks.

Bending slowly, she dabbed at the spill and deposited the wet towel in the hamper. As she stepped toward the closet to find a better shirt, Ev walked into the bedroom with concern written on his face. He stopped short when he saw her smile. In the closet, she grabbed a Mexican blouse, a frilly embroidered thing that a grateful client with a second home in San Miguel had given her and that she never wore. She never wore frills, but today was different. She slipped the blouse over her head and turned to him.

"Owen just called with news. He said they're pushing the app into the next phase and we'll be paid in a month. The next phase! We're solid."

"Are you feeling better?" He didn't look happy.

"I have a cold, but I'm feeling great. Let's celebrate when the staff gets here. Maybe you could pick up pastries? And fruit? Or should we cater lunch?"

"I think you should take it easy." He sat on the bed.

She sat beside him. "I was beginning to doubt everything I thought I knew about our line of work." She poked him in the shoulder, expecting a friendly tussle. He did not react.

"Have we been offered another contract?"

"One step at a time." She found his sobriety puzzling. Maybe he was stuck on a problem in the workshop.

"It's too soon to celebrate. Stay in bed. Get better. You don't need to rush."

She stood up quickly and the world spun. She sat down. "Still dizzy. I'll stay down. But I need my laptop."

He nodded and got up. "I'll get it."

Triumph tasted sweet, she thought. Triumph over the

chairman, and Owen, thanks to Myriam's intervention. A thought snagged her: how would the job proceed without Myriam? Could she find another way to navigate the client's bureaucracy? They'd been tangling with the Saudis for nearly a year, and she still did not know if the client would let them design something wonderful and bold. At least now they'd have the opportunity to try.

A knock on the door. Diane entered carrying Jo's laptop. She handed it over along with a bottle of Vitamin C. "Ev told me. Congratulations." She paused in the doorway. "You look nice."

"Thanks. In half an hour or so, I'm going to send some schedules to print. Would you bring them up to me? And bring tissues. They're in the supply closet." Her mind whirled through the changes she intended to make in the charts. She'd text Ev when she had results to show him.

Two days later, once she could maintain her balance going up and down stairs, Jo insisted on celebrating. She organized a party for the staff and their families to thank them for their grace under pressure, and, to tell the truth, to soften them up for another year or two of hassling with unpredictable deadlines and unknown conditions in the Middle East. She picked a Friday night and ordered Lebanese food—they drink alcohol in Lebanon—and a camel for the kids to ride. They set up a buffet table outside, on the patio between house and studio, opening both buildings for the Arabian-themed scavenger hunt that would follow dinner. Andy rigged up speakers to broadcast the playlist of oud songs he had compiled. The weather was mild and dry; they could see the sun lowering across the Bay.

Carlos brought his pretty wife and two little girls and his older son, who stood around looking bored. Andy brought a girlfriend, a pale teenager whom Jo had met once or twice before. Garth, Andy's buddy who had taken over Becca's newsletters, brought another buddy whose neck and arms were covered in multi-colored ink. Jo tried not to stare at the paisley design, not what you'd expect on a burly guy. And, of course, Diane brought Joey, almost six feet tall now, who grinned when he saw Carlos's girls. He broke away from his mother and lurched toward them. Diane watched him out of the corner of her eye as she poured herself a glass of Merlot.

A truck pulling a horse trailer parked across the street, and a man in a turban unloaded the camel. He positioned the gangly creature in the driveway and made it sit down, folding its legs underneath its body, which brought the tandem seat on its hump to chest height. Jo signaled "go ahead," and the handler beckoned the kids. The girls squealed and ran up to the camel. Carlos's boy followed, and then Garth's tattooed friend. Joey hung back, fear on his face. Diane gentled him forward, but he said aloud "no, no." Carlos's older girl stopped in her tracks. She called her sister and the two of them ran to Joey, each one taking a hand and urging him to approach the camel. The older girl asked the handler to help her sister mount and then Joey. She mounted last, sitting behind Joey and holding his waist. The handler gave a signal and the beast lurched upward, releasing a pungent cloud of dust. Everyone clapped and cheered as the handler led the camel down the street. They could hear Joey yelling, "Oh, oh, oh" as the camel swayed. The handler led the camel back, made it sit, and helped them dismount. Joey finally looked happy. He sought out his mom, who told him how proud she was of him and thanked the girls for their courtesy. Jo had to admire whatever it was that made the girls enjoy nursing a disabled boy twice their size. She felt a flash of sympathy for everything Diane had endured and would continue to endure as Joey grew but didn't mature. She felt grateful not to be so burdened.

Carlos's boy took the next camel ride, followed by his parents, riding together, Carlos cussing in Spanish as they bumped along. Andy, then Garth took a turn. Ev watched the camel but didn't ride. He seemed fascinated by the way its joints collapsed as it sat. Jo half expected him to run for his notebook, but he stayed with the company. When no one else wanted to ride, Jo asked for quiet. She stood on a chair and raised a glass.

"To the world's best design team! Even the government of Saudi Arabia recognizes your talent!" She took a sip. "Ev and I want to thank you for all your hard work. And I hope you find the work to come even more exciting and rewarding. Cheers!" The others cheered back. "Dinner is ready. Would the camel riders please sanitize their hands before helping themselves to food?"

She stepped off the chair and stood at the head of the buffet line with a box of wipes, doling them out liberally. The second time Andy passed, he thanked her for the vegetarian option. She had forgotten about his preference, but, hey, she'd take the credit. She surveyed the table: there was enough food for seconds all around.

Diane appeared at her elbow and leaned toward her ear. "There's a phone call for you on the landline."

Jo frowned. "I don't want to leave the party."

Diane spoke over the female voice trilling in the background. "Trust me, you need to take this one."

Jo handed her the wipes and stepped into the office. She picked up the receiver on Diane's desk. Myriam.

"We have a tragedy. The director's husband crashed his airplane. He is gone, and the director must leave the government. No one will contact you, so I tell you the museum project is over."

"How can that be?"

"Her husband's family is related to the king, not her family. No one in the government will listen to the director now. I am sorry."

Jo felt her gut shrink. She stumbled over her words. "I . . . give the director my condolences. I . . . I am sorry, too."

"It cannot be helped. I will not call you again."

Jo could not speak.

"Good-bye, my friend."

The line went dead. Jo hung up the receiver. She heard the singer, the oud, the chatter of the partygoers, the braying of the camel. She could not move. She could not rejoin the others to play a Middle Eastern game.

Diane poked her head into the office. "What did the lady say?"

"The director's husband crashed his airplane. The project is dead."

"Oh my god. I'm so sorry." She looked stricken. "Are your friends okay?"

Jo shrugged. "The project is dead." She was whispering now.

"Can you come back to the party? They'll miss you."

"I can't."

Jo turned and walked upstairs. She wanted to disappear. The thing she longed for, the prize for which she had been struggling, the world-class stage on which to present her credentials, ripped away. Her very bones ached in defeat.

She lay down on their bed. She knew she should feel sorry for the director, but she felt nothing, as if a switch had been thrown and a current had erased her mind. She knew she should feel sorry that Saudi girls would continue to be neglected by the Ministry of Education, but she did not. She knew she should regroup, but she could not. She had read somewhere that extreme joy felt like pain and extreme pain felt like joy. She felt neither; she felt nothing.

Ev knocked on the bedroom door and pushed it open. He stood over her. "Jo."

She didn't look at him.

"Why are you up here? You've thrown a wonderful party for some good people. Come join them."

She had nothing to say to him. He hadn't cared about the project, not the way she had.

He sat beside her. "Are you okay?"

"Go. Party."

He stood and walked to the door. She heard him go down the stairs. She heard Carlos call to him and the little girls shriek playfully. She heard a cascade of melancholy chords produced by a lone oud. Joey's laughter floated up the stairs. She stared at the ceiling. A year of hope and sweat and tears had come to nothing.

She didn't rejoin the party. The next week, she didn't return to her desk. She hung out in the bedroom and took slow, meandering walks. After a while, at Ev's urging, she got back on her bicycle, and it helped. After a while her appetite returned and she began to assemble light meals. At Diane's suggestion, she checked out the yoga studio down the hill. She didn't like it, but her headache faded. She began to brood less about what could have been. She began to read her mail. It did not stimulate her to look for new accounts, but she bent her will to maintenance tasks. She fell into the rhythm of the office, albeit with a dry mouth.

Then Phil Owen called, and Ev passed the phone to her. She put it on speaker.

"Well my dear, I've been told our final payment has been approved. I will cut you a check for the demo and travel, plus your share of the contingency and profit. I'd like a small consideration in return."

She had expected to bicker over pennies. She perked up.

"I want to show your mothers' club material to another international client as an example of culturally appropriate programming. The Saudis wouldn't know or care if I used their intellectual property, but you would, and I want to remain in your good graces. As a potential collaborator."

"I'm surprised. I thought you blamed me for opening Pandora's box."

"You closed it again. Tightly. The Saudi system killed the job, as simple as that." He paused. "What do you say to my proposition?"

Jo liked the idea of a fat check in the mail. They needed the cash. She liked Owen's asking to use their work rather than stealing it. She liked his placing blame on an authoritarian culture rather than an unlucky pilot or a warring design team.

"Sure, if you include D-Three in the credits."

They exchanged sign-offs and Jo hung up. Owen's behaving decently made her feel lighter, and she floated up from her chair. Ev gave her a questioning look and she hugged him. She'd never work with Phil Owen again—he'd called her a whining woman—but the wolf had been banished from their door.

Ev wrapped his arms around her. "*Now* are you ready to go back to work?" He gave her forehead a peck.

She whispered, "Almost."


On Saturday, Joey turned eighteen and aged out of the special school in which he'd been enrolled. Diane organized a "flying up" ceremony at her place, although it wasn't yet clear where he would fly to. She'd invited Jo and Ev, Joey's aides, and his best friend from school, Megan, with her aides and parents. Jo made an effort to look nice, her first since the plane crash, in honor of her nephew. She wore a dress with a diagonal, purple design and the dangling earrings Joey had played with as a kid. Ev wore a jacket over his jeans. He brought the present he'd purchased, the next video game in the children's series Joey liked, wrapped in three layers of washi. Joey liked to unwrap, and Ev liked the feel of washi in his fingers.

Diane had pushed a table to the side of the concrete slab in her backyard that served as a patio and covered it with a paper tablecloth in Joey's favorite yellow. She'd placed a karaoke machine at the other side—it was Joey's new favorite toy—and ranged chairs along the perimeter. Megan's parents sat stiffly on two adjacent chairs. The four aides, twenty-somethings, joshed each other and the kids, whooping and laughing. Ev went over to them to show them how to fold origami animals. Jo went to the kitchen to help Diane carry the spread outside: half sandwiches, cookies, cut fruit, slices of cake, chips and dip. Joey preferred peanut butter and jelly to everything else. The dog followed Jo's every move

As people helped themselves, Diane turned on the karaoke machine. She selected a slow, sweet Dolly Parton song that reminded Jo of their childhood. Wondering what Joey remembered about his life before Oakland, Jo approached him and took his hands in hers.

"Remember I taught you how to dance in your old house? Let's dance."

Joey grinned and withdrew his hands. "I want to dance with Megan." He loped over to his friend, who was talking to her mother, and took her hands. They held each other appropriately and shuffled to and fro in the middle of the patio. The aides clapped and whistled. The dog yelped at them. Jo realized Joey's being eighteen meant more than she had anticipated, and she felt a twinge at losing priority in her nephew's affections. She walked over to her sister as the song played on.

"I didn't know Joey had a girlfriend."

"The aides have caught them making out a couple of times. I don't think it's gone further, although he gets hefty hard-ons."

"How are you going to handle his love life?"

Diane held arms akimbo. "One day at a time." She turned to Jo. "You know, this is a plus. For him, something normal in a sea of abnormal. For me, too. "

"But it won't be normal?"

Diane's face took on the same piteous expression Myriam's had all those months ago. "This is Joey's version of the senior prom. He and I are both enjoying it, just as it is. I've learned to control my dreams."

"How do you do that?"

"I just do it. Joey's a great kid. He loves back."

The song ended. Diane put on her filigreed eyeglasses, saying, "Excuse me. Gotta find a fast one." She scanned the karaoke list.

Jo was stunned. She'd always considered Diane's sloppy, harried demeanor a sign of bad character. But Diane wasn't sloppy when it came to Joey. She was exacting and strong in a way Jo hadn't fully appreciated.

Jo drifted across the deck, past Joey and Megan holding hands as they waited for the next song to begin, and took the chair beside Megan's mother. An old George Jones tune began to play and one of the aides grabbed the mic and starting bellowing. The others gathered around him; someone clapped to the beat and the others joined in. Megan's mother, who looked pained, pointed to her daughter, still holding onto Joey, and said something to her husband. She turned to Jo.

"She's too young for this."

"How old is Megan?"

"Sixteen. Your sister shouldn't let them touch."

"They seem careful of one another."

The woman snorted. "She is going to be heartbroken when Joey goes away. Your sister said she'd bring him back to visit, but I don't expect it." She clutched her husband's hand. "I don't want Megan to regress." The woman's face twisted in what Jo read as hope battling fear.

"Can you send Megan to Joey's new school?"

"Not in another state. We can't afford to." She spat out her words. "We're not those kind of people." She leaned back and scrutinized Jo. "I don't know how your sister can afford it."

"She works hard."

"A single mother? You must be paying for it."

Nasty woman! "Good luck with Megan." Jo got up and walked toward the karaoke machine. Diane was bent over it, adjusting the volume.

"Megan's mother doesn't like you."

"She's having trouble letting Megan grow up."

Jo took Diane's arm, "When were you going to tell me you're taking Joey out of state?"

Diane removed her glasses and straightened up. Jo had her attention. "When you were back to your old self. I told Ev."

"Where are you going?"

"To either San Jose or Tucson. It depends on the financial aid package."

"Pick San Jose." Jo wanted to grab her and hold her in place.

Diane shook her head. "Even if we go to San Jose, I couldn't commute to Oakland." She lowered her voice. "I hate leaving you. But I have to take care of Joey. I'm not like you, Jo. I'm not engaged in the business. All I ever wanted was to be a mother. A good mother. I have Joey, and I'm blessed."

Jo fought to keep back tears.

Diane dropped the eyeglasses and embraced her. "We'll visit. You can't get rid of me, Big Sister."

"I don't want to." It was true! She wanted Diane near her. To care for her and to be cared for by her.

Diane gave a squeeze and let go. "Time for another song." She turned to the machine and picked up the playlist. "Maybe Joey will dance with you now."

Jo looked over her shoulder for her nephew. He was at the center of the karaoke crowd, still holding one of Megan's hands. She turned back. "I think not." She retrieved the eyeglasses and handed them to her sister. "I'll start to clean up."

She went into the kitchen to hide from the noise. Ev was at the fridge, scrounging a beer. He looked up.

"Ready to go?"

She nodded. Diane's announcement had broken her open, and the past month's events whirled in her head. She needed the calm of home to think. Someone else could clean up.


It was sweater cool on the patio that evening. She sat in the Adirondack chair the house's previous owners had left behind and watched Ev behind the studio glass. He was wrapping plastic around the last of his refurbished displays to transport to San Francisco over the weekend. A xylophone in the shape of a giraffe, where the high notes climbed higher up the neck. He had thought it would give users a visceral feel for pitch, but it had proved too cumbersome; kids didn't climb on the attached stepstool and raced past. Ev thought it might charm adults.

The lights went off in the studio. He emerged carrying his notebook and noticed her sitting there in the half light from the house. She gestured for him to come. He pulled a storage box over beside her chair and sat.

Jo said, "I've been thinking about sweaters." She stroked the front of hers.

Ev raised his eyebrows.

"When I was a kid I used to think a sweater made you warm. You put on the sweater when it got chilly, and the sweater made you warm. I didn't understand for years—for decades, until you said something about insulation—that *you* made you warm. *You* were the source of the heat. The sweater just kept the heat in." She paused. "I'm having a sweater moment."

He looked interested.

"For years I thought Diane was a purposeless flake. Uh uh. She's passionate about motherhood."

"Yeah. She copied you."

"Me?"

"She once told me she followed you around when you were kids, and she wanted to take care of things like you did. And then she named Joey after you."

Jo sat up. "No! She named him after his father, Jimmy something."

Ev shook his head. "You are stubborn." He stretched and arched his back. "Are we done?"

She nodded. He got up and headed for the house.

She leaned back in the chair. Oh my god, she thought, he's right. A wave of pleasure flowed through her.

Then she knew.

She hadn't been mourning the Saudi job, she'd been mourning justice denied. She'd expected acclaim about the job to make up for every slight the profession had given her, to make her glamorous at last. So puny an ambition compared to Diane's!

Or to Myriam's.

Another sweater moment. She didn't miss the Saudi job, she missed Myriam. She missed her wisdom and her power. No small feat to bore from within. She wanted to reach halfway around the world to celebrate sisterhood with her, with or without the veil.

It had gotten cold. There was a limit to how much comfort one thin sweater could provide. There was a limit to how many raw, pregnant thoughts she could entertain. She grasped the chair's arms and raised herself to standing. She went into the house to get ready for bed. She hoped Ev was already asleep since she was not prepared to talk.

Jo helped Ev carry the giraffe-xylophone from the truck into the
warehouse behind the gallery. The gallery staff—a pale young
man and a chubby woman who wore very good clothes—had
arranged all twenty-five of Ev's pieces along the rear wall. Eying
the giraffe, the young man began to slide a few pedestals together
to make room. He helped Ev maneuver the instrument into place
and then went to find the boss.

The young man reappeared, with Jack behind him and three
other men on his heels. Jack strode toward Ev and Jo, hand out-
stretched. Ev swaggered over to him—Jo's skin prickled—and they
shook hands. Jack swiveled to Jo.

"Good to see you again, Jo. Hope you don't mind my fishing
buddies. We're leaving for Montana from here."

He did not wait for a reply. He strolled along the wall, tweaking
a lever here and there. His friends followed. They peeled off separately,
each stopping in front of a display that caught his fancy. They man-
handled the displays, just like kids. They called to each other to come
see, just like kids, except in baritone. They regrouped and burst into
boisterous laughter. The staff stood at the sidelines, pen and clipboard
in hand, watching Jack's moves. Jo could not read their expressions.

Jack came to the end of the lineup and turned to face them.
He pointed to the pedestal that bore one of Ev's abstract pieces, a
multi-faceted cube suspended in a frame in which it twisted as if
on gimbals. The faces were made of dichroic glass that sparkled in

different colors depending on the angle at which light struck. Ev had attached an LED lamp to a gooseneck at the base so you could direct a spot of light anywhere you wanted.

"Now, that's a beauty," Jack said. "It's bright, whimsical. Has your name written all over it. But it could be even better." Jack motioned to the young man, "Eric, see if you can detach the lamp."

Ev took a step toward Eric. Jack held up his hand to stop him. "Easy, we're not doing anything, just investigating. I know my market. They like mystery."

"Tell him not to touch my stuff." Ev's back hunched.

"Sure." Jack nodded to Eric, who retreated to his place. "We're just looking."

"Why?" Jo stepped forward, sensing she must intervene.

"I can use half a dozen of these pieces as is. I want your husband to tweak the others. Lizzie will coach him. She's got great taste."

Ev blanched. "I already tweaked them. They're finished."

"Look, you're a newbie. After we make your name, you won't need suggestions."

Ev shut his mouth.

"I have a customer in mind who'd salivate over that piece if it had clean lines."

Jo said, "It does have clean lines."

Jack turned to Ev. "You realize you're contractually bound to improve the ones I want improved. In your own way, of course."

Jo looked at Ev in amazement. His face was blank. She turned to Jack. "What do you mean 'contractually bound'?"

Jack flicked his wrist and Lizzie produced a document from a folder on her clipboard. Jo scanned it. Bunch of boilerplate. Ev's signature at the bottom. He'd signed a contract without telling her. What a jerk! Then she saw an opening.

"You contracted with Dunhill + Dana + Design," she said slowly, "not with Ev personally. For deals over five thousand dollars, you need two signatures, Ev's *and* mine. This isn't valid." She handed the document back to Lizzie.

Jack's eyes narrowed. "Signature is a formality. Your husband agreed to the terms of the show."

"The formality would hold up in court."

He drew himself taller. "Do you want a show or not?"

She glanced at Ev, still silent and pale. "Not on your terms. But we'll be happy to negotiate a new contract."

Jack broke into a smile. "If you think you can satisfy me, I'll give a listen when I get back." He turned to his staff. "Consolidate the stuff. I'll be back end of the week." He turned to his pals. "Fishermen, let's go!"

At the door, he turned back and pointed. "Take that giraffe thing home. Too gimmicky. It'd turn off the serious collector."

The four men cleared out quickly. Lizzie and Eric began to push the pedestals into a corner. Ev's face turned from white to red.

"We can leave."

"Don't you want to talk with the staff?"

"Nope." He bent to pick up the plastic with which the giraffe-xylophone had been covered. "Help me bring it home?"

They wrapped the instrument and lugged it to the door. Lizzie stopped them to ask when they'd be back. Jo said when Jack was prepared to re-negotiate. Lizzie looked doubtful. Ev thanked the woman for her help and proceeded onto the loading dock. He and Jo tied down the giraffe and got in the truck. Ev backed away from the building and drove to the freeway with uncustomary speed. Jo raised her eyebrows but waited until they were well onto the bridge, past Treasure Island, before speaking.

"You're driving like me. What are you thinking?" She resisted the impulse to berate him for having kept a secret, the poor chagrined man.

"I'm going to build a menagerie of animal instruments. Paws and tails will control timbre and attack. Breath will control timing. Not a gimmick among them." He stared straight ahead, nodding yes.

"Sounds electronic."

"In part."

His jaw clenched. She waited for his words.

He glanced at her, then back at the road. "I watched Jack's friends behave like nine-year-olds, and I saw Jack didn't give a damn about the work. He has another agenda."

"He wants to sell, and he's probably good at it." She kept her voice neutral. "Why did you hook up with him in the first place?"

She could see him thinking.

"I wanted something different. A different platform for my work."

Warning flags fluttered in her head. "Are you unhappy at D-Three?"

She held her breath.

"I thought people would behave differently in a gallery and it would be thrilling. I thought I'd feel different about my work, and myself. I didn't."

"Jack and his buddies had fishing on their minds. Don't be too hasty."

He didn't respond. He maneuvered the truck into the right lane, checking the giraffe in the mirror. She wanted to draw him out.

"I'll negotiate with Jack if you want me to. Are you willing to give him an inch of control?"

He paled again. "I guess I expected everything to be on my terms."

"Jack could make you famous, if that's what you're after."

He shook his head. "I don't care about fame."

"Then what *do* you want? You've been fanatic about *something* for months."

He paused, as if collecting his thoughts. "I guess I wanted to go back in time. What if I'd gone to art school in West Virginia, what would I be building now? Who would be my peers?" He took his eyes off the road to look at her. "When Jack slammed the giraffe I realized I'd been deluding myself. You can't redo history."

She felt she could probe now. "Why didn't you talk to me about it?"

"I thought you'd be jealous."

"Of what?"

"You wouldn't want me to go out on my own." He paused. "I shouldn't have shut you out. You're the one who makes things happen. I'm an idiot without you. I can't talk to clients. I can't put first things first. You hold it together."

She felt a whoosh of relief. D-Three was safe. "If it makes you feel any better, I've been deluded, too. I went after the Saudi job for the wrong reasons."

"You went after glory."

"If you thought I was wrong-headed, why didn't you correct me?"

"You can be hard to dissuade."

True, she thought. It takes a plane crash.

He signaled to exit the freeway. "I'm sorry about Becca. She was so enthusiastic about the show that I let it go on. I should have listened to you."

"Apology accepted."

"Thank you."

She watched him steer the truck down the ramp and up the hill, careful and steady, a man who respected the rules of the road and the laws of nature. A genial soul whose vanity had run away with him. She could overlook vanity. He had demonstrated his constancy, the better part of love. He was a partner she could count on.

She decided to let him off the hook. "Speaking of Becca, Diane said she's coming to visit Joey. I'm going to help her get a good job."

He glanced at her. "Very generous."

Yes, she thought, now I can afford to be. "If we get busy again, maybe she'll come work for us."

He pulled the truck into their driveway. A eucalyptus nut clunked on the windshield as he turned off the engine, and they both laughed. She faced him.

"If you're really going to make a musical menagerie, I'm going to find you a buyer. Even if I have to cold call every museum in the directory."

He eased out of the driver's seat. "I'm not kidding." He slammed his door shut.

She slammed her door shut and spoke to him across the hood. "Neither am I."

The next morning in the studio, she watched him disassemble the giraffe-xylophone. He placed the pieces one at a time into cushioned slots in the wall of the crate he had built especially for the instrument. He handled them with delicacy, the same way he handled the cacti growing infinitesimally slowly on their kitchen windowsill. The same way he'd tuned and retuned the exhibits in Al Khobar.

Al Khobar flashed into her head, the mother–daughter meeting with Myriam's club. She pictured the women and girls sitting around her, eager and shy, having driven hours to hear from her. Back then, the mothers' hopes for their daughters, despite all the obstacles in Saudi society, had stirred Jo to the core. Their gratitude to her for serving as a beacon had been a gift, a small consummation of her desire to make a difference. She wanted to give Ev such a gift; she wanted to accommodate his deepest desires. She made up her mind.

"I've had a thought. You need another animal for your menagerie."

He looked up from the crate.

"Do you still want a dog?"

"What are you saying?"

"I want to get you a puppy."

His face lit up. "Are you sure?"

"I'm sure. I'm in no hurry to traipse around the world solving other people's problems. Time for something new."

He abandoned the xylophone and approached her.

She stood tall. "Only there's one condition. You're in charge. *You* worry about accidents and diseases. I don't drive to the vet in the middle of the night."

"I've thought about rescuing a mutt like Joey's."

"Okay, but . . ."

"I want a male with a problem," he interrupted. "Three legs. One eye. Terrible temper. I'll make him whole." He pulled her toward him and hugged gently. "You're going to love him."

"Whatever you say." She suspected they both thought she might not. But she was all in.

# READING GROUP GUIDE

I f your group wishes, the author will participate in your discussion by Skype or Facetime (or in person if you are in greater
Phoenix). Contact her via her website, www.sheilagrinell.com.

1. There are four contracts in play in this novel:
   1) the deal with the Saudi government to build a chil-
      dren's museum, which doesn't materialize;
   2) the subcontract D-Three is forced to sign with
      Owen Associates;
   3) the exhibition contract offered to Ev by the gallery
      owner; and
   4) the marriage contract between Jo and Ev.
   How does Jo feel about each of them at the start, and
   how do her feelings change?

274 ·ဆ· THE CONTRACT

2. Jo and Ev have such different personalities, yet they've developed a successful business together. How have they managed it, and at what cost?

3. Myriam follows the conventions of her society despite its restrictions. Jo finds those restrictions hugely burdensome. Yet Jo and Myriam develop a mutual fondness. What enables them to bridge the cultural divide?

4. Diane and Jo have been at odds for decades, at least in Jo's mind. Entrenched family relationships tend to persist, yet the relationship between these two sisters manages to undergo redefining. What makes this possible?

5. At the start, Ev and Jo disagree about the value of the Saudi job. As things progress, Ev grows further disenchanted and turns his attention elsewhere. What drives his interest in showcasing his work at an art gallery? Is there a subtext of resentment toward Jo? Is there a subtext to Jo's response?

6. Jo and Becca are both people who are set in their opinions. They disagree about the Saudi job, among other things, yet they work well together. What pulls them together? What forces them apart? Should Jo have fired the girl?

7. Jo pursues personal redemption in the form of business success until the plane crash forces her to re-evaluate her motives. Do you expect her to develop different pursuits as a result?

8. After years of disinterest in bringing another creature into their household, Jo decides to give Ev a puppy. What will it mean to each of them? How do you envision the future of their relationship?

9. Is there a pattern to the discoveries Jo makes as a result of her year of struggle in the Kingdom of Saudi Arabia?

# ACKNOWLEDGMENTS

I would like to thank museum colleagues in Saudi Arabia and the US for sharing their work and their worlds with me, especially Bushra Aldraihim, Ahmed Al-Shible, Robert Grover, Yasser Refai, Peter Wissa, and my consulting partner, the late Alan J. Friedman, PhD. Thanks also to Michael Damschroeder for suggesting that I write about my stint in Saudi Arabia in novel form. A few of the exhibits described here were inspired by the work of Doug Hollis, Norman Tuck, and the incomparable Bob Miller. I learned about tree root structure and function in Peter Wohlleben's *The Hidden Life of Trees* and about the equivalence of extreme joy and extreme pain in a story by Alice Munro.

I am grateful to my editor, Carol Test, and writing group partners, Pam Hait and Emily Hinchman, for sticking with me to the end. Three beta readers provided gentle course corrections: Jan

Goodwin, an award-winning journalist who looked behind the veils of Muslim women; Rachelle Marmor, poet, artist impresario, and healer; and Barbara Meyerson, a leading authority on children's museums. My thanks also to the other Finalists in Kevin Canty's section at the 2018 Tucson Festival of Books Literary Awards Masters Workshop for their comments on the opening chapters. I am grateful to Duffy McMahon, Ellie Sutter, Gillian Thomas, and Lois Zachary for taking a final read. Thank you, also, to Lauren Wise at She Writes Press for caring.

SG

# ABOUT THE AUTHOR

Sheila Grinell spent forty years developing science centers in the US and consulting on museum projects around the world, including in Saudi Arabia. She turned to literature in her sixties, publishing a debut novel, *Appetite*, in 2016. *The Contract* is her second work of fiction. Born in a taxi in Manhattan, she studied at The Bronx High School of Science, Harvard University, and the University of California at Berkeley. She lives in Phoenix with her husband, Tom Johnson, and their dog.

To learn more about Sheila, her work, and to subscribe to her monthly newsletter, see www.sheilagrinell.com.

If you enjoyed this book, please help other people discover it. Your comments on social media and your reviews on vendor sites can make all the difference. Please take a few minutes to:

- Write a short review and post it on Amazon or your preferred vendor's website
- Post your review on Goodreads or Instagram, or wherever you prefer to share comments about books
- Tell your friends.

Thank you!

To hear about readers' reactions to *The Contract* and Sheila's other work, subscribe to her monthly newsletter at www.sheilagrinell.com.

You can follow her on:

 bookbub.com/authors/sheila-grinell

@ sheilagrinell

Sheila-Grinell-author-778119465648171

linkedin.com/in/sheila-grinell-041b915

# SELECTED TITLES FROM SHE WRITES PRESS

She Writes Press is an independent publishing company founded to serve women writers everywhere. Visit us at www.shewritespress.com.

*Appetite* by Sheila Grinell. $16.95, 978-1-63152-022-8. When twenty-five-year-old Jenn Adler brings home a guru fiancé from Bangalore, her parents must come to grips with the impending marriage—and its effect on their own relationship.

*Play for Me* by Céline Keating. $16.95, 978-1-63152-972-6. Middle-aged Lily impulsively joins a touring folk-rock band, leaving her job and marriage behind in an attempt to find a second chance at life, passion, and art.

*Again and Again* by Ellen Bravo. $16.95, 978-1-63152-939-9. When the man who raped her roommate in college becomes a Senate candidate, women's rights leader Deborah Borenstein must make a choice—one that could determine control of the Senate, the course of a friendship, and the fate of a marriage.

*Shelter Us* by Laura Diamond. $16.95, 978-1-63152-970-2. Lawyer-turned-stay-at-home-mom Sarah Shaw is still struggling to find a steady happiness after the death of her infant daughter when she meets a young homeless mother and toddler she can't get out of her mind—and becomes determined to rescue them.

*American Family* by Catherine Marshall-Smith. $16.95, 978-1631521638. Partners Richard and Michael, recovering alcoholics, struggle to gain custody of their Richard's biological daughter from her grandparents after her mother's death only to discover they—and she—are fundamentalist Christians.

*A Work of Art* by Micayla Lally. $16.95, 978-1631521683. After their breakup—and different ways of dealing with it—Julene and Samson eventually find their way back to each other, but when she finds out what he did to keep himself busy while they were apart, she wonders: Can she trust him again?